UNCOVERING JUSTICE

ISBN-13:
ISBN-10:

First printing,
Cover design by Moon Dusk Designs

“It is slavery in the modern age. Every year thousands of people, mainly women and children, are exploited by criminals who use them for forced labor or the sex trade. No country is immune. Almost all play a part, either as a source of trafficked people, transit point or destination.”

–United Nations Secretary-General, Ban Ki-moon

One

Harper Matthews handed the twentyish-looking man his fourth flute of champagne. He mumbled a "thank you" as he set the glass on the tabletop in front of him. The passenger drew in a shaky breath, pushing it out with the same shaky breath. Chewing on his bottom lip, he clutched tight to a small, slim package as he looked out the window, then set it on the table. His hand lingered momentarily above the envelope before he snatched it back up with a startled gasp, looking around the plane. He cursed underneath his breath and closed his eyes. His mouth moved slowly as he counted.

The same actions he had done several times since they departed John F. Kennedy.

Harper paused before stepping away.

"Is there anything else I can get you, sir?"

He looked up and continued to stare into the blackened sky.

"Sir?" She touched his shoulder with a gentle squeeze.

As if woken from a deep sleep, the passenger shook his head and blinked at her.

"Di-did you say something?"

She offered him a warm smile. "I was wondering if there is something else I can bring you? Water, perhaps?"

He blinked again before forcing a tight smile. "I'm fine. Right? I-I'm okay. But thank you j-just the same."

The passenger tugged at the collar of his shirt as if it were a snake choking him. He set the package on the table, frowned at it, and snatched it up again.

"You say we're almost in Atlanta?"

Harper nodded as she checked her watch. As she did so, a strand of dark brown hair fell in front of her eyes. She tucked it behind her ear with a smile."We'll be landing in thirty minutes."

She sat in the empty seat next to him. Harper tried not to look out the window. Even the mere thought of being by the window, thousands of miles above the ground with no chance of escaping the small enclosure of the plane, Harper's heartbeat would quicken.

It quickened now, as she struggled to maintain composure, to calm a passenger who was obviously rattled.

"What are your plans in Atlanta?" she asked him. "Business or pleasure?"

The passenger appeared as nervous as she was, if not more. It'd taken her years to keep her own fears in check. She preferred to keep herself busy, force her mind off her thoughts. But, on the red-eye, when the passengers slept soundly, it wasn't an easy task. She decided this particular passenger needed to take his mind off whatever he seemed worried about. It was obvious from the moment Harper set eyes on him that something was amidst.

His right cheek twitched as he peered at her.

The passenger swallowed hard, glancing again out the window.

For a second, Harper thought he wouldn't answer, but when he did, it was in a soft, unsure tone.

"Business."

"What is it you do?"

"Huh, what?"

"Your job," Harper said, "What is your job?"

"A r-reporter," he stammered with a swallow.

"Nice. So what brings you to Atlanta? Anything I've heard on the news?" Her eyes flickered to the envelope. It wasn't something she intended on doing, but somehow, someway, it drew out more of her curiosity.

The passenger slipped the package out of sight without a word, but couldn't mask the slight tremble in his hands.

She chose not to press the issue of the envelope. Instead, Harper replied, "Why don't I get you that water? I'll be right back."

She moved away until he called her.

"Can I ask you a question?"

She stopped, noting the edge in his voice.

Turning, Harper stared at the back of his head.

"Of course."

He paused and took a sip of his champagne, following with another. "Have you ever had to make a choice? One you don't want to make?"

"Sure, I have," Harper replied. "I'm sure we all have at some point in our lives."

The passenger rose, turning to face her. His green eyes had grown dark, emanating an emotion she wasn't sure what make of. She stepped back.

"No," he said, keeping his voice low, "I don't think you have. I don't mean a choice between what movie to watch or what to eat. I mean between what's right and what's wrong. A choice where the answer is always wrong."

"I-I'm sorry, sir," Harper said, blinking her eyes. She felt her skin crawling. The blood running through her veins suddenly seemed cold. "I don't understand."

The passenger opened his mouth as if to speak, then clamped it shut.

He returned to his seat.

"I'm sorry," he said. "I shouldn't have said anything."

"Perhaps if you told me more," Harper prompted, "I can help you figure it out. Are you in trouble, sir?"

Turning to face her, he flashed another tight smile. "Thank you for the drink. That'll be all."

Harper remained planted in place after the passenger turned to face the window.

Should she prompt him for more information?

Should she alert the pilots?

Something in the pit of her stomach tightened, a voice telling her to let it go, another voice telling her something was gravely wrong.

The passenger continued to glare out the window, the reflection in the glass staring directly at her.

Another chill crawled up her spine as she decided to walk away.

Whatever was going through the passenger's mind, she knew she'd better not continue to bring up the subject.

Her mind replayed the conversation as she slipped behind the curtain.

"You okay?"

Harper glanced at her coworker before peering through the curtains at the passenger.

"Hey, Olivia, you see that man? I just had a weird conversation with him. I mean, scary weird."

"What's going on?"

Olivia set her magazine down and freed her thick brown hair from its ponytail. After running a comb through, she pulled her hair back into the rubber band. She listened with intent as Harper closed the curtains and relayed the short version of the conversation.

"Wow," Olivia breathed, her eyes wide. She bit her bottom lip. "It could be nothing, but maybe you should tell the pilots."

"He has seemed freaked out over something this entire flight. I don't want to cause him any trouble if it's nothing. But…he seemed…off."

"Like he's going to hijack the plane or something?"

"If he was planning on taking over the plane, don't you think he would have by now?"

"Maybe," Olivia muttered.

Harper drew in a deep breath and pushed it out. She closed her eyes, feeling the walls closing in on her.

Olivia chuckled. "You see the irony in this?"

Harper opened her eyes and said nothing as she reorganized the snack cart. She needed to focus her mind.

"He asked if you'd ever had to make a difficult choice," Olivia continued, "And here you are, making a difficult choice. If we alert the pilots, they must alert airport security, who will take him in for questioning. The process can be long and tedious, especially if he's just a nervous passenger. If you say nothing and he is a bad guy, you'll feel guilty, knowing you could've prevented whatever crime he intends."

Olivia brushed her bangs from her eyes.

"So, what should I do?" Harper asked.

Olivia shrugged. "Suppose you can play it safe. Talk to the pilots, let them make the hard decision."

After glancing once more at the fidgety passenger, Harper nodded her agreement, reaching for the phone. She waited until the co-pilot answered, then once again, explained the conversation.

"It's probably nothing," she ended, "But I wanted you to be aware."

"You did the right thing, Harper," came the smooth reply. "It sounds questionable. Thanks for the heads up. I'll go have a talk with him. I'll see if I can't feel him out. You say he's in first class?"

"That's correct," Harper acknowledged.

"Very well," the pilot said. "I'll keep you in the loop."

He ended the call and Harper replaced the receiver, unsure of how she felt about the situation. Her mind considered the puzzle, and she shook her head.

Picking up the magazine Olivia was looking through a few minutes ago, Harper thumbed through the contents, not really seeing the pages.

She jumped when a hand gripped her shoulder.

Harper blanched at Olivia.

"You okay?" her friend asked, eyes narrowing with concern. "Not about the passenger, but about…"

Harper gazed at her friend, but before she could answer, the curtains pulled back and the co-pilot appeared. The usual crisp white uniform had a stain from when Harper spilled coffee on him before leaving the airport hotel.

Jonathan Parker removed his pilot cap and scratched the back of his head.

"Well, I talked to the gentleman," he began. "He claims to have an important business meeting, and that's why he's nervous. He asked me to tell you he apologizes if he frightened you."

"So, you don't think he's a terrorist planning to murder us?" Olivia interjected, her hand on her hip.

Jonathan lifted his lips in a crooked smile. "No, I don't believe he plans to kill us." He returned his gaze to Harper, then put his hand on her shoulder. "Will you be okay?"

She cleared her throat and offered a weak smile. "Yes. I'm sorry if I troubled you."

"It was no trouble." Jonathan hesitated, watching her carefully. He squeezed her shoulder and offered a smile. "I better get back."

After Jonathan returned to the cockpit, Harper pushed out a breath.

"You must think I'm crazy."

"Not at all," Olivia protested. "I'm going to make a quick round, get the passengers prepped for landing. When we sign off, you wanna grab a drink before we go home?"

"No, thanks. I'm tired," Harper sighed. "I've been away for too long. I'd kill for one night in my bed. Raincheck?"

"Definitely."

Olivia offered a warm hug before she departed.

Harper closed her eyes, focusing her mind on her slow, steady breathing. Though she tried to empty her mind, her thoughts continued to drift to the strange passenger.

Though every thought she had told her to pass him off as just another nervous passenger, something continued to tug at her curiosity.

Have you ever had to make a choice? One you don't want to make? I mean between what's right and what's wrong. A choice where the answer is always wrong.

A choice between right and wrong.

Where the answer is always wrong.

What was he talking about?

Thoughts swirled in her head until Olivia's voice filled the intercom, instructing the passengers to buckle and prepare for landing.

Before taking her seat, Harper regarded the passenger.

He had his thumb and forefinger pressed against his eyes.

When Olivia made the announcement a second time, Harper hurried to her seat and latched herself.

She decided she'd try once more to talk to the passenger after the plane landed.

Olivia took her seat next to Harper.

It didn't take long for the plan to come to a halt at their destination, but during the bumpy landing, Harper gripped Olivia's wrist. Her friend said nothing despite the force of Harper's nails digging into her skin.

After ensuring all passengers left with their belongings, Harper gathered her things and headed for the ramp. She stepped into the airport and scanned the chaotic terminal, but the passenger was nowhere to be found.

She searched the baggage claims and didn't find him.

With a frown, she decided the issue would be better put to rest. In the distance, she spotted Jonathan Parker heading her way. She turned to

take him again."

Harper laughed. "I'll be home for the week. I fly out again next Thursday. But they're welcome to come over anytime they'd like."

"Don't tell them that. You'll never get them to leave," Ollie said. He shook his head once, his blonde waves bouncing slightly, then paused. "So…how are you doing?"

Ollie's voice turned to concern, but Harper opted to ignore it. She let her shoulder rise and fall, telling him she was fine.

"I don't know how you do it," Ollie said. "I admire you for being daring enough to fly as often as you do."

"It helps to keep busy," Harper admitted. She walked to the refrigerator and pulled out two beers. She handed a bottle to Ollie. "But, if I think too much, I can't breathe. My coworkers help. Especially Olivia." Harper stretched her lips in a smile, raising her bottle as if to toast him. "She's my Ollie in the air."

"I'm glad," Ollie replied, his cheeks turning a light shade of pink. He knelt to pet Collier, who continued to spin with the occasional bark. "I worry about you when you're up there."

"Well, a wise friend once told me if I want to get over a fear, I need to embrace it. So, embrace it, I do."

"Sounds like a smart friend," Ollie said. "Too smart for his own good."

"Maybe," Harper said. "But if it weren't for you, I don't know what state I'd be in. When my heart acts like it's going to burst, I think of you. It helps."

Ollie took a long swig of his beer. "You're amazing, Harper."

"That's only because I have an amazing friend."

They fell into a brief silence.

"Hey, guess what? I have new music," Harper announced. "Wrote it the other day."

"Well, what are you waiting for?" Ollie demanded, eyes wide and eager. "Aren't you going to play it for me?"

"Only if you don't judge too harshly," Harper said with a sly smile as she grabbed her messenger bag from the floor.

She set it on the kitchen table and opened it.

Her breath caught in her throat as blood pulsed through the veins as if to burst.

"Oh, my…"

"Don't say you lost it," Ollie told her with a snicker. When she didn't answer, he stepped to her side, his hand first on the small of her back, then her shoulder. "Are you okay, Harper?"

With slow movements, she reached into the bag, pulling out a small, brown envelope.

The same envelope the strange passenger had.

Her hands trembled as she recalled the conversation on the plane.

"Harper?"

"Um…I…" her words trailed off. "He must have accidentally dropped this in my bag."

"Who?"

"A passenger on the plane."

She considered whether to tell Ollie what had transpired between them. Harper decided against it with a shake her head and forced smile. "He was just a nervous guy. I talked to him, trying to keep his mind off whatever was bothering him. I'd accidentally bumped into him when I was leaving. He must have dropped it."

"And it just happened to fall into your bag?" Ollie's tone was laced with skepticism.

"I'll call the airline and track him down."

Ollie sat at the kitchen table as Harper pulled the cell phone from her back pocket. She searched for the number of the airline.

Once connected, Harper told the customer service desk the seat number and requested for the passenger's name and contact information.

A few minutes went by before the woman returned.

"His name is Daniel Clark," she announced before reciting the telephone number.

Harper thanked her, ended the call, then punched in the phone number. It rang until it reached the generic voicemail. Harper left a quick message, asking for Daniel to return her call.

She set her cell on the counter and released a sigh.

"He's not answering. But it is late. He could have gotten a hotel and gone to bed." She glanced at Ollie, whose gaze was on her as he scratched between Collier's ears. "I'll try again in the morning."

"Wonder what's in the package," Ollie said, a mischievous smile playing on his lips.

Harper scoffed. "Yeah, I'm not planning on finding out. It's his personal property."

Ollie held his hands in front of him as if to surrender. "I was just wondering. Relax."

Rolling her eyes, she fished out her sheet music and passed it over.

"Anyway, here it is."

"Wow, this is amazing." His eyes skimmed the markings and pushed to his feet. He returned the pages to Harper. "I demand a private recital."

"But it's like one o'clock in the morning," Harper protested with a yawn.

"Your point?"

"I'm tired."

"Try again."

"I don't know," she said. "What if it's terrible?"

"Harper Matthews," Ollie said, putting a hand on either of her shoulders. He shook her lightly. "I have yet to hear any of your compositions that are in the category of terrible. And, anyway, you don't have much choice. Play for me or I'll bug you all night. That's a promise."

Another roll of her eyes, Harper pulled away from him and removed her violin from the case.

"Fine. You win."

With the sheet music in hand, she walked to the corner of her living room where she'd set up her music station. She placed the sheets on the stand and sat.

Harper stared out the window, the bright city lights of Atlanta allowing no chance of a starry night. Regardless, she could see the hazy aura of the moon shining behind the clouds. Down below, traffic remained thick, but still not as awful as it would be in midday. There were great similarities between Atlanta and New York, and great differences.

Try as she might, she couldn't imagine living anywhere else. Home was in the busy life of Atlanta.

She waited until Ollie situated himself on the couch. Collier jumped on the cushions next to him, climbing into his lap.

Her heart gave a nervous jolt, and she reminded herself she was only playing for Ollie. He was her best friend, someone she shared the most intimate of secrets.

"Okay, here we go. Don't be harsh," Harper warned. "Promise me."

"Just play," Ollie instructed. He lifted the corner of his lips in a smile. "Please."

"Okay," Harper said. "Here goes nothing."

After three deep breaths, Harper lifted the violin to her chin.

As she played, she took notice of Ollie's reflection in the glass. His eyes were closed, listening to each strum of music she played.

Harper closed her eyes, allowing herself to surrender to the melody. The bow glided across the strings in slow, fluid motions. The world appeared to melt and there was only the sound of the violin's music calling to her.

As the rod stroked the strings, Harper felt as though she was being lifted from her seat. The music played, and everything that went wrong in the world no longer mattered.

When the music faded, she kept her eyes closed and the instrument resting underneath her chin.

Harper finally opened her eyes and turned to see Ollie smiling at her.

"That was the most beautiful piece you've ever written, Harp," Ollie praised. "Took my breath away. Are you sure you don't want to make a living out of it?"

Harper offered a shy smile. "This is just a hobby. An escape." She set the violin on its stand. "It's nothing magnificent."

"You underestimate the power of your playing," Ollie said, rising. "And how you feel playing. You're most at ease with the violin than anything else."

Harper stood. "No, I don't. I know I'm good. My playing is just…personal. I think if I shared it with the rest of the world, I'll lose the meaning."

Ollie nodded. "I understand. Still, you're too good to not let everyone hear."

"Thanks, Ollie. That means a lot."

He stood in front of her, opening his mouth as if to say something, then he seemed to change his mind with a shake of his head. "All right, well, I better leave. As you said, it's late. I know you're tired. I'm glad you're home safe and sound."

She kissed his cheek. "Thanks again for letting Collier stay with you. You're the best."

"Let's have lunch one day before you take off again."

"Sounds good."

Harper followed him into the hallway. After saying their goodbyes, she locked the deadbolt and set the chain in place.

She picked up the small brown envelope and eyed it with curiosity.

"Any guesses on what's inside, boy?" she asked Collier.

Still on the couch, the Sheltie tilted his head to the side, one ear hooked downward.

"Yeah, me neither," Harper said. She placed it back on the counter. "What I do know, though, is I can hardly keep my eyes open. It's been a long time since I've seen my own bed. C'mon, boy. Let's get some rest."

In answer, Collier jumped off the couch and trotted after her.

Three

Harper woke to the bed shaking.

With one eye open, she noticed the clock read ten twenty-five. With reluctance, she pulled herself from the pillow. Collier stopped scratching behind his ear, gazed at her, then shook his body, the movement creating another earthquake just for her.

He released a single bark, jumped off the bed, hurrying to the doorway. Collier stopped to look back at her with another bark.

"All right, boy, I'm coming," Harper assured him with a yawn.

She climbed out of bed and followed the Sheltie to the living room.

He waited by the door, spinning in circles, while she searched for the leash.

After slipping it on Collier, Harper grabbed her phone from the counter and they left the apartment.

She had to jog through the hallway and down the steps to keep up with the overeager dog.

Once outside, Collier searched for a spot to relieve himself. As she waited, Harper tried again to contact Daniel Clark.

"Hey, Mr. Clark," she said when the voicemail prompted her to leave a message. "This is Harper Matthews from the airline again. I'm just trying to get in touch with you about the package you dropped. I'd really like to meet with you to give it back." She recited her phone number for the second time before ending the call.

When Collier appeared more interested in barking at passersby, Harper tugged his leash, pulling him inside.

She spotted Ollie and his daughters descending the stairs.

"Good morning," Ollie said as the girls ran to pet Collier.

"Good morning," Harper echoed.

Ollie's daughters fell to their knees to give Collier their attention.

"Where are you guys off to?"

"Baylee and I have to get a present for our friend. Her birthday party's today." Emma, the oldest by two minutes, giggled as Collier lapped his tongue across her face.

"Cutting it kind of close aren't you?" Harper smiled.

Baylee rolled her eyes up at her dad. "Yeah, well, Dad's been too busy."

"Hmm. Shame on you, Oliver," Harper teased, swatting his shoulder.

Ollie held his hand in front of him. "I admit it. I'm a terrible dad."

"No, not terrible," Emma replied with a sigh. "But, you do have room for improvement."

Baylee nodded in agreement as Harper laughed.

"Hey, uh, did that guy ever contact you?"

Harper shook her head at her friend. "I tried calling him again and left another message."

"What guy?" Baylee asked.

"No one special," Harper answered. "He's somebody I met on the plane. He lost a package. I'm trying to return it."

"Is he cute?"

Harper giggled. "I guess you can say that."

"Mommy used to always say the first thing you do when you meet someone cute is to check to see if he has a ring."

"Is that right?" Harper said. "Well, I'm afraid I didn't take much notice."

"When you see him again, do it," Baylee pressed.

Harper nodded. "I'll keep that in mind *if* I do see him again."

"You should have a look in the package," Ollie suggested.

Harper regarded him. "Wow, you're nosy, you know that?"

"I prefer the term 'curious.'"

"Well, curiosity killed the cat, didn't it? You know, I can't open that package. It's his personal property."

"It might give you a lead on where to find him," Ollie said. "If you still can't reach him by phone."

"We'll see," Harper said. "I want to give it a while longer before I commit a federal offense."

"C'mon, Dad," Baylee urged. "We've got to go. It'll be time for the party soon."

"We're going, we're going," Ollie said, putting a hand on her shoulder. He gazed at Harper. "Keep me posted, will you?"

"Of course. I'll see you guys later."

The girls said their goodbyes to Collier and Harper before trotting away.

Collier led the way to the apartment as Harper searched her phone for Olivia's number.

"Hey, Liv," Harper said when her friend answered. "I didn't wake you, did I?"

"What?" she mumbled, then sighed. "Uh, no."

"You're a terrible liar," Harper told her. "Sorry. Listen, I'm calling because remember that guy from last night?"

"What guy?" Olivia said as she released a yawn.

"The one acting all weird and skittish and whatever."

"Oh," Olivia muttered. "Yeah. What about him?"

"I saw him again before I left the airport. He apologized for the way he acted, then when I got home, I found a package in my messenger bag."

"A what?"

"He had a package with him on the plane. It seemed important to him."

"And he handed it to you? That's weird."

"He didn't exactly hand it to me," Harper said as she reached her door. She unlocked it, freed Collier from the leash and gave him a treat from inside the pantry.

"What's in the package?"

"I don't know," Harper replied. She picked it up and studied it. It was small, slim and had no writing, no stamp. "It's his stuff. I don't feel right going through it."

A sigh. "Harp, he obviously wanted you to have it, right? He wouldn't have put it in your bag. And from the things he said to you, it's gotta make you wonder."

"It does," Harper admitted.

"Have you tried contacting him?"

"Yeah. I called twice and left messages. He hasn't responded yet. I just…"

"What?" Olivia said.

The sound of a drawer sliding open filled the phone line.

"I don't feel right about this. Ever since last night, there was something about him that wasn't right. It's not the feeling that he's a terrorist or something. But, I think he could be in trouble."

"Let's meet for breakfast," Olivia suggested. "Bring the envelope. We can discuss it then."

Harper hesitated. She heard water in the background.

"All right. Breakfast, then."

* * *

At J. Christopher's, Harper and Olivia sat at a table on the patio, looking over the menu. Harper settled on a stack of blueberry crushcake.

After they ordered, Olivia asked about the package. Harper removed it from her messenger bag.

"This is it," Harper said, passing it across the table.

Olivia accepted it with narrow eyes. "Curious."

"And, on the way here, I remembered something he said before he walked away," Harper began. She sipped her orange juice. "He said 'I made my choice. Now it's up to you.'"

Olivia regarded Harper through her eyelids. "I'm tempted to tell you to take it to the police. This whole thing is just…odd. But…I want to know what he's hiding."

Harper nodded. "I agree."

Olivia handed the package back to her. "Then open it. Let's see what he has to say."

Chewing on her bottom lip, Harper took the package. She hesitated before opening it.

By then, the food arrived.

When the waitress set the dishes in front of them and walked away, Harper pulled out the contents of the package.

She stared at the faces of young girls, all under the age of eighteen, Notes were attached to each of the photos.

"I recognize some of these girls," Harper said with surprise lacing her words. "I think from the news. They've disappeared. No one knows where they went." She read the first page to herself. "Here, it says a fifteen-year-old went to the mall with her friends. She was separated from them and never heard from again. That was almost two years ago. Last week, a thirteen-year-old was supposed to go home after school, but never showed."

Harper handed Olivia a page.

"Wow," she breathed. "What do you think this means? Is he a private investigator? Was he searching for these girls?"

"I don't know," Harper said. She picked up a photo of a young girl, studied it, then showed it to Olivia. "I know I've definitely seen her. She's from California. I don't know much. Only saw her face. But I remember catching the news at the airport, maybe two weeks ago. The reporter was talking about the girl having a boyfriend. She'd snuck out of her house one night. The authorities questioned the boyfriend but didn't have anything to hold him on."

Olivia said nothing as she continued to study the contents of the package.

Harper frowned, still glancing through the stack of photos.

Haiti. New Jersey.

Brazil. New York. Texas.

Georgia.

"Geez," Harper muttered as her mind spun in many different directions. "None of these girls are older than fifteen. What if this guy's involved with these girls' disappearances? What if he's forcing them to…" Harper trailed off, a knot forming in her stomach.

Olivia eyed her. "What are you saying?"

"I think you know."

"What I'm thinking is I've lost my appetite." Olivia frowned into her barely touched food. "What I'm thinking is impossible. It can't be."

Harper fished her phone from her back pocket and ran a search through the girls' names. There were news reports about their disappearances and many conjectures, but so far, no one had any clue where they may have been taken.

Harper set her phone on the table.

"There was something about this guy, Liv. Something was scaring him. What if he was somehow involved in taking these girls and selling them off?"

Olivia chewed on her lower lip. "Harp. Maybe this Daniel guy really was nervous about a meeting. It could be many things. I wouldn't worry about it too much."

"But these girls," Harper protested. "No one knows where they are."

"What are you going to do about it?" Olivia wondered. "I mean, you don't know where to find *this* guy. You don't know who these girls are. You're a flight attendant, not a cop." Olivia paused, her eyes clouded with sadness. "You can't save everyone, Harp. What you should do is take it to the lost and found at the airport. If the package is important to him, he'll be looking for it."

"Then he would call me back, right?"

Olivia let her shoulder rise and fall. "What I think is we're both tired. We've been going back and forth across the states for over a month. We're jet-lagged. You spoke to some nervous guy who probably hates flying. He may be a reporter. A private investigator. Who knows? This isn't something *you* need to worry about."

Harper's lips turned to a frown. "I guess you're right. I'll give him one more call, then I'll take it to the lost and found."

She watched as Olivia picked up a strip of bacon and bit off a piece. Harper lost her appetite, but to mask it, she saturated her breakfast with maple syrup.

As hard as she tried, Harper couldn't push the feeling that there was something more to the contents of the package.

She had to find out what it was.

She had to find Daniel Clark.

Four

"To what do I owe this pleasure?"

Harper stepped inside Jonathan Parker's hotel room when he opened the door wide. She glanced around at the messy area before answering, her eyes examining the clothes strewn about. When her eyes met his, she released a sigh.

"Sorry to bother you, John," she began.

He put a hand on her shoulder and smiled.

"You can bother me anytime you'd like," he assured her. Jonathan leaned close to her, kissing her forehead. "Anytime."

Before she had the chance to protest, he took her lips to his and brought her in for a deep kiss. She allowed his tongue to search hers before pulling away.

"C'mon, Harper, don't be like that."

Harper stepped back, crossing her arms over her chest, narrowing her eyes. "You think for a second I'm going to allow you to sweep me off my feet after what you did?"

"Harper, Harper," Jonathan teased. "That's what you always say. Somehow you always seem to end up in my bed."

She plastered a fake smile on her face. "True. But that was before I found *you* in someone *else's* bed."

Jonathan frowned as he made his way for the mini-fridge. He took out an opened bottle of beer and set it on the counter.

"I hope you've managed to remove that coffee stain from your shirt," she continued, "It's not befitting a pilot with a dirty uniform."

"That's over now," he protested. "It was a one-time thing. I promise you. You're the only one I care for. You know that."

"I know you *say* that, John. But…" Harper hesitated as she avoided his eyes. "I need time to think things through, okay? Even then, I wasn't ready for a relationship. You knew that from the start. Right now, I think the best course of action for me is to take a step back."

Jonathan cleared his throat and took a sip. The room fell into a cold, uncomfortable silence.

"So, if you're not here to forgive me, then what can I do for you?"

Harper moved to sit at the kitchen table, reminding herself she hadn't come to fight.

"You remember that passenger from the flight?"

"Yeah, the nervous bloke? What about him?"

"Did he tell you where he was going? Where his meeting would be held? I need to find him."

Jonathan narrowed his eyes. He studied her, setting his beer on the counter. "Why?"

"Because he dropped a package. It seemed important to him. I'd like to give it back to him."

"Take it to the airport lost and found. That's where he'll go if he looks for it."

"Well, I kind of wanted to talk to him," Harper admitted. "The contents in the package are…strange…considering my conversation with him."

Jonathan grabbed his beer moved to sit in the chair across from her.

"You looked inside?"

She nodded. "I was hoping to find more about him, so I can locate him."

"Did you?"

She wavered her head to say she didn't.

"What was in this package?"

"A few photos of young girls. And notes about them."

"Curious," Jonathan said. "That's a bit odd, don't you think? Do you have them with you?"

"Yeah." Harper reached inside her messenger bag and pulled the package out, passing it to him.

She waited as Jonathan removed the contents and studied each page, his brow knitting together.

"Why did he give it to you, I wonder?"

"Not sure. I spoke to him after we got off the plane and when I got home, I found it in my bag. I called the airline. They said his name's Daniel Clark. I have the phone number he used to purchase his ticket. I tried calling and left him messages, but he hasn't gotten back with me. I was hoping he told you why he was coming to Atlanta, you know, since you spoke to him on the plane."

Jonathan shook his head. "Sorry, he didn't say anything other than he was here on business."

Harper pushed out a breath as she replaced the papers inside the envelope. "I thought it was a longshot. Thanks anyway."

She reached her hands out for the photos.

"I can take it to the lost and found if you'd like," Jonathan offered.

"That's okay," Harper said. "I can do it. I'm going to give him a few more chances to contact me."

Jonathan nodded slowly. "Okay, as you wish."

He handed her the photos, brushing his hand against hers, creating a jolt of electricity. She tried to mask it as she rose.

"When can I see you again?" Jonathan said, touching her arm.

Harper gazed at him, hating herself for wanting to be near to him. She reminded herself Jonathan was not the kind of man she wanted to be with, but, still, his charismatic smile seemed to make her knees weak.

"It's not a good idea," she told him. "I'm sorry."

"Harp…what happened…"

"Was my fault," she whispered. "I knew better than to trust you. I can't allow myself to fall into that trap again."

Jonathan shook his head. "You can't run from all men for the rest of your life, Harper."

"I have to go. I'm sorry. Thank you for your time."

Without waiting for a response, Harper left the hotel room.

She tried to ignore the twinge in her heart as she walked, but the more she tried, the more she thought about it.

At her car, Harper hit the hood with the heel of her hand with a curse. She ran a hand through her hair before climbing behind the wheel.

She used her cell phone to search for Daniel Clark's name on the internet, only to receive more results than she wanted. Harper added "reporter, New York" to the search and found what she was looking for.

Daniel Clark wrote several human rights articles for the *New York Times*. She found a photo of the same, nervous-looking man she met at the airport. However, in the picture, he was erect with confidence, rather than fear.

She found the "contact me" page and dialed the number. Her finger lingered over the "send" button. Her heart seemed to thrum in her chest and her hands felt clammy. Wondering if she should do what was suggested and drop the envelope off at lost and found, an image of one of the young girls flashed across her mind.

"Harper, you're insane," she whispered to herself. She realized it was possible whoever she spoke to probably wouldn't give her Daniel's whereabouts, especially if he was one of those undercover reporters. Harper said a silent prayer and pressed "send."

"*New York Times*, this is Brenda, how can I help you?"

"Uh, yes," Harper stammered. "My name's Harper Matthews. I was inquiring about a reporter for *The Times*. His name's Daniel Clark. May I speak to him?"

"Daniel's not in at the moment," Brenda answered. "He's away on assignment."

"Mr. Clark and I were supposed to meet this afternoon," Harper lied. "However, I'm afraid to say he didn't. I tried calling his voicemail but had to leave a few messages. Have you by any chance heard from him? Has he mentioned changing his mind?"

Brenda hesitated before replying. "What is this regarding?"

"I'm afraid I cannot disclose that information," Harper said, biting her bottom lip. "Mr. Clark was adamant that I don't say anything. I have a package for him. A very important package I must give him. However, Mr. Clark seems to have vanished."

"I see," Brenda said, slowly.

"If you can tell me what hotel he's staying at, I can leave it for him at the front desk. He can decide whether or not to make contact."

"I don't know, Miss Matthews," Brenda said. "I'm not sure I'm allowed to give out his information without verifying who you are. Is there anyone that can do that?"

"I'm afraid not. For my safety, Mr. Clark suggested I keep my involvement a secret." She paused. "I'm at risk just trying to find him. Please. It's important that I give him this package."

A pause.

"All right," Brenda said with a sigh. "Let me see if I can find his information."

Harper waited until Brenda returned. After she relayed the information, Harper thanked her and ended the call. Satisfied her fib worked and she found Daniel Clark, she steered the car toward the Hilton Atlanta.

Five

Harper rapped her knuckles on the door and waited. When no one answered, she knocked again.

She was about to leave, feeling discouraged when a voice on the other side of the door inquired who was calling.

"Uh, Harper Matthews," she said.

"Who?"

"Harper Matthews. We met on the plane last night."

"We did?"

"Yes. I'm the flight attendant."

A second later, the door opened a crack.

Harper saw only parts of Daniel Clark's face. His sandy brown hair was out of sorts, his eyes glassy and bloodshot. She could tell if he managed to sleep at all, it wasn't very restful.

"What are you doing here?"

"You're a tough man to track down, Mr. Clark," Harper told him.

"Obviously not tough enough. Why are you here?"

She fished the package from her messenger bag. "You accidentally left this with me. I thought you might want it back."

Daniel neither took the package nor did he open the door.

"That's not mine. But thank you for your trouble."

He made to shut the door when Harper jammed her feet in the doorframe.

"Wait. A minute, Mr. Clark. What's going on with you? Ever since we met, you've seemed strange. Not the usual kind of strange. Are you in trouble?"

"No," Daniel said, his tone laced with annoyance and uncertainty.

"Are you into something illegal?"

"No." His tone sounded genuinely appalled at the suggestion. "Of course not."

"Then what is this?" she pressed, stuffing the envelope in his face.

He didn't respond.

"Look, I went through a lot of trouble in finding you to return this package. I think I deserve to know what it is. Who are these kids? Do they mean something to you? Did you kidnap them?" She released a gasp. "You killed them, didn't you? What, do you have a sick fan—."

"I'm sorry to have troubled you," Daniel interrupted. "It was a mistake. That's all."

Before Harper could react, he snatched the package from her hand and slammed the door.

"Hey!" Harper exclaimed, banging on the door with her palm. "Open the door right now before I call the cops!"

When Daniel didn't respond, Harper cursed him and hit the door once more before walking away in a huff.

Stabbing her index finger against the elevator button, she waited for the door to slide open. Stepping inside, she chose the lobby button and waited until the elevator began to move before slumping against the wall. Mired with frustration, Harper tried to forget Daniel Clark as she stepped outside the hotel.

She hesitated before making her way through the parking lot to her car. A part of her wanted to return to Daniel's room and insist he explain what was going on. Another part told her she needed to stay out of it. Whatever he was involved in, she wanted no part.

When the sane part of the war waging in her mind won, she began to walk until a shout came from behind.

"Miss Matthews!"

Harper turned to see Daniel jogging after her.

"Look, I'm sorry," he told her as he neared. "I shouldn't have gotten you involved."

"I'd appreciate it if you wouldn't be so cryptic with me, Mr. Clark. If you're in trouble, I'd be happy to help you in whatever way I can. Unless, of course, it's illegal, then I will go my way."

"I know," he replied. "Call me Daniel."

He extended his hand, and with hesitation, she said, "Did you do something to those girls?"

He shook his head. "No."

She finally accepted his still-outstretched hand. "Harper."

"I'm sorry," Daniel reiterated. "I think I better explain everything. And after you hear what I have to say, I'll let you decide." He released a heavy breath. "Let's go back to my hotel room."

Harper shook her head firmly. "Uh-huh. Not a chance. For all I know, you'll kill me to keep me from talking to the cops."

"Fair enough," Daniel said. "I'm a journalist...I only wanted to bring to light an issue, but the closer I've come to the truth, the worse it became for me. What I've found led me to Atlanta. And, so, I came. Even though it meant putting the lives of the ones I love around me in danger."

"Go on," she urged when he stopped talking.

"On the plane, I was having second thoughts on what I should do. It didn't matter what choice I'd make, nothing good would come out of it."

She felt a chill encase her as she remembered the unnerving question Daniel had asked her.

Have you ever had to make a choice...one where the answer is always wrong?

She cleared her throat. "Did you decide?"

He nodded. "I decided if I don't speak out, then who will? It's not an issue people are willing to discuss. Those involved are either killed or they do the killing. There is no in between. It's not a pretty world and not enough people are doing anything about it."

"What about the police? Can't you tell them without risking your life?"

"I tried. They wouldn't help. I don't think can trust them enough anyway." Daniel rubbed the back of his neck, looking around them.

"You gave me the package," she reminded him. "Why?"

Daniel's eyes moved to the ground. "I was desperate. I needed a new way in. But, after I walked away, I started wondering if I did the right thing. You're not a cop. You aren't even a reporter. You're a flight attendant. And I was going to ask a complete stranger to risk her life? What kind of person does that make me?"

Harper continued to watch him, unsure whether to stay or go. She considered the photos of the young girls in Daniel's envelope. The missing girls. They were the key to whatever frightened Daniel. They were defenseless. They needed someone to speak for them.

"It has to do with the girls in that package, doesn't it?" she asked. She stepped closer to him, her voice above a whisper. "They're being trafficked, aren't they?"

Before Daniel could respond, screams erupted in the air surrounding them.

Loud, loud noises sounding like cars backfiring swallowed the screaming.

People in each direction dove for cover, men protecting the women and children.

Harper fell to the ground and felt someone tug at her.

Daniel.

His mouth was moving. He was saying something.

Run!

Scrambling along the ground, Harper found safety inside the hotel lobby.

A mother hid behind a sofa, the entirety of her body covering two young boys.

A young man fell back against the lobby doors, his eyes wide, chest unmoving. Blood oozed from his chest. The tears of a little girl standing next to the fallen man caught Harper's attention. Without thinking, she rushed to the girl's side, grabbing her arm to pull her out of harm's way.

As she did, a bullet grazed Harper's shoulder, but she held the little girl's head against her chest for the child's comfort, as much as her own.

Almost as soon as the fiasco began, it ended.

A harsh silence filled the air, and Harper looked around for a sign of Daniel. He was nowhere to be seen.

"Are you okay?" she asked the child, peering into her fearful eyes.

The girl didn't answer, only cried harder, her blonde pigtails falling into her mouth.

"Call nine-one-one!" a faint voice called from outside. "Somebody help!"

Feeling her blood pulsing in her ears, and her heart hammering against her ribcage, Harper passed the child to a nearby hotel employee.

"Stay here. Take care of her. I'm going to check outside."

The elderly man, eyes clouded with fear, nodded and set the child in her lap. Despite his own needs, he consoled her.

Once Harper realized she could stand, she peered outside the lobby doors. A crowd of people scattered around the entrance.

"Did anyone call the police?"

"What just happened?"

A sick feeling erupted in Harper as she stepped outside the lobby. She pushed through the crowd, scanning the fallen people.

Then she saw him.

"Daniel!"

Harper pushed between a man and a woman, falling to her knees. She grasped Daniel's hand in hers.

His chest gushed blood, riddled with bullet holes. His breath short and shallow came out in choking gasps. He coughed up more blood.

"Hang in there, Daniel," Harper told him. "Please. The ambulance will get here soon. Just hold on."

"P-please. S-save her."

"Who?"

"P-p…" Daniel couldn't finish his words. He released one more bloodied cough before his chest stopped heaving.

"Daniel?" Harper said. "Don't do this to me. Daniel!"

His eyes rolled to the sky, remaining open. Empty.

He was gone.

Six

"Harper!" Ollie came running to her. "Are you all right?"

Without answering, she reached her arms out to hug him tight. She let loose the tears she'd kept bottled up.

When she finally pulled free, she regarded Ollie's face, his forehead crested with concern.

"He's dead, Ollie. He's dead."

"Who? What happened? Harper, what are you doing here?"

Harper wiped her eyes free of the tears before answering. She took his hand and pulled him away from earshot of people nearby.

"Daniel Clark was the man from the airplane. The man who dropped the package in my bag. He was a reporter working on a story. He was about to tell me everything when someone shot the place up."

Ollie released a curse and attempted to pull her away from the scene. "Come on. I'm taking you home. We'll get your car later."

"No, wait, Ollie, please."

When he faced her, she glanced toward the hotel lobby and then at him.

"Before the ambulance came, I took his key card. I want to go to his room and find that package. And anything else he was working on."

"What?" Ollie gasped. "Are you insane? If whatever he was talking about was what got him killed, then it could happen to you if you get involved."

"Whatever is going on meant a lot to him. He was trying to uncover something. I think it has to do with trafficking children."

Ollie's eyebrow rose before he ran his hand over his face.

"This is crazy, Harp. You almost got killed. You aren't thinking straight. Let me take you home. This does *not* concern you."

Harper shook her head with determination.

"No, Ollie. I have to do something."

"Fine," he retorted. "Just tell the police what you know. Let them sort it out. It's not worth your life."

Harper shook her head. "I can't do that, Ollie. Okay? You've got to trust me on this. Daniel didn't trust the cops. Maybe I shouldn't either."

"Not trust the cops? Harp, you knew this guy for all of one night. What makes you think you can trust *him*?"

She paused a beat.

"It's this feeling I have."

"Really?" Ollie spat. "This isn't the same feeling you had when you started sleeping with Jonathan Parker, is it?"

Harper glared at her friend, then cursed him before walking away.

With the police busy collecting statements, Harper slipped into the building unnoticed. It wasn't until she pressed the button in the elevator that she realized Ollie had followed her.

"I'm sorry, Harp," he said. "It's just when you called me about what happened, I was worried."

"I know," Harper said. "I'm sorry I worried you. I just can't let this go. These are kids. If their lives are really in danger, I need to do something to help."

"Like what?"

She remained silent, unsure of what to tell him.

Ollie grabbed her arm and didn't speak until she looked at him.

"Is it really worth dying for?"

"It was to him."

The elevator slid open on the seventh floor. She stepped off, Ollie close behind her.

They walked in silence, and when they reached Daniel's hotel room, she turned to face Ollie.

"About Jonathan…"

Ollie waved his hand as if to erase the slate. "Forget about it. I shouldn't even have said that."

"No, I'm sorry," she muttered. "I really am."

"We're fine," Ollie insisted. "Okay? No matter what, you and I will always be friends. Nothing will ever change that."

She wanted to say more but decided against it. There would be time later.

Harper used the key card to unlock the door, and they stepped inside.

"Whatever you're looking for, we better find it quick," Ollie suggested. "It won't take long before the police come to search his room."

"Right," Harper muttered.

She found the package on the glass coffee table, the faces of several young girls, including a few she hadn't seen before, spread out. She gathered the photos, slipping it back into the manila envelope.

"Is it wise to take anything?"

"He originally gave it to me," Harper reasoned. "He wanted me to have it. So I'm just taking what belongs to me. Do you see anything else?"

Ollie stepped out of the living area, into another room as she searched the kitchen.

She found his cell phone on the coffee table and looked at the screen. It was locked, but she could read the previous message: *Leave Atlanta today, or I will return her in pieces.*

"Hey, Ollie," Harper called. "I've got a message on his cell phone. Someone threatened him. Says they'll 'return her in pieces.' If he doesn't leave Atlanta."

"Who?" Ollie asked, returning to the living room.

"I don't know." Using her phone, she snapped a photo of the screen. "But, he said his investigation was putting the people in his life in danger. And before he died, he asked me to 'save her.' He didn't tell me who, though. Whoever he was investigating must have someone he cared about."

"This is one reason why the cops should handle this," Ollie pointed out. "Can we go? There's nothing here. He doesn't even have a suitcase. Just a carryon and a laptop."

"Anything on the laptop?"

Ollie shook his head. "Password protected."

"Can we take it with us?"

"Are we thieves, now? I think we need to let the cops do their job."

"But…"

"Harp. Whatever this guy was into isn't worth your life. If he wanted to die for it, then more power to him. But you don't know him. You don't know what he was involved with. Why do you have to make it your responsibility?"

With a frown, Harper nodded her agreement. "All right. I guess you're right. Let's go before the cops get here."

"Thank you," he replied with undeniable relief in his sigh. He took Harper's hand and led her into the hallway. "I want you to know I appreciate your valor. You have such a big heart, Harper. You always have. But I don't want anything to happen to you."

"I love you too, Ollie," Harper said. "Thanks for staying with me."

Harper clutched Ollie's hand tight as they passed a group of police officers in the hall. When they reached the elevator and pressed the button for the ground floor, she pushed out a breath.

"You all right, Harp?"

"I'm fine."

"The girls are staying at their friend's house tonight after the party. Want to go out? Have a nice dinner?"

With a smile, she regarded him. "You're relentless. You realize that, right?"

"I prefer to think of it as heart-struck."

She leaned in to kiss his cheek. "The time isn't right, Ollie. Not right now."

He frowned at her. "The time's never right with you. But, somehow the time's always right for creeps like Jonathan Parker. I'm getting the feeling you enjoy having your heart stomped on."

"That isn't fair."

"It may not be fair," Ollie said as the elevator doors slid open, "but it's the truth. One day you'll come to me, realizing you could have had it all. Only I won't be around."

Harper remained silent as she watched Ollie walk away.

"I already realize that," she muttered.

She stepped outside and pushed through the crowd when her cell phone pinged.

Harper fished it out of her back pocket to look at the text: *Can we meet?*

Frozen in place, Harper replied: *Who is this?*

The three dots on the phone indicated the sender was typing out a response.

We have a mutual friend: Daniel Clark.

What about Daniel?

Meet me at Woodruff Park in one hour.

Not until you tell me what's going on.

I know what Daniel was working on. I know he contacted you. We were working together. If you want to help, come to Woodruff Park.

Harper frowned at the message. Who was texting her? And why? Should she go to the park? After a brief consideration, she decided it was safe enough. It wouldn't take too long for the park to get busy even though it was in the middle of the workweek.

How will I know how to find you?

Three dots appeared, and then: *I'll find you.*

Seven

Harper walked along the trail, keeping her eyes open for a sign of the text sender. So far, no one had approached her, and she began to wonder if the person would show. Looking at her watch, she realized it was lunchtime.

She'd give the mysterious texter ten more minutes before she left.

Harper crossed the park to sit at a nearby bench. The shops and restaurants slowly began to spread thick with customers. A teenage girl pushed a double stroller along, the trail, calling after two boys running toward the swing sets. A man and his dog jogged at a steady pace.

She didn't notice a man in a hooded sweatshirt approach. It was only when a shadow fell over her, she realized she had company.

He lowered himself on the bench next to her.

"Thank you for meeting me. I assumed you'd prefer to meet somewhere public."

Harper twisted her body to look at him.

The stranger was older than her, possibly in his late forties. Because of the hood, she couldn't see his hair color, and part of his face was hidden by sunglasses. He had a hint of a goatee underneath his chin, barely hiding the birthmark.

"Who are you?"

"Someone who wants to help. My name isn't important."

"Daniel's dead," Harper said. "He died a little while ago from a shooting at his hotel."

"I know."

"You were there?"

I arrived a few minutes before the shooting. "I saw him talking to you. I assume he told you what he was working on?"

"Not exactly," Harper said with hesitation. "He started to. Most of what I know are assumptions."

"Such as?"

"He has pictures of young girls. He's been investigating them because they've disappeared. Someone kidnapped them or something."

"You aren't far off."

"What is happening with them?"

He paused a beat. "I think you know."

"Tell me."

"Come with me. I don't want to discuss this here."

"Where? Why should I trust you?"

"You'd be wise not to," he admitted. "The fact is, in this business, anybody can be involved. Even that friend of yours. The one who went back into the hotel with you after the shooting."

"Ollie? What does he have to do with anything? He knows even less than I do."

"This is a business that makes billions of dollars. Like I said, anyone can be involved. Including those close to you…your friends, your neighbors…anyone. And they will stop at nothing to be sure their money will keep coming. Even kill."

"I don't understand," Harper said.

"If you come with me," he said, "I'll tell you everything you want to know."

"Why me? What makes me so special?"

"Daniel. He was a good judge of people. He could see you are a smart, strong, resilient woman. He didn't trust too easily. But he felt drawn to you. Like you'd help."

"Before I go anywhere with you, I want you to give me a reason why I should trust *you*."

"I suppose I can tell you a little, then explain in detail later. Those young girls in the pictures weren't just kidnapped. They've been trafficked. Do you know anything about that? What happens to the victims?"

"A little," Harper said. "I'm ashamed to say not much."

"Many people don't. Many people prefer to believe trafficking happens only in third world countries. But, the truth is, there are places everywhere in the world where women and children are trafficked. Even boys and men, but it's usually the females. And it happens here, in the United States. Daniel was investigating a few men who are involved in a trafficking ring. It brought him to Atlanta, the man he was looking into."

"Who was it?"

"I don't know. Daniel never told me."

"What do you have to do with all this?"

He hesitated before continuing.

"Daniel's sister was trafficked. I was the one who contacted him."

Harper rose and stood face to face with the stranger. "You contacted him? Why?"

"She asked me to."

"You've seen her?"

"Come with me. I promise you'll understand everything."

"Understand?" Harper released an uneasy laugh. "How can I understand a thing like this?"

"I'll rephrase. Things will become clearer."

Harper hesitated. "At least tell me your name."

"Craig."

"Where are we going, Craig?"

"We need to go somewhere with privacy. You can follow me to my home. Let's get going. I'm afraid too much time has already been wasted."

"I haven't said I would help you."

"No, you haven't," he agreed. "But you wouldn't be here talking to me now if you didn't want to help."

Without saying more, he walked away. Harper watched him before she followed.

Eight

Harper contemplated calling Ollie to tell him what had transpired, but she decided against it. He was probably still upset with her and she didn't want to pour salt into the wound. Her next choice would be to talk to Olivia. After she pulled into Craig's driveway, she texted her friend to let her know where she was, and Craig's address. She ended the message promising to call her in an hour with details.

Harper climbed out of the car and met Craig at his front door. He unlocked it and allowed her in before him. He offered her a drink, which she declined.

It didn't take her long to learn who Craig was.

"You're a cop," she said, staring into a photo of him holding a plaque with two other men in dress blues.

"Yes," he said as he booted his computer. "I'm actually an undercover cop. I met Daniel's sister at a brothel two weeks ago. I went in there under a guise. Daniel's sister, Adaline, was the one assigned to me. It was obvious the child was frightened. But, she would do what was told of her. If she didn't, she'd be severely punished."

"How? They'd beat them?"

"Yes," Craig replied. "And sometimes, they'd rape those unwilling over and over until they've been broken in. That's the fear factor. And they control them through drug use. Many of these girls come already vulnerable. They use mental manipulation to keep them in line. Adaline was trafficked only because Daniel asked questions to the wrong guy. She was taken more as a warning for him to back off."

"Geez," Harper said. "How old is she?"

"Twelve."

"You're kidding!"

"Unfortunately, I'm not. The ages of these girls range from thirteen to seventeen. However, there are also quite a few older women who fall victim. The ones involved learn pretty quickly who to target."

"So, who are these people?"

"I don't know. That's the problem. The ones involved could be someone you see every day. Someone you work with. Go to movies with.

They could be a teacher. Your dentist. It's like a serial killer. They're normal, day-to-day people. You never truly know a person."

"That's sick."

Craig nodded. "I agree."

"How does it work? Once these kids are stolen?"

"There are brothels everywhere. Some are dumps, some have Jags sitting in front of large houses. When the buyers go to the girls, it's called an in-call. Sometimes the girls are taken to the buyer. When a girl is bought, they're forced to do whatever is requested of them. If they don't, they'll have to face the consequences."

Harper swallowed hard, her throat feeling dry.

"Every day, they must meet a price quota set by the trafficker."

"I think I'll take that drink now." She walked to the refrigerator and pulled out a bottled water and wet her throat with several large gulps. She cleared her throat and wiped her mouth.

"The worse part is sometimes the cops tend to arrest the wrong people. They arrest the girls and women for prostitution rather than their johns."

"Even if they're underage?" Harper gaped.

"If they're underage, the johns will go to jail, but they tend to not stay there for long."

"That's not right."

"Again, I agree with you."

"How can it be so easy for strangers to walk up to you and convince you to do something you wouldn't normally do?"

"You did," Craig pointed out.

Harper opened her mouth for a rebuttal, then realized he was right.

"Point taken."

"But, in all honesty, it *is* easy. Scary easy. These guys are pros. They know who to target. You wouldn't try to sell a credit card to someone with no credit. For the credit card companies, they're too much of a risk not paying back what they've borrowed. The favorites and low-risks are the ones with low self-esteem, the ones who have no one to love them…outcasts. All anyone wants is to be accepted. You try convincing a fourteen-year-old with a distorted self-image she has a model face.

She's not sure about it, but you give her a business card and urge her to give you a try. If they go, the fake photographer will start by being subtle. Gentle. Next thing you know, this girl is posing naked because she thinks that's what it takes to be a model."

"What can *we* do about it?"

Craig regarded her.

"I'm not sure if you'll be up for it, but it's the best course of action. It's very dangerous. It was Daniel's idea, actually. I was against it at first, but eventually, he convinced me. However, he couldn't do it. They knew who he was. I'm deep undercover, but it's going to be a long stretch to bring the whole operation down in one fell sweep."

"I still don't know what you need me to do."

Craig frowned with hesitation. He turned to the computer screen to look at the photos of the young girls. He shut off the monitor with a sigh and turned back to face her.

"I could put you on the inside."

The water bottle slipped through Harper's fingers and clattered to the floor.

"What did you just say?"

"Before you say no, let me assure you I'm wholly trusted by the ones involved. I'll be there to protect you. Okay? I won't let anything happen to you."

"You're asking me to willingly go in there and let men take advantage of me? That won't work. There are rules about putting civilians in any kind of situation. Especially this."

Craig watched her, searching her eyes.

"But you're not just any civilian, are you?"

Harper's eyes grew and she took a step back. "Wh-what?"

Craig removed a folder next to the computer monitor and opened it. "Harper Matthews. Age twenty-five, been a cop for some years. Took classes in going undercover. She's an expert marksman, a black belt." He set the folder down, looking up at her. "Why'd you leave the force?"

Harper pulled in a shaky breath. "I grew up with violence, got into a career with violence just because I wanted it to stop. It never did. I don't know that it ever will."

"Maybe not," Craig agreed. "However, it's becoming increasingly more difficult knowing who to trust."

Craig let his words sink in as he rose and made his way to the fridge.

"What are the odds that a journalist investigating a human trafficking ring getting on the very flight an ex-cop is attending? Slim, right? He knew he was in over his head. He also knew when you were a cop, you were good at what you did."

"I haven't been a cop for years. I'm out of touch."

"Then you'll get back in. Because that's what you are. Daniel saw it. And I see it now."

Without answering right away, she knelt to retrieve the water bottle from the floor. Using the kitchen towel hanging on the sink, she mopped up the small spill.

"What I'm asking you is to go in there and play the part. I will request you be mine and no one else's. They won't touch you."

"How do you know?"

He remained quiet for a few minutes.

Harper could hear the clock ticking on the wall.

"Like I said. It'll be dangerous. I won't force you to go in there against your will. I will do everything to make sure you aren't harmed. I think this is the best way we can bring down a small part of a larger ring."

"I'm not sure I like this idea."

"I completely understand. That's why I was against it at first. It's not an easy task to take over. Listen, why don't you sleep on it tonight? Take a few days if you need it. I want you to go in this knowing everything you need to know. I want you to decide without hesitation."

"Okay," Harper said after a long pause. "I'll think on it."

"One more thing."

She eyed him.

"You can't tell anybody about this. Not even your friend who was with you at Daniel's apartment. You can't tell anyone. It'll keep you and the people around you safe. They must not know."

"I won't." She glanced at the door. "I think I should go."

"Here's my number," Craig said as he scribbled on a scrap piece of paper. "Call me day or night for anything you need to help make your decision."

"Thanks." Harper accepted the paper. "Guess I'll be talking to you soon."

Nine

"You're going to *what*?"

Olivia had begun making coffee when Harper filled her in about her meeting with Craig. The coffee grounds spilled onto the floor when Olivia spun to gape at her friend.

"I know," Harper said. "Crazy, right?"

"Try *insane*. This seems fishy, Harp. You're not actually thinking about doing this, are you?"

Harper let her shoulders rise and fall in a shrug as she knelt to clean the coffee mess.

"You are, aren't you?" Olivia demanded. "This is so like you. The moment someone is in trouble, you can't help but fly in on your silver white horse to save the day."

Harper dumped the grounds into the trash with a sigh.

"It's just those girls are so young. They're vulnerable. And Daniel's sister is among them. How can I walk away? All I've ever wanted was to change things in this world. What if I can actually help these people?"

"Are you sure about this?" Olivia asked. She put her hands on Harper's shoulders. "Are you absolutely sure? I don't know a lot about what happens behind the scenes. Yes, I know it happens, but I'm still clueless. What I do know, Harp, is this is dangerous. *Very* dangerous. Are you willing to put your life on the line for people you don't even know?"

"Men and women do it every day," Harper said, her voice above a whisper. "They're fighting for our freedom outside this country as we speak. What about the freedom of the people in *this* country? What about protecting the innocence of children who don't have a voice. Daniel risked everything. Even the life his own sister. And he died trying to get to the truth of this. And his sister is still with those…*people*."

"You don't have to convince me, Harp," Olivia said. "No matter what I say, when you have your mindset on something, you have to see it through. You've got such a big heart. I wouldn't want to change you for anything."

"That's what Ollie said." Harper busied herself by finishing the coffee.

"It just scares me," Olivia said.

"It does me too," Harper admitted. "But I've spent my youth running away. I can't do that as an adult. I know the risks involved."

"Have you mentioned this to Ollie? What does he have to say?"

Harper scoffed. "I can't tell Ollie. He's mad enough at me as it is. Craig didn't want me to tell anyone about the idea. But I couldn't even think about this without letting someone know what I was planning, in case something went wrong. And Ollie…he'd be so angry at me for meeting a stranger who texted me out of the blue in the first place."

"Yeah, about that," Olivia said from behind Harper. She rested her chin on Harper's shoulder. "Never do that again."

Harper laughed. "Deal."

"Promise you'll stay safe," Olivia said. "I don't want to lose my best friend."

"Don't worry about me, Liv," Harper told her. "I'm a big girl. This is a big decision and I'm not going to give him an answer before I've gone home and thought everything through. Just…don't tell anyone. Okay? That includes Ollie."

"Of course not," Olivia promised.

On the counter, Harper's phone rang, the photo ID revealing Jonathan Parker's face.

"Hey, John," she answered.

"Have you checked the news?" he demanded.

"No, why?"

"That guy from the plane…he's dead. Along with four other people at the Hilton. There were several injuries. You weren't there, were you?"

"I—," Harper stopped short before speaking. If she told Jonathan she was there, she'd have to explain more details than she wanted. "No, of course not. You're saying he's…"

"Dead. Yeah. Thank goodness you weren't there," Jonathan told her. "You could have gotten hurt or worse. I know you were searching for him."

"Yeah, I was," Harper said. She looked into Olivia's eyes as she spoke. "I was, but I decided that it would be next to impossible to find him. So, I…uh…took the package to lost and found."

"Good," Jonathan replied. "I'm glad to hear that. I'm also pleased you're safe."

"Me too," Harper agreed. "I'm sorry about Daniel, though."

"Yeah," Jonathan said. "Okay, well I just wanted to check in with you and be sure you're all right. I have to go now."

"I'm fine, John. Thanks for caring."

Harper ended the call and leaned against the counter. She accepted the coffee mug Olivia handed her.

"I hate lying."

"What's going on between you and Jonathan, anyway?" Olivia asked.

Harper raised her shoulders, then took a small sip. "Nothing much."

From the look Olivia gave her, Harper could tell she didn't believe her.

"We had a little fling," she admitted. "But it didn't take long for him to have a fling with someone else."

"Wow. What a jerk."

"To top it off, I'm afraid I'm ruining every chance I have with Ollie," Harper confided. "He's a wonderful catch. He's been my friend since forever."

Olivia lifted the corner of her lips. "I can tell the poor guy cares deeply for you."

"He once told me he loved only two women in his life. Me and his late wife." Harper blew into her coffee, then sipped. "These days I would just feel like I'm replacing her."

"Have you talked to him about it?"

Harper shook her head.

"Maybe you should. Lay everything out so you're both on the same page. I know you feel the same about him, by the way. I see it in your eyes when you mention his name, so don't try denying it. You deserve happiness, Harper. You've been through a lot in your life. After everything your dad did…you deserve to find someone who can help you rise above that."

Harper paused, not wanting to think about the ordeal she'd been through with her father.

"You're right, I guess."

"Of course, I am."

"I'll talk to him. But, first, I need to sort out this thing with Craig."

Olivia nodded her response and leaned in for a hug.

"Thank you for the talk," Harper said. "I'll keep you updated as much as I can. And I'll tell you what I decide before I do anything. In case something happens, I want someone on the outside to know where I'll be."

"Be sure you do that."

Harper finished her coffee, then left, feeling more apprehensive than before.

Ten

Harper prepared to make a decision by reading information on the internet about human trafficking. She found many websites which assisted in helping victims and watched talk show clips of survivors discussing their ordeal.

She had an idea of how bad it was for the victims, but she had no idea.

The victims are beaten, drugged, starved…the list went on with each website she visited.

A knot grew tighter and tighter in her stomach the more she read or listened. And Craig and Daniel wanted her to help them bring a close to a small part of the trafficking operation.

She couldn't help but wonder, why her? Why did they choose her to risk her life?

But did it really matter?

She'd called Craig several times during the course of her research to ask questions: will they drug her? What exactly would they do?

He promised to protect her the best he could.

The more she learned, the more she wanted to take part in helping the victims.

She refused to sell herself on a lie…she understood the risks involved. Regardless, Daniel's voice echoed through her mind.

If I don't speak out, then who will?

The fact was there were people taking risks in speaking out against human trafficking. But, there weren't enough. Not nearly enough.

Something had to be done to protect the innocent.

Harper closed her laptop and set it to the side. Deep in thought, she scratched behind Collier's ear as he slept next to her.

"When I was little," she said to the Sheltie, "My mother told me taking risks is worth it, especially if it meant saving the lives of others." She pulled in a breath and pushed it out as she gazed at an old photo of her with her mother. Young Harper had a beaming smile spread across her face, pink cotton candy in her hand. In the backdrop was a roller coaster. Her mother knelt behind her daughter, planting a kiss on her cheek. Her eyes shone with excitement and adventure, as they always did. It was one of the last memories she had of her mother. "I think in this case, she wouldn't have needed to think about the risks involved. She would have done it the minute Craig brought it up. What do you think?"

In answer, Collier lifted his head and tilted it to the side with a soft whine.

"I wish I could be more like her. Be brave. But, what I'm considering is terrifying. Anything could happen to me. And I may even be killed. It cost Daniel his life. It even cost his sister's innocence—that is, if she's even still alive. And the saddest part is she's only one of the thousands. If not millions."

Collier barked twice, his tongue rolling out of his mouth.

She got to her feet and walked to where she'd set up her violin station. Harper lowered herself to the chair, picked up the violin and played.

She played the new music she'd performed for Ollie only yesterday.

Had it only been one day since she met Daniel Clark?

It seemed like a lifetime ago.

She ignored the sound of barking.

The music took her to a place where she always felt carefree. A place where her mother was alive, where her dad couldn't get in.

But, as the music continued, her dad did get in. He'd grabbed her by the hair, pushing her in the closet because he was fired from another job. Harper heard the chair scratch along the hardwood floor as he positioned it under the knob. Her mother tried protecting her. Harper couldn't hear what was happening.

Little Harper cowered in the corner of the dark closet, unable to get out, unable to see.

Her breathing stopped, and she began hyperventilating.

She dug her nails into her flesh until she couldn't stand the pain any longer. Harper found the doorknob and tried pushing the door open, but it wouldn't budge.

The yelling hurt her ears.

Always yelling.

But, no, Harper was grown. Her mother was dead, her father, somewhere hidden in the world.

As she played, Harper forced the memory from her mind. She was safe in her apartment.

Then the music stopped.

Harper found herself thrown back inside the closet. She couldn't breathe.

It took her a second that seemed like hours to realize something was covering her head.

She wasn't inside the closet.

Someone had broken into the apartment.

Harper scratched at the plastic preventing her from breathing. Her heart thrummed against her chest as she gasped.

A harsh voice, one she didn't recognize, spoke to her.

"Where is it?"

Harper couldn't speak. She couldn't breathe. She reached further behind her head in hopes to scratch her attacker. He wore gloves and a long sleeve shirt, but she couldn't find skin.

Harper pushed with her feet and together, she and her attacker flew backward to the floor. It was enough for him to lose grip of the plastic that had cut off her breathing.

Harper coughed for air, but not enough would enter her system before her attacker grabbed her again. He pulled at her hair and she felt cold, sharp metal pressing against her throat.

"Where is it?" he demanded, his throat a guttural growl.

"I don't know what you're talking about," she forced. The hot tears fell from the corners of her eyes and her heart drummed in her ears. Her body shook violently and she struggled with a silent prayer.

Please, God, don't let him kill me.

He jerked her head with such force, she felt her tendons tear.

The intruder cursed her, driving the weapon he held a bit further into her neck, enough to break the skin, but not enough to take her life. He demanded the same question.

Who was he? What did he want?

Then, she realized he may be after Daniel's notes.

"C-closet," she stuttered. "I-in my bag."

He pushed her to the floor, his knees on her back. She felt him bind her hands together tightly, then her feet. Finally, she heard his footsteps recede, and minutes later, she heard the door shut.

Harper struggled with her hands, trying to free them to no avail.

She heard Collier bark twice, then the smell of dog breath assaulted her nostrils.

Someone knocked on the door.

Moments later, she heard Ollie's muffled voice calling to her.

"Ollie!" she exclaimed. "Ollie, help!"

The door opened and Ollie appeared. "Harper! What happened?"

He rushed to her side, pulled out his pocketknife and cut through her bindings. Ollie said nothing as she wrapped her arms around his neck, tears streaming down her face.

"It's okay," Ollie whispered in her ear. "You're safe. You're okay."

When Harper could speak, she pulled back to see his face.

"What happened?" Ollie asked, rubbing her tear-stained face with his thumbs.

"I'm not sure," she said, her throat still harsh. "I think he came for that package Daniel gave me."

Ollie cursed under his breath. "I told you it was trouble. Why didn't you just listen to me?"

Harper narrowed her eyes. "What are you doing here, Ollie?"

"What do you mean?"

She pushed to her feet, using a nearby table for support. Harper scanned the room as if looking for something. The only mess as a result of the struggle was the overturned chair at her music station.

She met Ollie's eyes.

The words of Craig burned through her mind.

The ones involved could be someone you see every day.

"Why are you here, Ollie? Did you just attack me?"

"What?" Ollie exclaimed, his mouth falling open. "No, of course not! Why would I want to attack you?"

"I don't know," she spat. "To get that package? To teach me a lesson? I don't know!"

"Will you listen to yourself, Harper?" Ollie demanded. "You're becoming paranoid!"

"Get out. Now. Get out!"

"Harper, I'm trying to—"

"Get. Out. Of. My. Apartment!" Harper jabbed her finger toward the still-open door.

Ollie hesitated before nodding. "All right. If that's what you want. I'm just—"

"Go! Now!" Harper shoved him toward the door. "Out!"

When he was in the hallway, Harper pushed the door shut with force, the framed artwork on the wall rattling.

She locked the knob, turned the deadbolt and slid the chain in place before resting her forehead against the surface. Unable to maintain her balance, she slid to the floor, sobbing.

Eleven

"Do you want anything to eat or drink?" Olivia asked, covering Harper's hand over her own. "Water? Wine? Something stronger?"

Harper shook her head.

"I completely lost it on Ollie, Liv."

"You were scared," Olivia replied. "Considering what you told me, you had every right to be."

"But to accuse one of my closest friends of attacking me?" Harper blinked back a tear. "He may never speak to me again."

"Did you call that Craig guy yet?"

Harper nodded. "While Collier and I drove here, I did. He's now having second thoughts about using me to infiltrate."

"Good," Olivia said with determination. "Whoever attacked you has to be involved."

"What am I supposed to do, Liv?" Harper asked. "Am I supposed to walk away? Daniel died for this. I could have died."

"That's my point," Olivia said. "You could have died. Someone knew you were in possession of vital information that proves these girls are being trafficked. If you go in there, that puts you at even more of a risk."

"But there has got to be a way to bring these people down. I can't let them get away with this, Liv. Not now. Not when someone broke into *my* home and attacked me because of this."

Olivia frowned but didn't protest. "What are you going to do?"

"I'm not sure. I'm going to talk to Craig again tomorrow. We'll figure something out."

They fell into silence, which became disrupted by Collier's barking by the door.

Harper's body jerked and she released a gasp when she realized it was likely nothing. She covered her mouth, afraid she may get sick.

"He probably has to go out," Olivia told her. "I'll take him."

Harper nodded as Olivia rose to get the leash.

"We'll be right back." She knelt to slip the leash on the collar. "Won't we, boy?"

Harper said nothing as her friend led Collier out the door.

She rose to go into the bathroom. The marking from the knife was still visible.

Releasing a gasping sob, she leaned against the sink, allowing her tears to stream down her face.

After seconds passed, Harper stepped to the living room to fish her cell phone out of her messenger bag and call Ollie.

He didn't answer, so she left a message.

"Hey, Ollie," she began. "I wanted to tell you I'm so, so sorry for going off on you like that. If you only knew what I've been thinking about…well…I would say you'd understand how I reacted. But the truth is, you'd be furious with me. And, honestly, I understand that." She paused, blinking back tears. Her voice broke as she continued the message. "I hope you'll forgive me. I'll have to figure a few things out tomorrow. I don't know when or if I'll be able to talk to you again. Give my love to the girls, okay?"

She ended the call and dropped her phone into the bag.

"This is the best dog I've ever known," Olivia announced when she opened the door. "He's so sweet and loving."

"He is," Harper agreed. "Liv, if you don't mind, depending on what happens tomorrow, I may need you to take care of him for a while."

Olivia's lips turned to a frown.

"You realize we're both supposed to fly out in a week, right?"

Harper nodded with a sigh. "I have vacation time I've racked up. I might as well use them."

Olivia shook her head as she released Collier from the chain. "Well, I know I won't be able to change your decision, so be careful, whatever you do."

"I will. I promise."

Twelve

Harper spent the evening and the next day looking more into human trafficking, trying to learn all she could. She also found some of Daniel's articles about normal people like her infiltrated the trafficking ring. She was amazed at her bravery and wondered if she could even come close.

Her memories of her mother were few, but Harper knew she wouldn't have wasted time thinking about it. Her mother would have jumped in headfirst at the mention of others needing help.

Harper decided even if it didn't end completely, at least she could do her part and help end a small part, however small it is.

After her decision was made, she went to visit Craig.

She could tell Craig was relieved to hear her willingness.

He grabbed two bottles of beer and they sat at the kitchen table discussing into detail what they would do.

The plan was simple. At least, Harper told herself as such.

Craig would tie her up and take her to where he worked.

From there, she would build a rapport with the girls. There were a few who dealt with the top men involved. Craig had mentioned he once tried to gather the information they needed, but the girls were too afraid, in part, since Craig was considered one of them, and in part, since they were conditioned to fear anything and everything.

Bringing Harper in would give them a better chance at finding who the top boss was.

Craig no longer asked if Harper was sure about going under. There was no need.

Instead, he went into detail on what she should expect.

He'd do what he could to protect Harper, but there was no guarantee he'd be around every time something happened. Although it had been some time since she'd been a police officer, Harper continued her martial arts training for her own protection. Her short years as a cop was something she didn't like discussing. It only drew up memories she'd prefer to forget. She hadn't even told Olivia.

However, each time she closed her eyes, Harper couldn't keep the images of the girls away. As her mother's child, she'd been bred to help people, and as her father's child, she refused to let anyone destroy her.

The only problem was she wouldn't have a phone, and she wouldn't have access to a weapon.

Craig told her if she needed to make an escape, to do so at night. There would be fewer guards around. Most of the time, the girls would be too weak or too scared to think about an escape, so the doors to their rooms would be unlocked.

There was always a guard in the main room. Getting past him would be the only thing keeping her from freedom.

The alarm to the door would be changed every night, so the guard would have the code inside a book in his pocket.

Get the code, input it, then leave.

Once outside, all Harper needed to do was escape to the nearby gas station where Craig would have a phone waiting for her in the back, behind a dumpster. She'd call the police and tell them everything she knew.

Harper still hadn't heard from Ollie. She didn't like the idea of not making amends with him before going off the radar. She had tried to reach him again but to no avail. Harper decided she'd have to deal with it when, and if, she returned.

"Are you ready for this?" Craig asked, breaking the silence. He sipped his beer.

She regarded him before answering, forcing all thoughts of Ollie from her mind.

"Yes, I think so," she replied.

"Don't forget I will be there with you. I'll do all I can to keep you safe. But, if I'm not around…just trust yourself."

Harper smiled. "I'm still wondering why Daniel chose me. Why you still want me to do this."

"Because you're tough. You're willing to put yourself out of your comfort zone to protect others. When Daniel told me about you, he said he noticed you were afraid about something. He said it wasn't a normal, everyday fear."

"It's an everyday fear if you ask me." Harper released a sigh, took a sip of her drink, then nodded. "He was right."

"What was it?"

She drank again before responding.

"When I was younger, my dad would lock me inside the closet when he was angry. It didn't matter why he was upset. I could spill a drink on the kitchen floor, or he'd lose another job. Anyway, it was small and dark. He made sure of that. There was a light on the ceiling, but he'd removed the bulb. He taped underneath the door in case the room's light was on. He wanted me to be in complete and total darkness."

"That's terrible," Craig said.

Harper nodded. "He'd push me inside, saying he didn't want to look at me. I'd have to stay there until he figured out the best way to punish me. I'd hear him beat my mother. She'd tried to get me out of the closet, but he wouldn't let her. When I was eleven, he'd hit her and she fell. It was several days before anyone found me. The doctors said she'd died instantly from hitting the edge of the dresser."

Harper scratched the back of her head and closed her eyes at the memory.

"It wasn't until I was a freshman in high school I realized I had a fear of enclosed spaces. I'd always been the quiet type. Unfortunately, it didn't make me invisible. I was bullied all the time. Once, as a joke, the cheerleaders pushed me inside my locker. That was when I met Ollie. He saw what they'd done. He got me out, and stayed with me, helping me through my panic attack. We became friends and he urged me to get past my fears. It took years to get the courage. But, I did. At least partly."

"By flying?"

"Yes. After a lot of therapy sessions, I decided I wanted to push myself. I didn't want to live the rest of my life in fear. As it was, I was afraid my father would come back. So, I got a job as a flight attendant. If I'm millions of miles away in the sky, I'd have no choice but to force myself to work on my issue."

"That's very brave. Your mother would be very proud of you."

"I hope so. She's part of the reason I want to do this. My mother was like Mother Theresa to me. She always tried helping people worse off than her. She wouldn't even have needed to think about it. She'd already be undercover."

They slipped into another silence as they sipped their beers.

"When do you want to bring me in?" Harper asked. She glanced out the window and was surprised to see the sun was going down. When she looked back at Craig, she noticed he was doing the same thing.

He took a long swig and set his beer on the table.

"Now."

Thirteen

Harper rode in the back of Craig's car, hands tied behind her back. She didn't mention the rope he used was cutting into her skin, rubbing against the sore from the when the attacker tied her. She decided it needed to be authentic enough, so she ignored the pain it caused.

It took an hour and twenty minutes to arrive at their destination, and she counted every second, preparing herself to lose her freedom. With each passing sign, she'd begun feeling anxious.

When Craig finally pulled into the long driveway of a large house, Harper scanned the area to become familiarized. If she needed to make an escape, she needed to know where she was, and the ideal places to hide.

The house, three stories high, appeared to be a centerfold out of *Country Living*. The four pillars holding the roof above the front porch offered an elegant touch. The grass was neatly cut, its fresh scent reaching Harper's nostrils through the cracked windows.

There were cars scattered along the yard.

Men stood on the porch with mugs in hands, talking amongst each other. As Craig slowed, the men turned their attention toward them.

A young Mexican girl stepped out of the house with a coffee carafe and refilled one man's cup. He leaned over, tapping his finger to his chin. She kissed him before moving to refill the mug of another. He also leaned over for her to kiss.

"Who's that girl?"

"Bonita. She arrived from Tijuana three months ago. She speaks very little English."

"She's so young," Harper muttered. "Is this where it all happens? It's so beautiful. It's hard to believe."

Craig released a grunt. "I'm afraid it's not as glamorous as it appears. This is the grooming house. They'll dress the girls, do their hair, makeup, the works. Basically, they get them ready to be sold. Then once a girl is bought, they'll begin the work. They very often are rotated, never staying in one place for more than a month. It keeps them under the radar."

Craig stopped the car and turned off the ignition, then looked back at Harper.

"Stay here. I'll come around and get you. And keep your head down. If you look at another john, they might stake a claim on you. So, only look at them when I tell you."

She lowered her head as instructed, while Craig climbed out of the car.

"What do we have here?"

Looking up through her lashes, Harper watched as a thin, bald man wearing a black t-shirt lean into the car. The steam from his coffee clung to the window.

"That's a fine piece of—"

His words were cut off when Craig placed a hand on his shoulder.

"That one belongs to me, Rocco. You hear?"

Rocco frowned and straightened himself, puffing out his chest. "What you sellin' her for? I'll buy her right out."

"She ain't for sale. I've seen her with that girl's brother—Adaline. I was going to give her up, but, you know, I decided I wanted her to myself, hear?"

Rocco leaned in to regard her again.

"Hey, honey, you want Rocco to be your new daddy? I be mighty good to you."

With force, Craig pulled Rocco to the ground.

"I said, she's mine." Craig kicked Rocco's stomach before walking around the car. He pulled the door open and grabbed Harper's arm.

"Get out of there, what are you waiting for?"

Harper gasped at the force Craig used on her.

"But you said—"

She stopped short when he slapped her. "I give you permission to speak, huh?"

Before she could answer, he pushed her toward the house.

She fell up the short steps and sharp pain erupted in her knees when she landed on the wood.

"Get up," Craig growled. He pulled her by the arm the rest of the way inside. He scanned the front room. "Where's Juliette?"

"Upstairs," a man sitting in a cushioned chair said. He peered over the top of his newspaper. "Found yourself a new date, Craig?"

"Sure did," Craig sneered. "Pretty little thing, don't you agree? I've seen her talking to that Daniel fella. You know, Adaline's big brother. I decided I had to have her. I'm thinking I'll keep her for a while."

Craig pulled her closed to him.

The man in the chair narrowed his eyes. "Adaline's brother? You sure it's wise to bring her in here?"

Harper bit back a whimper as Craig, nuzzled her ear.

"Why not? This girl's sweet. Sweeter than that sister of his," he continued, "We're gonna head on up the stairs so sweet Juliette can make her all good and pretty for me."

He pushed Harper toward the stairs.

"Bring me a scotch on the rocks, why don't you?"

The man in the chair responded to the statement, but Harper couldn't hear.

"Do you have to grope me?" she hissed.

"If you want it to look real," he replied, his breath hot against her ear. "Juliette! Where are you? I've got some business for you!"

Harper saw a tall, dark-skinned woman appear in a doorway. Her short leather skirt barely covered her hips. She swayed in their direction, a smile on her lips.

Harper kept her eyes lowered, feeling embarrassed to look at even Juliette, wearing a revealing top. It didn't seem to bother Juliette. Harper wondered what her role was.

"And what have we here, darlin'? You tradin' up on me?"

Juliette put a hand on Craig's cheek and leaned into him for a kiss.

"Never, my dear," Craig told her. "This is just a little side project, hear? Unless, of course, I get to have you and all of you to myself."

Juliette tilted her head back, with a smile.

"You keep bringing home new girls, I just might get jealous enough, daddy."

"That's the plan, sweet Juliette." Craig regarded Harper. "Fix her up nice and pretty, why don't you? Then escort her to my room."

"As you wish," Juliette said. "Come along dear. Don't be afraid.

Juliette will fix you up nice and pretty like."

As Juliette led Harper to another room, she looked back, wide-eyed at Craig.

Instead of giving her assurance, he turned and walked in the opposite direction.

"This your first time?"

"Huh, what?"

Juliette motioned for her to sit in the chair.

"It'll be okay, dear. You're in good hands with Craig. He'll take real good care of you long as you don't disobey his rules."

Harper cleared her throat as Juliette ran a comb through her hair.

"Rules?"

"Each john has their own set of rules. If Craig hasn't given you his yet, then he will before long. Just do what he says and you'll be just fine."

"How long have you…been here?" Harper asked as Juliette picked up the curling iron.

"About fifteen years or so."

"Do…do you like it here?"

Juliette said nothing as she wrapped a strand of hair with the curling iron.

"I'll be blunt with you. I like surviving."

"If you don't like being here, why stay? Can't you find out a way to leave?"

"Darling, those types of questions are liable to get you a good whuppin'." She sighed. "My advice to you is to learn to like it here. Because there ain't no gettin' out. Of course, I suppose if you made your quota, then you can ask to leave."

"What's a quota?" Harper searched her mind but realized it was blank. She knew she'd heard the term before. She silently scolded herself. She couldn't keep blanking out on the important details. It was imperative she remember as much as she possibly could if her mission would succeed.

Juliette offered a small smile. "A quota is the amount of money you earn from the Johns."

"What's the quota?"

"It varies."

Harper fell silent, watching as Juliette finished fixing her hair and her makeup. After it was done, she almost didn't recognize herself. Her normal straight blonde hair was now curly, her eyelashes long and dark. Juliette had painted her lips burgundy, her cheeks a soft pink. She now wore black lace undergarments and a half top with dark brown mini-skirt. A chill enveloped her and she struggled not to shiver.

Harper swallowed hard as she took in her reflection. She'd never imagined in her wildest dreams she would wear clothes so revealing.

She felt degraded.

But, of course, that was the point, wasn't it? They needed her to entice the men—or Johns—in order to make money off her.

"You'll get used to it," Juliette assured her, after watching her for a few seconds. "Crying's not going to help you. The best advice I can give you, dear is to toughen up. Come on. I'll deliver you to Craig now."

Harper followed Juliette to Craig's room, walking with her arms covering as much as she could.

At the stairs, they ran into Rocco.

Harper averted her eyes, well aware of his sneer, his eyes ogling her.

"You sure you don't want to come to my room tonight? We'll have a mighty fun time, sweetheart."

Harper ignored him as she ascended the stairs.

Juliette led the way down the hall, knocked twice at the door. A second later, Harper was relieved to see Craig in the frame.

She noticed his eyes skimming her body.

"Y-you do great work, Juliette," he stammered. "As usual."

"Let me know if I can do something else for you, daddy," she replied.

Craig nodded once, pulled Harper inside and shut the door.

"You okay?" he said, his voice soft.

"I will be if you stop looking at me like that," Harper replied, removing her arm from his grasp. "Do I really have to wear this?"

"Here." He walked to his closet, pulled out a dress shirt and passed it to her. "Here."

Harper slipped her arms through the sleeves and began to button the shirt. "This is so demeaning."

"It's only going to get worse," Craig reminded her. "We both have to play the part if we're going to find answers."

Harper nodded, letting him know she understood. She reminded herself that she was doing what was needed to do to help the victims.

"What now?"

"Now, you're going to rest. It's late. I'll get you up in the morning. You'll be able to eat, mingle with the other girls."

Harper scanned the room.

"There's only one bed."

"Are you okay with that?"

"Guess I'll have to be."

Craig put a hand on her shoulder. "Thank you for this. Because of you, Daniel's death won't be in vain."

Harper sat on the edge of the bed, running her hand along the silk comforter.

"Do you know who killed Daniel and those other people at the hotel? Was it a coincidence? Or was he the target?"

Craig wavered his head that he didn't know. "It's on my list of things to find out. These aren't the most trusting people. After all, there's a lot of money involved. It's the root of all evil."

"Right," she muttered.

They fell int a brief silence before Craig broke it with a sigh. "Get some rest."

With a nod, Harper pulled the covers down and climbed inside. She closed her eyes, but she didn't sleep.

Fourteen

The next morning, Craig gave Harper a t-shirt to wear before going downstairs for breakfast. She'd earned little sleep but hoped she'd be able to mask it. She knew her first day at the grooming house was going to be a long one. All night, her mind reeled over the documentaries and survival interviews, and admitted to herself that she was terrified.

Craig pulled Harper by her arm into the dining room where several girls sat in silence around the table, pushing their food around the plate more than eating it.

Craig looked from girl to girl with a blank stare before tilting his head in her direction. "This is Harper. She arrived last night."

Harper recognized the Mexican girl, Bonita, from when she first arrived. She had a swollen lip and a black and blue eye to match.

"Why don't you have a seat, Harper?" Craig continued as if having a friendly conversation. "Have a bite to eat. You'll need your strength. After you've eaten, I want you to wash the dishes."

Harper did what she was told. She watched as Craig left the room, then turned to face the girls and forced a smile.

"Um, hi. I'm…Harper."

The girls blinked at her, then lowered their heads to their plates.

"What are your names?"

"Jenny," the blonde across from her said, her voice above a whisper.

Between Jenny and Bonita sat a redhead named Katie. Another Mexican girl, Maria, sat on one end while Keiko from Japan sat on the other. Next to Harper were Vietnamese girls, Mai and Nghia, and Astrid from Norway.

Harper learned that Astrid had arrived last night, shortly after Harper and Craig.

Mai and Nghia were transferred from Bangkok a year ago. Mai spoke very little English but was able to tell Harper she was stolen from her home during an invasion. She and her mother were raped before they shot both of Mai's parents. They separated her from her older brother before she was sold to a woman running a brothel. It wasn't long until Mai had become considered too old, so Mai was sold to come to the

United States.

"I'm so sorry," Harper told her. "That's so awful. Do you ever get to contact your brother? Is he still alive?"

"They send small money to Chi."

"Do you know where Chi is?"

Mai shook her head.

"What about you, Nghia?" Harper asked.

"She does not know your language," Mai said. "I speak for her. I translate. Her papa sold her…four years ago."

Harper's eyes grew. "You're kidding. How could he possibly do that to his own child?"

"He need money. To pay debt. So he sell her. He sell her sister. They say, once debt is paid, she go home."

"How long until her debt's been paid?"

Mai asked Nghia in Vietnamese. After Nghia responded, Mai frowned and regarded Harper, her eyes clouded.

"Nghia say debt paid three weeks ago."

Harper blinked. "Three weeks? Why is she still here, then? Doesn't her dad want her?"

"They make promises," a voice from behind said. "But that doesn't mean they'll follow through."

Harper turned to see Juliette step into the kitchen.

"But, that's not—"

"Fair?" Juliette finished. "Not right? Girl, life ain't fair. And the daddies don't care what's right. If you wanna live, you give them what they want. You do what they want. Don't ask no questions. Don't say 'not tonight.' Then you live. Some even take care of you. Like yo' man. You give Craig good sex, he'll give good life."

"What happens if you protest?" Harper asked. "They'll hit you? Is that what happened to you, Bonita?"

Bonita shook her head, but Harper wasn't sure if it was an answer, or if Bonita couldn't understand her.

"Rocco got rough with her last night," Maria explained. "He wasn't in a good mood."

"I'm sorry, Bonita." Harper frowned. "I'm sorry about all of you.

Girls everywhere."

"Who are you?" Juliette asked. "Rich dame who thinks you owe your sympathy to us? You think you better?"

"N-n-no, that's not what I'm saying at all."

"Like I told you last night, baby girl," Juliette said. She grabbed a toast from Kelly's plate and bit into it. "You get used to it."

"Do you know who is in charge?"

They all shook their heads in answer.

"We call him The Ghost," Katie said. "Even the daddies don't know who he is. The Ghost never comes on the property."

"That ain't exactly true," Juliette said. She leaned against the counter, inspecting her long fingernails. "He came by yesterday to get Adaline."

"A-a-adaline?" Harper stammered. "The Ghost has her?"

"Sure does," Juliette confirmed. She narrowed her eyes at Harper. "You know Adaline?"

"No, no, I don't," Harper said quickly. "But I do know her brother…knew…her brother. Daniel."

"Really? I heard about good old Danny boy," Juliette said.

"He's dead. He died the other afternoon. Some men shot up his hotel."

"Really? Shame," Juliette said. "Guess Adaline's big brother can't save her after all."

"Daniel was trying to find her," Harper insisted. "Where do you think The Ghost would take Adaline?"

Juliette scoffed. "Where would he take her? You planning on finding her? You going to take good ol' Danny boy's baby sister from The Ghost? You dreamin' baby girl."

"She doesn't deserve to be treated like an object!" Harper hissed. She glanced at the girls sitting around the table. "None of you do."

"And what do you think you're going to do about that, baby girl?" Juliette scoffed. She stepped around the table and leaned in close to Harper. Harper could feel Juliette's hot breath on her neck. She smelled the strong scent of cheap perfume. "You gonna save all of us? You? You just got here last night, and you decided you're going to play savior?"

With a swallow, Harper glanced at the table. The girls hung their heads, avoiding her eyes, eating in silence.

"Don't you want to leave, Juliette?" Harper glanced back at her. "Look at them. They're only kids. Keiko's gotta be…what…thirteen? Nghia and Bonita can't be more than seventeen or eighteen themselves. All of them, yourself included, are forced to sleep with more than one man every day and night. How can you be used to it?"

"I love how rich newcomers think they can waltz in here and then waltz outta here when they feel like it," Juliette said, a smirk on her lips. "Don't worry, baby girl. Keep that attitude, and you'll find your place soon enough."

With that, Juliette sauntered out of the room. Harper could hear her voice carry down the hall, "Hey, Rocco, baby. Wanna get some lovin…"

Fifteen

"Line up!" Rocco's voice boomed.

"What's going on?" Harper asked Katie.

"It's time for the men to choose who they want for the hour. We must hurry. If we don't do what they say, they punish us."

Harper turned on the sink as if she was in the middle of washing the dishes and waited a few seconds before she walked to the entranceway. She had a good view of the living room, so she wanted to observe the scene.

As the girls lined up, four men entered the room. One went straight to Nghia and took her hand, leading her up the stairs. Another studied Katie and Jenny before settling on Katie.

Harper watched as Katie went with the man without protest. Before she disappeared up the stairs, Harper caught Katie's eyes, laced with fear and pain, the youthfulness that was once there gone.

Harper's attention was diverted to a man wearing a business suit. He looked Keiko over, turning her around as if choosing a Rolex.

He glanced in her direction, back at Astrid, then again at Harper. The businessman made his way toward her. Her heart seemed to leap in her chest and she turned, praying Craig would come in and protect her. But she hadn't seen Craig since earlier that morning, after he left her in the kitchen. And now, she was unsure of what to do.

"I want that one." Harper didn't turn around, mostly out of fear. If she understood correctly, she was supposed to belong to Craig—could one of the men just take her?

"She ain't for sale." Rocco's gruff voice rang loud and clear.

"I'll pay double," the businessman offered.

"Sorry. Orders from The Ghost."

Harper willed herself to turn in time to see Rocco grab Keiko's arm, pushing her forward. "Take this. I'll give her to you for half the price."

The businessman considered the offer, then smiled. "You got yourself a deal."

The last man grabbed Astrid by the waist, pressing her against his big belly. "Is this one fresh?"

"Sure is," Rocco sneered. "Ain't never been used, came off the truck last night."

"Please, no," Astrid said, shaking her head. She tried to pull away, but her strength was no match for the john's.

"Come, little lady," he replied, tossing her over his shoulder. "Time to break you in."

Squeezing her buttocks, he left the room, carrying her along with him, her cries floating up the stairs.

"Don't let him do this!" Harper protested to Rocco hurrying for the doorway. "Please!"

He responded with a smile. "Your time will come 'fore you know it. Don't be jealous."

"Please, don't let him hurt her."

"As long as she does what she's here to do, she'll be fine," Rocco said, his words almost drowning from Astrid's screams.

Harper cursed Rocco, who grabbed her neck.

He opened his mouth to say something, then decided against it as he walked away with a whistle.

She remained in the doorway for a good few minutes, trying to control herself. She forced Astrid's screams from her head, only to be shattered with another cry.

Her legs feeling like jelly, Harper moved to sit at the kitchen table, waiting.

Waiting for what, she didn't know.

A part of her wanted to search around for Craig, but another part wanted to be available to check on Nghia, Katie, Astrid, and Keiko.

She remained in the same spot for what seemed like hours. Maybe it was, maybe it was mere seconds. She didn't know, neither did she care. She only prayed a silent prayer for the girls to survive their abuse.

One by one, the girls finally entered the room.

Nghia, dazed, couldn't walk. Harper saw the hand marks on her arms and legs, the fingernail scratches. She asked if she was all right, but Nghia didn't answer. When Mai entered, she devotedly went to sit next to Nghia wrapping her arms protectively around her, speaking in soft Vietnamese.

The kitchen remained in harsh silence, only the faint laughter of men greeting their ears. Their laughter only gave rise to the chill Harper had fought.

Finally, Katie and Keiko entered at the same time.

Katie blinked back her tears and Keiko's body shook.

"Are you okay, Keiko?" Harper asked, her hand on her shoulder. "Katie?"

The girls exchanged glances. "We will be," Keiko whispered. "It will pass."

"Where's Astrid?"

"Still in the room," Katie answered. "I think he left her a little while ago."

Harper jumped from her chair and rushed out of the room, ignoring the calls after her.

It didn't take long for her to find Astrid's room. After a soft knock, she turned the knob, pushing the door open.

"Astrid?"

She found Astrid curled into a ball, sobbing against her pillow. Her clothes had been torn from her, tossed carelessly along the floor.

Harper stepped into the room. "Astrid?"

She put a hand on her shoulder and retreated when Astrid jerked away.

"It's okay." Harper's empty assurance tasted like lead in her mouth. "You're safe now."

She looked at the other girls crowding into the bedroom.

"We're going to find a way out of this. I promise all of you. We will get out."

"How?" Mai asked. "There's no way."

"Just trust me," Harper said. "Can you do that?"

Glancing at one another, they nodded.

"Have any of you seen Craig?"

Before they answered, Rocco appeared in the room.

"He's in the next room. Asking for ya."

Jumping from the bed, Harper ran into the room next to Astrid's, ready to yell, punch him, possibly even strangle him if she could actually get close enough.

But the room was empty.

She turned to see Rocco standing in the doorway.

"Where is he?" she demanded.

He remained silent, his lips curved in a sneer.

When Harper tried to push past him, he grabbed her arm pulling her close to him.

"You don't go anywhere until you give me what I want."

He clamped his hand over her mouth when she tried to scream. He tossed her onto the bed, forcing her head to connect with the headboard. White light exploded in front of her eyes and she fought against the pain.

"Somebody help me!"

Rocco locked the door and turned to face her.

"Stay away from me," she hissed.

Without answering, he began to undo his pant buckle.

"This will go a whole lot better for you if you behave," he told her. Rocco slid his pants down his legs and stepped out of them.

Harper rolled off the bed, toward the window. She tried to open it, but it was locked. She jiggled the window with frustration and fear bubbling inside her. Harper banged her palm against the window, crying out. No one seemed to notice her.

Rocco grabbed her arm and jerked her back onto the bed. He climbed on top of her, forcing her legs apart.

Harper thrashed her arms, but he jammed something sharp in the side of her neck. Within seconds, her limbs began to relax. The room wobbled, and she felt her strength leaving her body. She fought to keep her bearings, but it was a fruitless effort.

He leaned close to her neck, nipping at her skin with his teeth. She felt his hand go between her legs as he kissed her.

She couldn't move. She couldn't cry out.

She couldn't even breathe.

Harper was frozen, her heart beating against her rib cage.

She felt him tear away her lacy underwear. He rubbed against her and Harper heard his soft moans.

"That's it," he whispered against her ear. "That's a good girl. Tell me you like it. Tell me you want…"

His voice faded into the distance.

She closed her eyes, then forced them to reopen, but her eyes closed again. Sound became distorted. Even his touch seemed far away.

It took a second for Harper to register something that sounded like gunfire. A blurred version of Rocco slumped on top of her, pinning her to the bed.

She blinked but didn't move. Her vision was clouded, unstable.

A figure of a tall man stood before her. He put a hand on her face and stroked.

She blinked again but she still couldn't make sense of her surroundings.

"You're okay," the voice whispered. "I've got you."

She recognized the voice but couldn't tell who it was. Was it Craig? Rocco?

"Where were you?" Her voice sounded weak to her ears. "You left me here alone."

"I'm here now."

Harper tried to pull herself from the bed, but her body felt heavy. She heard more distorted voices and saw two men standing in the doorway. A woman stood behind them. Had she seen her before?

"Get rid of Rocco's body," the voice echoed. He held something in his hand as he spoke. She saw a blur move to her neck and then a pinprick. "Take her to the van."

Harper tried to remain awake to see what was happening, but soon, she'd passed out.

Sixteen

Harper woke with a migraine. She heard a loud humming, and the hard surface she laid on moved up and down. She released a moan and gripped her forehead.

"How are you feeling?"

Harper opened her eyes and tried to adjust her vision.

Her heartbeat quickened, and she realized she was in a dark place.

No windows.

No light.

Closed in.

"I have to get out of here." Harper scrambled and felt for a door handle but couldn't find anything. She banged her palm against the metal surface.

"Let me out! Please!" Harper's tears caught in her throat. "I can't breathe! I need air! Please!"

Harper turned to see eyes staring back at her. The darkness swallowed their features.

"Where's Craig? I need to see Craig. Please help me. I can't stay in here!"

Her chest rose in quick successions as the tears spilled from her eyes.

She shook her head and banged on the metal wall again. "Please! Please! Help! Please!"

The jumping slowed to a stop, followed by the loud humming. Seconds later, the doors opened, and Harper jumped out, stumbling to her knees.

Someone grabbed her arms, preventing her from running. She pulled in two deep breaths, but despite the open area, it didn't help calm her.

Harper fell to her knees, her gasps coming in sobs.

A man she'd never seen before knelt in front of her and gripped her chin with force, studying her, his eyes cold.

"She'll do, I guess. I don't know why The Ghost insists on me having this one. But, she's pretty enough. I'm sure she'll make us plenty of cash. Take her inside."

He moved to the girl next to her.

Nghia.

"You're a pretty one. Where are you from?"

A man began to drag Harper away. She looked back, hearing Nghia speaking in Vietnamese.

The man glanced at one of his men. "She speak English?"

"No, sir."

"She's of no use to me, then. Trash her."

The man he spoke to cocked his rifle. Nghia began speaking fast, her words laced with tears.

"No!" Harper screamed as the man aimed his rifle at the girl. "Please! Don't hurt her!"

She was pulled inside the house when the gunshot echoed in her ears.

Harper cursed the men surrounding her, slapping the one who dragged her inside.

He retaliated, knocking her to the ground. He grabbed a fistful of her hair, jerking her neck back.

"Hit me again and you're dead," he spat at her with a curse.

When he released her, she sobbed into the ground.

"Get up." When she didn't move, he kicked her in the stomach. "I said, 'get up.'"

Her legs like lead, Harper forced herself to climb to her feet.

"Where's Craig?"

"Not here," he said. "You've been sold."

"S-sold? Harper exclaimed. "How? I'm supposed to be with Craig!"

The man raised his shoulder, letting it fall as he smirked at her. "Don't worry, I'm sure you'll find another john."

"What happened to me?" she demanded. "Why am I here? I was just talking to Nghia and Juliette and the other girls a minute ago. Why did that man kill her? Why isn't Craig with me?"

"Don't know," the man sighed. "Guess I can find out for you if that'll keep you in line."

"Please," Harper said.

"Okay," the man said. "But, you'll need to do something for me." He grabbed himself. "Because I have an itch."

Harper cursed him, resulting in him slapping her. She fell again to the hard surface.

"You've got a mouth on you," he told her. "That's not going to go over well here. You're going to have to learn to tame it if you want to live, Harper Matthews."

She looked up at him with wide eyes.

"That's right. I know all about you." He smiled at her, then pulled out his phone. "'Harper Matthews, born May twenty-fifth, nineteen eighty-one. Occupation…flight attendant.' Oh, lookie here. You're claustrophobic."

He frowned at her.

"I'm sorry. Had I seen that before, I would have let you ride with me up front instead of closing you up in the trailer."

He smiled, then returned his attention to the phone.

"Your mother is dead, father is somewhere in the world. He was abusive, making you have daddy and men issues. Understandable. Hmm. You have a close friend who works with you. Olivia. Pretty name. She must be a pretty girl."

He paused as he stared into Harper's eyes, lips curved into a grin. "You care about her, don't cha?"

He paused as if waiting for an answer.

"That's what I thought. In that case, you'll do everything you're told. Isn't that right? Because if you don't, I will find Livvie and I will do things to her you've never heard of…and I'll let you watch. Then I'll put a bullet in her skull."

"You don't scare me," Harper said through her teeth.

"Good," he replied. "Because I would love to meet our pretty friend Livvie."

Harper gazed at him, her insides burning with anger, confusion, and fear.

"By the way, Miss Matthews, you can call me Granger. Now that we've got the introductions out of the way, let's get you something to eat."

He pulled her to her feet by her shoulders and guided her into the dining room, shoving her against the table.

"Enjoy."

Harper watched as he walked away before looking back at the girls sitting around the table.

One of the girls pushed her plate toward her.

Harper wasn't hungry, and wasn't sure if she muster the energy to eat. Her mind ran in circles as she tried to remember what had happened before coming here.

Did she see Craig? Did he betray her? Does he know what happened to her?

"Eat."

Harper looked at the girl who spoke.

"I don't think I'm very hungry," she forced herself to say.

"You must eat to keep your strength."

Harper regarded the other girl but couldn't muster the energy to protest.

"What's your name?"

"H-Harper."

"I'm Blair. This is Adaline."

Harper glanced at the brown-haired girl and studied her. Her face faintly resembled someone she used to know. "Adaline? You're Daniel's sister."

Adaline's eyes grew, her eyes shining with joy. "You know my brother? Is he coming for me? I knew it!"

Harper's heart squeezed in her chest and she released a choking sob. She looked at Adaline, sickened to have to tell her the news.

"Adaline," she said in a low voice. "I'm sorry to tell you this, but Daniel's dead. He-he died a few days ago."

"No." Adaline's eyes filled with tears as she shook her head. "That can't be real. Danny will come for me. He promised."

"I'm sorry," Harper told her. "I'm so, so sorry. He was trying to find you. He wasn't going to give up until he brought you home."

Adaline gripped the necklace she wore and sobbed. Blair wrapped her arms around Adaline's shoulder.

"I'm so sorry," Harper repeated.

After a few seconds ticked by, Adaline raised her head and forced a smile. “It’s not your fault. I know Danny would get me if he could. Danny will always be here.” She placed her hand over her heart.

Harper wanted to say again how sorry she was, but she couldn’t find the words. Instead, she picked up a piece of stale bread and ate.

Seventeen

No matter how hard Harper tried to remember what had happened, she couldn't. She didn't know where Craig was, and she didn't know where she was taken. She didn't even know what day it was. She could have been passed out for ten minutes or ten days.

All she knew was that Nghia was transported to this new place with her and they'd killed her for no reason other than not speaking English.

Where were the other girls? What happened to them?

How could people be so cruel?

The question echoing in her mind made her stomach tie in a knot.

All she knew was she was in trouble. Without Craig, she had no way out. Without knowing where she was, she was lost. She had no way to contact Olivia. Even if she could, it wouldn't do her any good if she didn't know where she was.

Harper paced the room given her.

The windows were barred. She had already tried to jimmy the metal contraption loose, but it wouldn't budge.

Harper stared out the window, looking as far as she could see. Trees surrounded her. The grass was dead. Two men and a woman sat at a white round picnic table drinking what appeared to be beer from a bottle. A white pickup was parked in front. She saw no sign of the van that had taken her and Nghia to this strange land.

She curled her fingers around the bars, and with all the strength she had, Harper pulled, trying to force it loose.

She screamed, angry, frustrated, frightened. So many different emotions swam in her body.

Harper grabbed the lamp by her bedside and tossed it against the wall. It shattered into several large pieces as her door opened.

The man who called himself Granger frowned at the broken lamp.

"That's going to cost you." He tilted his head toward the hallway. "Let's go."

"Where are you taking me?" Harper crossed her arms, determined not to move.

"You have a customer. I expect you to do as you're expected. Don't forget our deal about your friend."

Harper frowned but complied. Somehow they seemed to know things. She didn't want to chance anything happening to her. Or Ollie, or even his girls.

"Can you at least tell me what day it is?"

"Monday."

So, she was missing a day. She'd gone undercover on Friday night.

Granger grabbed her arm, leading her down the hall as she recited in her mind what the day was. She didn't want to lose track of time.

Granger took her to the showers where a man waited.

He smiled when he saw her.

"Yes, she will do very nicely. Thank you."

Granger nodded, pushed Harper further into the showers and backed out. The door closed behind them.

"My name's Greg. What's yours?"

Harper bit her lip.

Greg offered a warm smile.

"I won't hurt you."

"So, you'll let me go?" Harper crossed her arms, hoping the expression on her face wouldn't betray her fear.

"I don't have a lot of time. I'm on lunch. If you don't want to share your name, I'll respect that. We can get down to business."

He turned on the faucet, tested the water, then turned on the showerhead. Turning back to her, he unleashed his black tie.

"Go ahead and undress."

Harper hesitated.

She'd agree to be a part of this. She couldn't allow her friends to be dragged into the mess. Harper knew going in she would have to do things she didn't want to do. No matter where she was now, where Craig was, as far as Harper was concerned, she had a mission.

She would set out and finish what Daniel had started.

Greg seemed to notice her hesitation. With a smile, he gently tugged her shirt off. Harper covered herself the best she could after stepping out of her skirt.

Greg took her by the arm and they stepped into the shower. The warm water pulsed against her skin as she allowed Greg to kiss her neck, her lips.

She felt the pressure of him pushing her to her knees.

"Please," she whispered. "I don't want to do this."

He ignored her.

Harper closed her eyes until it was over.

After Greg left, Harper remained in the shower, fighting back tears, scrubbing her skin until she was raw. She startled after hearing someone bang on the door.

"You've got a customer!"

"I just-I just f-finished one," Harper stammered. "I can't do-do another right now."

"That's fine, Harper," Granger called through the door. "You have yourself a rest. I'll give Livvie a call in your place."

Harper shook her head.

"Wh-wait," she stammered. "Can I have a second? Please?"

"Sure thing, darling. I'll wait for you here."

Harper stepped out of the tub and pulled on her clothes. Granger knocked again to urge her to hurry.

She hesitated, sucking in a deep breath before turning the knob.

Granger grabbed her arm and led her to a bedroom where a dark-skinned man waited. Granger shoved her to the floor, forcing her on her knees.

"Enjoy."

"On the bed," the man instructed.

"I can't do this. Please."

He grabbed her by the hair and dragged her to the bed. With a yelp, she clamped her hands over his, attempting to pry the hold he had on her loose.

"Stop, please! Let me go!"

He climbed on top of her, pinning her wrists together in one large hand. With his free hand, he jammed his hand underneath her damp shirt.

She jerked her knee toward him, forcing him to lose his balance. Harper pushed him off her, running for the door. He recovered, grabbing a fistful of her hair, pulling her back.

Harper elbowed him, resulting in a soft grunt. She landed a sidekick at his kneecap. When he fell, she kicked his groin.

Without waiting for him to make a recovery, Harper pulled the door open and ran into the hallway. She wasn't sure where she would go, but she knew she had to get out of there. She had to save herself.

Harper made it to the front door and struggled with the lock.

A sharp pain crossed the middle of her back. She fell against the door and again, felt the pain.

She forced herself to look behind her to see Granger recoiling his belt. He cursed her as his hand sliced the air and the belt made contact with her neck.

Harper released a sharp gasp. She blinked, trying to clear her cloudy vision.

He grabbed her throat, forcing her to his feet. "You're going to wish you hadn't done that. Let's go."

Harper clawed at his hands, gasping for breath.

He tossed her inside a closet.

"I'll let you think about your consequences while I go pay your friend a visit," Granger growled. "Maybe next time you'll think twice before you disobey."

The door closed behind him, cutting off any light.

Eighteen

Harper sat in the corner of the dark closet, her knees to her chest. She closed her eyes, trying to focus on her breathing. Her chest tightened as her heart thrummed against her ribcage. The room seemed to close in on her.

Harper counted slowly to ten.

Ollie had once told her to picture a place where she was happy. Where she felt safe.

She reflected on a day where she had gone on a picnic with him and his daughters at the lake. The girls were laughing, playing in the water.

She and Ollie had lain on the blanket, the warm sun swallowing them in its light.

It was the first time Ollie had confessed his feelings for her.

She'd recently ended a relationship, so at the time, Harper couldn't return her love. She couldn't tell him she loved him the same way. At the time, she wasn't sure how she felt toward him. Her heart had been crushed and trusting men wasn't easy.

It never was.

"I'm sorry, Ollie," she whispered, her voice quivering. "I'm so sorry I couldn't tell you how I felt."

Harper's heartbeat slowed, her breathing studied.

She opened her eyes.

She was still in the closet, still in the darkness.

She wasn't sure how long she'd been inside. It seemed like hours but could have only been a few minutes. There was no way to tell.

But she was no longer afraid.

At least that was what she told herself.

Her hands shook as Harper felt along the walls and the floor, searching for something she could use to get out of the enclosed space. Something she could use as a weapon.

She couldn't find anything.

Her chest clutched tightly as a gasping breath escaped her lips.

She had to focus.

Breathe, Harper, just breathe.

Harper climbed to her feet, using the wall for support. She found a shelf above her head and ran her fingers along the edge until she tapped something.

She pulled the object down. On the side was a single latch so she flipped it open.

When she found a flashlight, she clicked it on.

Her heart skipped a few beats, thrumming faster.

The room began to close in on her again.

Harper inspected the hammer but put it to the side—too bulky. Next, she studied the mini screwdriver—maybe.

Next to the box of nails was what she needed—a switchblade. Harper grabbed it, pressed the button and the silver blade popped out. It was rusted but would do the trick.

"Have we learned our lesson yet?" Granger called through the closed door.

With a gasp, Harper replaced the tools in the box, put it back on the shelf and slipped the knife and screwdriver underneath her clothes for safekeeping.

She turned as the door opened.

"Well?"

"Yes," Harper told him. "I'm s-s-sorry for what I did."

"I figured a little bit in timeout would do the trick." Granger smiled, reminding Harper of Norman Bates at the very end of *Psycho*. A chill crawled up her spine. "Let's go. Food's ready."

Harper stepped out of the closet and followed Granger into the kitchen, where Adaline and Blair sat at the table.

She sat, realizing how hungry she was. She hadn't had a full meal since before Craig brought her to the other house. Even then, she didn't eat much.

She looked up at Granger. "You said you'd find out where Craig was for me. Did you?"

"Oh, right," Granger said. "He's dead."

Harper blinked.

"Wh-what did you say?"

"I said…your cop boyfriend is dead."

"How?"

"That's the cost of an undercover cop thinking he could bring in a civilian to trap us."

"What's going to happen to me?"

"That depends on you," Granger replied. "The Ghost has requested nothing happen to you. But, like any good businessman, he understands that I will do whatever I need in order for you to stay in line. You do what's required of you, you won't have anything to worry about."

"What about Olivia? You won't hurt her?"

"As long as you comply, sweet Livvie will be fine. Now, sit. Eat. Enjoy."

Harper did as she was told. She gripped her fork and, unable to stand the hunger anymore, she stabbed two pieces of meat, sticking it in her mouth. As she chewed, she heard Granger's footsteps retreat.

After a quick glance behind her, she regarded Adaline and Blair.

"Are you girls okay?"

Blair nodded.

"I'm a little sore," Adaline admitted, her words soft. "The men I was with were rough."

"Men?" Harper echoed. "You had to deal with two at the same time?"

Adaline didn't respond. She gazed into her plate, her cheeks rising in color.

"I'm going to get us out of here," Harper whispered. "Okay? I promise."

"How?" Blair asked. "They'll kill our family if we try to leave."

"Just trust me, okay?" Harper pleaded. "I'm going to close down this entire operation. Adaline, one of the girls in the first place I stayed at told me The Ghost came and took you from there."

Adaline raised her eyes and nodded.

"Do you know who he is? His name?"

"I don't know his name," Adaline said. "They put drugs in me, so when I came here, I didn't know what happened."

"Did he speak? Would you recognize his voice if you heard it again?"

She raised her shoulders. "I don't know. His voice sounded funny. I'm sorry."

Harper reached across the table and put her hand over Adaline's.

"Don't be sorry, sweetie. It'll be okay."

"What did they do to you?" Blair asked. "I heard you screaming."

Harper frowned. "I tried to escape. Granger locked me in the closet."

"Were you scared?" Adaline wondered. "I would be scared."

"I was very scared," Harper admitted as she stuffed a forkful of mashed potatoes in her mouth. "I'm…claustrophobic. I can't breathe when I'm in a small space. Someone must have told Granger. So I guess he thought it'd be fitting to punish me by putting me in the closet."

Blair bit her bottom lip.

"It's okay, though," Harper assured them. "When I'm scared, I think about a place that makes me happy. Somewhere I've always felt safe. Then I'm not scared anymore."

"Will that help with us?" Adaline asked.

Harper nodded. "Of course."

"Then I'll think of my brother next time. He took me to Disney World a few years ago for my birthday. It was really fun."

"That sounds great. What about you, Blair? Is there any place you can think of?"

"I guess my aunt's ranch. She has a lot of horses. She used to let me ride them. But she died. They sold the ranch and the horses, so I can never go back."

"The mind's a wonderful thing," Harper told her. "It can always take you back to where you were happy." She paused, looking into their eyes. "Remember that feeling, Okay? Until I can get the three of us out of here, the next time you feel scared, I want you to think of those places. Being at your aunt's farm. And being with your brother at Disney World. Before you know it, the pain will pass."

Harper allowed the conversation lull as she considered a plan to get the three of them out of the house.

To get them to safety.

Nineteen

Harper realized if she was going to get herself and the girls to safety, she would have to spend a few days devising a plan. That meant she was going to have to do whatever she needed to do to survive. Even if it was unthinkable.

She hid her switchblade underneath the mattress for safekeeping. She would only use it when they made their escape. Pulling it out any other time would result in severe consequences.

During the times she didn't have to be with men, she studied the inside of the house. Like the one before, there was an alarm code. She wasn't sure if they armed it at nighttime but assumed they did. Her father used to have a friend who was an electrician. When Harper was younger, the friend explained how the wires worked, and which ones to cut to disable the alarm. Although she didn't remember which wire to cut, she figured slicing them all would get the job done.

As the days waned on, Harper and the girls each had daily chores to complete. She was in charge of washing the dishes and cleaning the downstairs while Blair scrubbed all the floors by hand, and Adaline had to clean upstairs.

Harper wanted to have a look around outside to scout the area, but she wasn't allowed out of the house. At least, not by herself.

An opportunity was presented to her after Granger escorted her to her room to greet an older man.

After she finished pleasing him, Harper leaned close to his ear.

"I hope you're satisfied, daddy," she said. She'd become practiced at not showing how it'd sickened her to refer to the johns as "daddy." It was a phrase they preferred, though she never understood why. It was wrong on so many levels. "Are you enough satisfied with my services to do me a tiny favor?"

"What's that, little lady?"

The john kept his eyes closed, his chest rising and falling with content.

"I just feel so cooped up inside this house all day." As she spoke, she massaged his shoulders. "I would love it if you could give me a tour outside. So, I can have fresh air."

"Would that make you happy, little lady?"

Harper smiled down at him.

"That would make me very happy."

The john propped himself up with his elbows. "Then, let's have a look around."

Harper giggled playfully and climbed off him, pulling on her clothes.

She noticed his cell phone had slipped from out of his pant pocket when he tossed it onto the floor earlier.

Harper glanced at the john to see his back to her as he stretched his limbs. Using her foot, she slid the phone underneath the bed, hoping he wouldn't realize it was missing.

After they dressed, she allowed him to take her hands and lead her down the stairs and to the front door.

They stepped outside, and for the first time in what seemed to be a long time, Harper felt the warmth of the sun against her skin. She closed her eyes at the feeling.

"It feels great," she muttered.

"Yes, I suppose it does," the john agreed.

They walked around the house, surrounded by trees in each direction. In the distance, she heard vehicles. There was only one thin slip of dirt road to allow people to come or go. She wondered how far away the main road was.

"Where is this place, anyway? What city?"

"Conyers," he replied.

Harper smiled to herself, pleased they were just outside of Atlanta, where she was familiar.

"What do you do?" Harper asked.

"I'm a lawyer," he answered.

"A lawyer?" Harper raised an eyebrow. By now, she wasn't surprised a man in such a prestigious profession paid for sex. "What kind are you?"

"I've been a criminal defense attorney coming on twenty-eight years. I plan to retire next year."

"Do you have any plans?"

"The wife wants to travel around Europe, so that may be what we do."

"Sounds lovely," Harper said. "I've never been to Europe."

"It's nice, I suppose. I've been there a few times." He glanced at his watch. "I've got to get going. I have an arraignment scheduled shortly. Ready to go back to the house?"

She nodded and followed him to the living room. After he kissed her cheek, she watched as he walked out of the house. Harper ran to the window and waited until the lawyer's car pulled away.

"Harper?"

She turned to see Adaline holding her stomach.

"I feel sick."

"Is it your stomach? A cramp?" she asked. When Adaline nodded, Harper put her hand on her shoulder. "I'll see if they have medicine to give you."

Harper searched the rooms until she found Granger in his home office on the bottom floor.

"Adaline needs meds for her stomach. Do you have any?"

"It'll pass," Granger said, not looking away from his computer.

"That's all you've got to say?" she snapped. "Adaline won't be able to do your services if her stomach's hurting."

"She'll have to," Granger replied. He looked at her. "Unless she wants punishment."

"Please," Harper said. "Have a little bit of sympathy. She's just a kid. I'll-I'll do whatever you want if you will just tell me where to get her the medicine."

Granger turned to the computer without speaking. Then in a sigh, he said, "Upstairs in the last bedroom, there's whatever you need in the bathroom."

"Thank you," she said.

Harper found Adaline in the kitchen with Blair, and she told them to follow her.

"Wait in my room, okay? I want to talk to you guys. I'll go see what meds Granger has."

Harper hurried to the bedroom and searched the medicine cabinet where she found the Tums. She took the container and hurried back to her room where the girls waited.

"Here, take one of these." Harper passed her two pills.

They were instructed to never close the door unless they were with a john, but she did anyway. It wouldn't take long for her to discuss with the girls her plan of escape, and she didn't want Granger or anyone else to hear the conversation.

"Adaline, when you're cleaning Grainger's office, is someone watching you?"

"Someone's always outside the door, but he doesn't watch. He just stands there. He usually reads or talks on the phone."

"Do you think you can find the spare keys to that truck?"

Adaline shrugged. "I don't know. Maybe."

"Okay. Try to find it. If you do, take it and give it to me when no one's around."

"Are we leaving?" Adaline asked.

"Yes," Harper said. She knelt and reached underneath the bed. Once she wrapped her fingers around the phone, she pulled it out. "I took this from that lawyer I was with."

Blair's eyes grew. "Harper! If Granger sees that, he'll punish you!"

"We won't be here long enough for that to happen, Blair. All right? You, me, and Adaline…we are leaving. Tomorrow night. When everybody's asleep, I'm going to send a message to a friend of mine. If Adaline can find the keys to that truck, we'll sneak out while everyone's sleeping. We'll drive out of here. If she doesn't find the keys, we'll go on foot. Either way, we're leaving."

"But somebody's always watching," Blair protested. "They'll stop us."

"I've spent the last few days watching Granger and the others. They're creatures of habit. They do the same thing day after day. As long as you do exactly as I say, we'll be fine. I'll protect you."

Harper pulled the switchblade from underneath the mattress.

"Where did you get that?"

"From a toolbox," Harper said. She slipped the knife and the phone underneath the bed. "When Granger stuffed me in that closet, I found it."

"I'm scared," Adaline whispered.

"I know," Harper said. She put a hand on her shoulder. "I am too. But we've got to do this. Okay? Tomorrow. It can't be a moment later. It's only a matter of time before that lawyer shows up here, looking for his phone."

Blair bit her bottom lip.

"Do we have a deal?" Harper glanced between the two girls.

Adaline regarded Blair, who hesitated.

"I'd rather die than stay here anymore," Adaline said as if trying to convince Blair. "Some of the men are really rough. They think it's funny hurting me."

After seconds ticked by, Blair finally nodded. "Okay. I'm in."

"Good. Don't mention any of this to anyone," Harper warned. "Tomorrow, we have to do everything normally. Then when it's lights out, I'll come for you and we'll leave."

Harper reached her arms out to hug the girls, then ushered them out of the room before Granger came looking for them.

Twenty

Harper waited, staring up at the ceiling as she laid in bed. She'd said many silent prayers that she could get herself and the girls to safety. Even if Harper didn't make it, she wanted Blair and Adaline to find their way home.

She climbed out of bed to retrieve the cell phone she'd stolen from the lawyer. Even though Harper knew Olivia would be asleep, she dialed her number. Her heart surged in her chest when she heard the ringtone in her ear. She kept one ear out for any sounds within the walls of someone who may barge in.

A few rings went by before Olivia answered, her voice tired.

"Liv, it's Harper." She kept her tone hushed.

"Oh, my goodness! Where are you?" Harper frowned at her friend's slurred words. "Are you okay?"

"No, I'm not," she said. "Everything Craig and I planned backfired. He's dead, and I've been transferred to a different house in Conyers."

Harper felt her cheeks redden as she considered what she'd been forced to do in the past week.

"It's so good to hear your voice, Liv," Harper interrupted. "You have no idea what I've been through. What I've seen. What I've done. I've been so trapped, Liv." Harper cleared her throat as the words cracked.

"Listen, Harp, something's terrible happened. I need to tell you…"

"I can't talk long, okay? I need your help."

"Okay…what's going on?"

Harper hesitated before speaking. "Tomorrow night, I want you to meet me at the Walmart in Conyers, okay? Eleven o'clock. I'll be there with two girls…Adaline and Blair."

"Adaline? Daniel's sister? You've found her?"

"Yes. We need you to take us to the police. Can you do that?"

"Of course."

Harper heard a sound in the background. It sounded like talking.

"Sorry, I didn't mean to wake you," Olivia hissed. "Go back to sleep. I'm about to hang up."

"Is someone there with you?"

"Oh, um…"

Harper shook her head, "It doesn't matter. I just need you to meet us. Don't be late."

"I won't."

"Good," Harper said. "There's a chance I may not be able to call you again."

"I wish you'd tell me what's going on. I've been so worried about you. And I don't want to make matters worse, but—"

Harper narrowed her eyes. "You didn't tell anyone where I was going, did you?"

"Harper, I…"

Harper hushed her when she heard a sound from the other side of her room. She saw the light fill the crack underneath the door, then the movement of a shadow passing. When it returned, it paused.

Without saying goodbye to Olivia, Harper ended the call and slipped the phone underneath her mattress. As her bedroom door open, she fell against the pillow, eyes closed, praying that whoever it was didn't hear her.

When the door closed, she waited a few minutes before reopening her eyes. The light under the crack had gone dark and the house once again fell into silence.

With a sigh of release, she turned to her back to stare at the ceiling. She

Twenty-one

The next day, Harper kept things as normal as she could, despite Blair's and Adaline's frightened demeanor and her own racing heart. She didn't have much of a plan other than run as fast and quietly as possible, hopefully as she drove the white truck. If not the truck, then they would have to use the woods to reach the road.

By lunchtime, Adaline returned from her chores at the house across the yard…with a set of keys.

She seemed pleased with herself at having found the keys without issue or being caught.

Harper ended the day by having to pleasure nine different men. She did so with the hope that it would all end soon. She, Blair, and Adaline would be safe, and she hoped the police would charge Granger and his men, as well as free the girls from the first house she stayed at.

When it was ten twenty, Harper used the screwdriver to remove her doorknob. She carefully stepped to Blair's room and did the same. She didn't bother with taking the time to replace it.

Blair sat on her bed, waiting. When she saw Harper, her eyes grew. Harper put a finger to her lip and motioned for her to follow.

Next, she broke her way into Adaline's room.

Daniel's sister lay curled in her bed. Harper crossed the room to her side and sat down.

"We don't have much time, honey," Harper whispered. "We have to go."

"I'm scared." Harper had to strain to hear her.

"I know you are. I am too," Harper admitted. "But, we'll be fine. You just have to trust me."

"I wish Danny was going to be there if we get out."

"I know, honey. But it's for Daniel that you must come with us. The longer we wait, the less chance we have."

After a brief hesitation, Adaline nodded and pulled back her covers.

"Good girl."

Harper held both girls' hands as she peered out the bedroom door, looking in both directions. When she saw it was clear, she guided them out of the room.

When they made it to the front door, Harper used the screwdriver to remove the alarm cover. She cut the wires with the switchblade. Once the cover was back in place, Harper opened the door, ushered the girls outside, then closed it.

They waited for a beat before running across the field to be sure the night was free of shadows. She heard faint voices around the corner of the house. Harper motioned the girls to keep as quiet as possible but to hurry.

As they ran, the leaves crinkled beneath their feet.

Harper used the key fob to unlock the truck.

"Hurry, get in. We're almost out of here."

She fumbled with finding the correct key, then dropped them when Adaline and Blair released bloodcurdling screams.

Harper's door pulled open and Granger grabbed her arm, pulling her out of the truck.

He punched her in the face, cursing her. She fell to the ground and he rammed a steel-toed shoe into the pit of her stomach.

"Run!" Harper shouted to the girls. "Run!"

"No!"

Granger raised a handgun in the air and fired.

"Run and you die!"

Harper pulled her switchblade from the back of her pant pocket, activated the knife and jammed it into Granger's ankle.

Above his howl, Harper again told the girls to run and get help.

Without hesitation, Blair pulled Adaline away, leaving Harper to fend off Granger.

She pulled the knife from his ankle and swiped at his leg, forcing him to fall to his knees.

"You're dead," he growled, his teeth clenched. Granger threw a punch at her, catching her by surprise.

Harper fell back, and Granger climbed on top of her, squeezing her throat.

She clawed at him, but his grip around her neck was too strong. Harper began to lose consciousness. She prayed the girls would find safety.

Granger cursed her through his teeth as his hands gripped her tighter, tighter.

Then a loud bang echoed in the still air.

The weight of Granger crushed her as he fell over her body

Harper pushed Granger off her, coughing for air. She looked at the shooter.

Blair, her eyes wide, still held the gun in an aim, her hands shaking. She tried not to cry, but the tears still came.

Harper looked at Granger, who gripped his neck, wincing in pain.

Forcing herself to find the strength, she climbed to her feet, wrapping Blair in a brief, tight hug.

They didn't have time for a breather.

Shouts came from the house, followed by gunfire.

Harper yelped as a bullet whizzed passed her and she instructed the girls to climb into the truck. Once the doors were closed, Harper pulled away from the house, dirt, and rocks flying in their wake.

"Get down!" Harper barked as the glass in the back of the truck cracked from another bullet.

"I can't believe I shot him," Blair said softly, her body folded toward her lap.

"Are you okay?"

She answered with a nod.

"Adaline? Are you?"

She also nodded, but when Harper glanced at her, she saw the tears streaming down her face.

"You girls did amazing," Harper said. "But the next time I tell you to run, I mean run. Don't wait for me, don't come back for me."

"But he was going to kill you," Blair protested.

"My concern is for you, okay?"

"Are you mad?"

She shook her head. "Of course I'm not mad. Like I said…you did amazing. Thank you."

"What's going to happen next?" Adaline asked.

"I have a friend who is going to meet us. We can't keep this truck, so we're going to a Walmart. It's the most public place I can think of. It's open this time of night and there will be people. We'll be safe there. After we find Olivia, we're going to the police to tell them everything."

"I'm hungry," Blair announced. "Can we get something to eat?"

"I don't know," Harper said. "We really don't have a lot of time, but…"

She hesitated, realizing she was also hungry. Harper pulled out the phone.

"I'll call Liv and make sure she's going to meet us. I'll have her buy some hamburgers."

When Olivia answered, she agreed to buy the hamburgers and again pressed for information. Harper promised to tell her in detail when they were together again.

She ended the call and continued to drive in silence. She'd been to Conyers a few times when her mother was alive, but she hoped she remembered the area enough.

During the drive, her eyes flickered to the rearview mirror, half expecting to see one of Granger's men following them.

But the people and vehicles were scarce.

Adaline and Blair huddled tightly to one another, fighting sleep, every so often, craning their necks to look out the back window.

When Harper pulled into the Walmart parking lot, she turned off the ignition and they stepped out of the truck.

Holding Blair's and Adaline's hands, she led them to the entrance. She scanned the store until her eyes rested on the back of Olivia's head, sitting at a table in a fast-food restaurant. She kept her head down at her hands, staring at her cell phone.

"Liv!" Harper exclaimed.

Olivia turned, her eyes wide. She pushed her chair back to stand.

"Oh, my…Harper!"

Releasing the girls' hands, Harper rushed into Olivia's arms, holding her tight.

"I was so afraid I'd never see you again," she cried.

"Honey, what happened? You look awful." Olivia pulled back from the hug and regarded Harper. "You've lost weight, your neck is red, face swollen. What did they do to you?"

"I'll tell you," Harper promised. "First, I want you to meet Blair and Adaline."

"Hi," Olivia said with a forced smile.

Adaline reached for Harper's hand and held on tight. Blair seemed to shrink a few inches as she hid behind Harper.

Harper gazed at Olivia, shaking her head, closing her eyes. "What I've been through doesn't even compare to them. Or the other girls."

"Listen, there's something I need to tell you," Olivia said, her eyes clouding over. "I tried to tell you over the phone…I just…couldn't."

"Can you tell me on the way to the police station? We have to get going." Harper looked around them. "It's not safe here."

Olivia gripped Harper's forearm to stop her from moving. "Harper…Ollie's dead."

Feeling the color drained from her face, Harper gripped the edge of the table.

"Oh m…wh…" She blinked back tears. "H-how?"

"He was in a car accident a few days after you left with Craig."

"No," Harper said, her bottom lip quivering. "That can't be."

"I'm so sorry," Olivia said, reaching her arms out for a hug. "I hated to tell you that after everything you've been going through…still…going through."

Harper shook her head as if it would rear her back to reality. Tears fell from her eyes and she could have sworn her heart began to crumble. "Come on, we need to get to the police station. I'll tell you everything on the drive."

"Okay," Olivia agreed. She motioned to the table. "I got the food."

Adaline's eyes grew as she hurried to the table, Blair following close behind.

"Grab the bags," Harper insisted. "We'll eat in the car."

Twenty-two

Harper walked into the police station and looked around. She didn't see anyone, even behind the glass window. Harper pressed a button on the wall that appeared to be a doorbell. She glanced behind her at Olivia, who talked softly to Adaline. Blair remained at Harper's side.

"Maybe no one's here," Blair suggested, pressing her nose on the glass as if it would let her see through walls.

"This is a police station," Harper told her. "Someone's always here. Even it's a graveyard shift."

"How do you know if we can trust the cops?" she asked. "Sometimes cops come to be with us."

"Would you prefer I ask for a woman officer?" Harper looked at Blair and studied her tired eyes.

She nodded.

"Okay, then that's what I'll do." She rang the bell again. "Don't forget. You and Adaline needs to tell the truth about everything that happened to you. Starting from when they kidnapped you."

"Okay."

Harper put an arm around Blair's shoulder, hoping to give her comfort. She knew they were all tired, but they couldn't wait until the morning. Either Granger would come searching for them, run away, or both.

"Harper?"

"Yes, Blair?"

"Why do they want to hurt us? I mean, I never met the guy who took me away from home. Did I do something wrong?"

Harper knelt so she could be at eye level.

"You didn't do anything to deserve this, Blair. You, Adaline, the other girls…well, you're victims." She sighed. "There are a lot of bad men in this world." Harper wrapped her arms around her for a hug. "It'll be over soon. You'll be back with your family again."

"But I won't forget, will I?"

Harper pushed out another breath, feeling the hot tear clinging to the corner of her eye.

"Probably not," she admitted, pulling away. "But, you will be able to move forward."

"How?"

"We'll get you some counseling. I won't lie to you. It won't be easy, and I imagine it won't be quick. But you'll be able to put the pieces of yourselves back together. Adaline, too."

She heard a door open and pushed to her feet. The desk sergeant appeared.

"What can I help you with?"

"We need to speak to someone. A woman."

"I look male to you?" the desk sergeant narrowed her eyes. "Or do I look like a rat? You afraid of rats?" She regarded Blair. "What about you? You scared of rats?"

"No, no," Harper said as Blair moved behind her. "We only—,"

The desk sergeant lifted the corners of her lips in a smile. "I was kidding. Didn't mean to frighten your daughter."

"She's not my daughter," Harper corrected. "We're…we're all in trouble."

The sergeant narrowed her eyes, carefully studying Harper, then the other three.

"What kind of trouble, miss?"

Harper bit her lip.

"Some man wants to kill us," Blair's quiet voice interjected. "Because we don't want to have sex with their friends anymore."

The desk sergeant looked from Blair to Harper. "What is she talking about? She leaned to the glass and mouthed, "Trafficking?"

Harper nodded. "I escaped with the girls a few hours ago. We're tired, but we can't let the night end before we tell someone what happened to us. Is there anyone that can help?"

"I'll get Lieutenant Rice out here, right now. If you'd like coffee, there's the machine over there. It ain't the best but does the trick."

She sat in her chair and reached for her phone.

Harper turned to Olivia.

"I don't know how long this will take," she told her. "If you want to get some rest, I understand." She considered Granger's threat. "But I would feel better if you stayed at a hotel instead of going back home. Granger…threatened…you if I didn't comply with what he wanted."

"No," Olivia replied. "I'm not leaving you."

Harper felt relief flood through her.

"How's Collier?" Harper asked.

"Missing you," Olivia replied with a roll of her eyes. "Like always. But he was excited when I told him you called."

"Ma'am?"

Harper looked up to see the desk sergeant stepping around her glass booth.

"Lieutenant Rice will be here shortly. She instructed me to let you wait for her in her office, so if you'll all follow me, I'll take you."

The sergeant led them through the police station into the vast array of offices until they reached Lieutenant Rice's.

"Give her about twenty minutes or so. She's coming from home."

Harper thanked her and told the girls to sit in the office chairs.

"Can I sit in that chair?" Adaline asked, pointing to Lieutenant Rice's chair.

"I guess it can't hurt, but you'll have to move when she gets here. Don't touch anything."

A smile spreading across Adaline's face, she plopped into the chair.

Blair curled herself into a ball in the corner of the room, eyes closed.

"She's so tired," Olivia acknowledged. She glanced at Adaline, then Harper. "All of you are. Are you sure you don't want to wait until morning? We can leave a message for Lieutenant Rice."

Harper shook her head firmly. "It's got to be tonight. Granger could be looking for us as we speak. If he finds us, there's no telling what he'll do. Kill us, or worse."

Harper walked to the window and peered through the closed blinds, looking around at the quiet streets. A car pulled into the lot and her heart jolted until it made a U-turn and turned back onto the streets.

Olivia wrapped her arm around Harper, startling her.

"I understand," she said. "You're here now. That's all that matters. You're safe."

"I need to find who's in charge, Liv," Harper said.

Olivia pulled away with a frown. “How are you going to do that? They’ve done nothing but prove they’ll do anything to remain anonymous and keep their ring alive. Daniel’s dead, Craig’s dead…you could be next.”

“If I don’t find out,” Harper insisted, then I’ll be spending the rest of my life looking over my shoulders. My memories of my dad are sweet in comparison to the last couple of weeks.”

“Shouldn’t you let the police handle it? You’ve done all you can do, which is more than you should have done, Harper. You can’t save everyone. But you saved Blair and Adaline. Can’t that be enough? You saved Daniel’s sister.”

Harper glanced at Adaline, who had fallen asleep in Lieutenant Rice’s chair, head propped against the desk.

Blair’s eyes were still closed, her breath rising and falling with steady movements in her chest.

Harper thought of Mai and the other girls. She remembered the gunshot echoing when they killed Nghia.

She shook her head. “I may not be able to save everyone, but I’m going to save as many as I can. I’m now a survivor. I won’t let Daniel’s, Craig’s, even Nghia’s death to be in vain. There are other girls in Atlanta. In our city, Olivia. Our home. And don’t forget all the other women and children in this country—and this world. How can you ask me to let it happen?”

Olivia turned her lips into a frown. “I’m not asking you to do that.”

Before Harper could reply, the door opened and a tall, slim woman stepped inside.

“I’m Lieutenant Charlotte Rice,” she said, extending her hand.

“I’m Harper. Harper Matthews.”

After she shook the lieutenant’s hand, she introduced Olivia and pointed out the girls.

“I’m sorry, Lieutenant. Both are wiped out. It’s been a long day.”

Lieutenant Rice nodded with a smile. “I understand, Miss Matthews. We’ll let them rest. Why don’t you tell me everything you know? Our desk sergeant told me these girls have been victims of human trafficking. Is that right?”

"Yes," Harper said. She cleared her throat. "I suppose, so was I. But I'm an adult, so I'm not so sure that label would fit me."

"It's not as uncommon as one would think," Rice said as she sat on the edge of her desk. "Why don't we start with your story? Give me as much detail as possible."

Harper lowered herself in an empty chair.

Then she relived the events all over again.

Twenty-three

"That's quite an ordeal you've been through."

After Harper went into detail on what had happened to her, the office filled with silence before Lieutenant Rice spoke. Her eyes had switched emotions as the story progressed.

Harper couldn't glance in Olivia's direction. She felt shameful and embarrassed to have her friend to her the details.

"You're a civilian. Why did you of all people go undercover? Surely you knew it was risky."

"I used to be a cop," Harper admitted. She ignored Olivia's surprised gasp. "Daniel apparently knew that. He couldn't trust actual cops, so he sought me out. I didn't want to do it at first, but…I suppose the cop part of me still lived."

"I see. And this undercover cop," Rice began slowly. She was scrawling something in her notepad, "You're positive he's dead? How do you know for sure?"

Harper considered the question before answering. "Well, I hadn't seen him around since that morning. Those men are capable of anything. Even murder. I've witnessed it firsthand. I truly believed he was legit. I mean, don't they go after people they see as troubled or gullible? I'm neither. At least I don't think I am. I find myself in bad relationships with men, but…" Harper trailed off, realizing she was beginning to babble.

"The way things work is they'll find someone they think can earn them money. There are really no set targets. You're a very pretty lady. Clear skin, fit, eager. When they approach you, they'll give you an offer that's almost impossible to turn down. Those involved are trained to know the smallest details that could hook women and men."

"But it was Daniel who brought me into all this in the first place. He was a reporter. He was trying to close this whole thing down. His sister was trafficked because he came close to finding the source. He wouldn't have done all that."

"Why not? Because his sister was stolen?" Rice glanced at Adaline, still sleeping peacefully. "You mentioned another girl…the one who was killed…Nghia. You told me her own father sold her for money. What makes you think Daniel wouldn't do it to his sister?"

Harper paused before speaking. The realization finally settled into place and the room slowly began to spin.

It couldn't have been, could it?

"I knew you shouldn't have gotten involved," Olivia said softly.

"No," Harper said firmly. For the first time since telling her story, she looked at Olivia. Her friend's face had lost all of its colorings. "I'm sorry, but I don't agree with that. Liv, I may not be the best judge of character when it comes to men, but I do believe Daniel meant well. He wanted to end this. He wanted to find Adaline."

Lieutenant Rice didn't respond. She didn't need to. Harper recognized the look in the other woman's eyes.

The thought crossed her mind briefly.

However, when Granger told her Craig was murdered because he was an undercover cop, she'd accepted it. But she never saw the body. She had not heard from Craig since he introduced her to the first girls in the dining room. And she was transferred that night.

"Oh my…" Harper trailed off, feeling sickness rise within her. "I can't believe it. I don't believe it. It can't be true, can it?"

She blinked back tears as she raised her eyes to look at Lieutenant Rice.

"I fell for it?"

"I'm not saying this man wasn't undercover," Rice said, her voice low. "However, it's very possible he was involved. I'm sure you can understand that, Miss Matthews. These men know who to target. As for Daniel, we may never know. But in my opinion, it makes sense that Craig knew Daniel was getting close. Human trafficking is one of the top moneymakers in the world. And people kill for less. How long before Daniel was killed did this cop contact you?"

"Excuse me," Harper said, ignoring the question. She jumped to her feet, ripped the door open and followed the signs to the women's bathroom, where she barely reached the toilet to empty her stomach.

She remained on her knees, facing the toilet in case more stomach contents arose.

After she was sure her physical sickness passed, she rose to her feet, using the stalls for support. Harper rinsed her mouth, gasping with tears she tried to keep from escaping.

But, the floodgates had already opened, and she fell to the floor, resting her head against her knees.

How could she be so stupid?

Craig didn't really use her, did he?

But, there was no other explanation.

"Miss Matthews?"

Harper heard the knock on the bathroom door and then footsteps. She felt a hand massaging her shoulder, so she looked up to gaze into Lieutenant Rice's deep blue eyes.

"I thought I was doing a good thing," Harper forced through her tears. He told me not many people want to acknowledge it. He told me what I needed to expect. Everything he said what would happen was the truth."

"You did do a *great* thing," Rice assured her. "And he's right. Now many people will acknowledge it. Yes, people do know it happens, but they don't know the truth about it. They don't know the gory details because they don't want to think there are people evil enough to do these things. And they don't know that anyone can be a victim."

"Even me?"

"Victim or not, you fought back," Rice told her. "Whether or not Craig did trick you into this…and we may never know for sure…they underestimated your strength. All of them did. Not only did you escape yourself, but you saved two young ladies."

"That's small assurance," Harper said, wiping at her tear-stained face with the back of her hand. "I can't stop thinking about the other girls. No one's saved them yet. No one."

"Then work with me," Rice said. "Let's find a way to bring these men to justice."

"What do you need me to do?"

"First, we need to find Granger and bring him in."

"I don't know the address," Harper said.

"Would you remember how to get there?"

Harper considered the drive from Granger's house to Walmart. It was only twenty minutes, maybe less.

She nodded.

"I think so."

"Good," Rice said. "I already rounded up a team. With your help, we'll find the house. It's possible Granger won't be there after your escape, but we may find evidence of where he could go, where the other house is…even the identity of The Ghost. Deal?"

Harper bobbed her head up and down.

"Deal."

Twenty-four

Lieutenant Rice agreed to set Olivia, Blair, and Adaline up in a hotel for the night. Harper had requested they go to Olivia's apartment to get Collier but was told it wouldn't be a good idea. Since Harper was warned of Olivia's life, it was possible someone was watching the apartment.

The girls hadn't woken since Lieutenant Rice first appeared at her office, so she told Harper and Olivia she'd collect their statements later.

Harper was relieved because she knew firsthand the girls hadn't had a good night's rest in a long while. She was also relieved that in addition to Olivia keeping an eye on the girls, Lieutenant Rice agreed to have officers keep an eye on all of them.

In the meantime, the morning after her escape, she rode with Lieutenant Rice and mentally prepared herself to return to Granger's house.

A part of her hoped the bullet wound from when Blair shot him killed him. Another part hoped he was still alive, in pain, unable to make his escape. A final part of her hoped he wouldn't be there.

Harper watched as trees and building blurred by as they drove to the Walmart parking lot.

As they neared, she pointed through the windshield.

"That's the truck!"

Without responding, Rice spoke into her radio, informing her men of the truck, then pulled up beside it.

"Stay here," Rice instructed.

She climbed out of the car, went to the truck, then walked to the truck, using her flashlight for a closer look. With her gloved hand, she opened the driver's door and shined the flashlight inside.

Harper watched as another officer opened the passenger side and leaned in. A second later, he pulled himself out, holding a gun. He passed Rice a slim black book. She pointed the flashlight on the contents and returned it to the officer with a nod. Her mouth moved as she spoke.

Rice walked to the car and got inside.

"The truck's registered to a Harold Granger," she explained. "We're going to run a background check and look into the gun's serial."

"What now?" Harper asked.

"Now while my guys prepare it to be towed, we'll pay Mr. Granger a visit."

Harper said nothing as the car pulled from the parking lot.

When they pulled into a familiar dirt road, Harper's heart clutched tight in her chest.

The lights were out, so Harper wondered if they'd left.

In case Granger showed up at a hospital, Rice had alerted the nearby clinics of his name and description. Harper and the lieutenant both agreed it was unlikely. Gunshot wounds would only raise suspicions and have the police called. No, Granger likely had someone with medical knowledge to assist with his injuries.

Airport securities were also aware of the situation and the police were setting up barricades.

Rice instructed Harper to remain in the car. She happily obliged, not knowing whether or not her feet would be able to carry her.

The memories of the past week with Granger surrounded her and she closed her eyes.

Two loud gunshots jarred her eyes open.

Then another rang out.

Harper's heartbeat in her chest and she gripped the door's handle.

She waited and breathed a sigh of relieve when officers led two men and a woman outside. Rice followed, dragging Granger with her.

From what Harper could see, he was in pain.

She led him to a police car, said something to her prisoner.

Granger spat in her face.

With a frown, Rice pulled a tissue from her pocket, wiped away the spittle. She pushed Granger into the car. It appeared to Harper she purposefully made him hit the side of his head against the top's edge.

Rice returned to her own car and climbed in.

"They were in the process of getting ready to leave," Rice explained. "But he couldn't go anywhere too fast. The gunshot made him lose a good amount of blood."

"Good," Harper grumbled. "I'm going to have to give Blair the biggest bowl of ice cream when this is all over."

"They deserve it," Rice said. "You all do. I can only imagine what you've gone through."

"Their lives will never be the same again, will they? Neither will mine for that matter."

"If you think about it," Rice said as she pulled away, "no one's life is ever the same. People make mistakes, they have regrets and the get into situations they can't control. It's part of life. Maybe it's not all bad, but our lives are forever changed with each second. It's how you let the change affect you that defines your future."

Harper smiled at her. "Thank you for being so good to us. I really appreciate it."

Rice let her shoulder rise, then fall. "It's my job, Miss Matthews."

"Possibly, but I still think you're a good person and I appreciate everything you're doing for us. And, please, call me Harper."

"I have a daughter of my own," Rice told her. "When my desk sergeant called me and told me a woman and two girls escaped from a man who had trafficked them, the first thing I did was look into her bedroom. I had to make sure she was safe."

"I can imagine when you're dealing with a case having to do with children, it makes it hard, personally."

Rice nodded. "Yes, it makes it almost unbearable. Sometimes I'm not sure if I can get through the case. But I have to because the child reminds me of my own. I would want someone else to do the same thing for her."

"How old is she?"

"Five," Rice said. "Her name's Stephanie, and she's the most energetic five-year-old I've ever known."

"I'd love to see a picture of her sometimes."

Rice pulled into the parking lot of the hotel. She reached into a compartment by the steering wheel and passed a photo to Harper.

Harper took it and studied the dimpled redhead, her hands in her lap. Her poster was straight as she beamed for the camera.

"She's beautiful," Harper said.

"Thank you."

After Harper returned the picture, she pushed the door open and stepped out. The hotel door opened, and Olivia leaned against the doorframe. Harper leaned in the car.

"You'll call me tomorrow about Granger?"

Rice nodded. "Would you like to listen in?"

Eyes wide, Harper said, "Can I?"

"We don't usually allow civilians to take part, but I think I'm willing to make an exception if that's what you'd like to do."

"I'd love that," Harper told her. "I've already invested a lot in this I'd like to see it through."

"Okay. I'll have an officer escort you to the station in the morning I'd also like the girls to make a statement if they feel up to it. And I'll make some calls around Atlanta. Check to see if they ever had a cop named Craig and let them be aware of where you were. You'll have to talk to them, let them know where Craig took you."

"I can do that," Harper said.

"I know you can," Rice told her. "It's late. Get some rest. You're going to need it. It's not over yet, but soon it will be. I promise."

Harper nodded. "Thank you, Lieutenant."

"Goodnight."

Harper closed the door and stepped into the hotel room.

Both girls continued to sleep soundly.

"They haven't woken yet?"

"No," Olivia said. "They've barely moved since we put them to bed. They need a shower, but I thought sleep would be best."

"They also need a change of clothes. We can try to get something for them tomorrow. I don't have money, can I—"

"Of course," Olivia interrupted.

"Thanks." She regarded Olivia. "I mean it."

Harper was aware Olivia watched her as she lowered herself to the chair at the table. She placed her head in her hands with a sigh, too tired to cry, but too sad to do anything else.

For a brief minute, she allowed her mind to think of other distress.

"I can't believe Ollie's dead." She pulled in a shaky breath. "I…I was going to tell him how I felt about him. And now it's too late. He'll never know."

"He knew," Olivia said softly, her hands resting on Harper's shoulders. "Why else would he have stuck around for as long as he did?"

"You didn't tell him anything, did you?"

Olivia shook her head. "Of course not. I told you I wouldn't. I only told him you were called away for something you couldn't get out of, and you didn't have time to give me details. He didn't like it, but I guess he accepted it. Still, he called me, asking if I've heard from you."

Harper pushed out another shaky breath. "I wanted to be honest with him, but I didn't want him to think less of me. When we last spoke, we had a disagreement. We never made up. How can I be so stupid?"

"Like I've said before…you have a big heart." Olivia looked at the sleeping girls. "And you're a hero. Ollie knew that."

"I don't think of myself as a hero," Harper told her.

"You're a modest hero," Olivia replied with a smile. "I can almost guarantee you that when those girls grow up, and they're able to put all of this behind them, they'll remember you. The light that took away the darkness."

Harper lifted the corner of her lips in a faint smile, then released a long yawn.

"I'm tired. I think I better try to rest."

"Yes, I suppose we all should."

Harper rested on her side, facing Blair and Adaline. When she closed her eyes, she drifted into a deep sleep.

Twenty-five

The next morning, Harper returned to the police station with Olivia and the girls in tow. They were once again led to Lieutenant Rice's office. The police officer knocked on the door twice and opened it, announcing their arrival. Harper saw Rice motion with her hand for them to come in as she spoke into the phone.

"Yes, they just walked in…yes, Lieutenant, I'm going to take their statements…right, I've already told Miss Matthews…thank you so much, I'll touch base with you soon."

Placing the phone on the table, Rice offered a warm smile.

"Good morning, ladies, I hope you got a lot of rest last night."

Adaline nodded as Blair bit her lower lip.

"Yes, thank you," Harper said as she lowered herself to a chair.

"Would you like some coffee?"

"That'd be great."

"That was Lieutenant Quintos," Rice said as she poured two cups of coffee. "He's the one who's going to talk to you when you get back to Atlanta." Rice passed them to Harper and Olivia.

Harper acknowledged with a nod as she blew into the coffee.

"Okay, now, I'm going to start by running over the basics with Blair and Adaline. Let the girls know what we're going to be doing." Rice studied the girls carefully. "We need to ask you girls a lot of questions. It's important for us to have as much detail as possible about what happened to you."

"What kind of questions?" Adaline asked.

"Who first kidnapped you, when they did, what they said. Uh, we'll go into more details on what they did." The lieutenant paused. "You know, sometimes it's tough revisiting trauma. So, if you need to take a break, that's what we'll do. Just let us know. Can you do that?"

The girls nodded.

Rice reached for her phone and instructed an Officer Jones to come to her office.

A few minutes later, an officer knocked and stepped inside.

"Blair and Adaline, this is Officer Jones. He's going to take you the two of you to an interview room where they'll talk to you. Separately."

"What about Harper?" Blair asked. "I want to stay with her."

"Me too," Adaline said.

Harper got out of her seat and kneeled in front of the girls. She took their hands into hers.

"You'll be okay, I promise. I'll be right here. Lieutenant Rice needs to talk to me herself, okay?"

"You won't go away?"

Harper brought Blair's hand to her lips and kissed her. "I'm not going anywhere. If you need me, tell the officer and I'll come."

When the girls finally agreed, they left the room with Officer Jones.

"They'll be fine," Rice assured Harper. "Kids are stronger than they seem."

"I know," Harper said. "I'm just worried. Blair was with those people for a long time. I'm not sure when Adaline was taken, but she knows they targeted her because of Daniel. And she knows he's dead because he didn't stop his investigating. They've been through a lot."

Rice nodded. "So have you, Miss Matthews."

Harper cleared her throat, closed her eyes. She pushed the sick feeling down, not wanting to discuss it. "When are you going to question Granger?"

"Right now," she said. "Do you still want to listen in?"

Harper replied that she did.

"So, what should I do?" Olivia asked. "Stay here?"

"Yes," Rice told her. "Would you like something to drink while you wait?"

Olivia wavered her head to say she didn't.

"All right, well, we'll be back as soon as it's over. I'll have someone come check on you." Rice regarded Harper. "Let's get going."

Harper followed Rice through the police station. With each stride, she felt as if her legs were going to fall underneath her. It would be the first time she'd seen Granger up close, hear him talk, since she escaped.

Rice took her into the room where she could watch and hear everything said. Before Rice stepped into the interview room, she put her hand on Harper's arm and squeezed.

Rice stepped into the room and closed the door behind her.

Granger sat at the table, legs apart, leaning against the back of his chair. His lawyer next to him wore a clean pressed suit and a smirk that sent chills up Harper's spine. She wondered if the lawyer was involved somehow. He seemed fishy enough.

"Good morning, Mr. Granger," Rice said as she pulled back a gray folding chair. She sat, her eyes never wavering from his. "Hope you slept okay."

Granger grunted in response.

"Do you mind if I record this?"

"I have a choice?"

"No."

"Then why ask?" Granger crossed one leg over the other, leaned back and laced his fingers behind his head.

"Habit," Rice told him. For the recorder, she said her name Granger's name, and the date and time. "Mr. Granger, why don't we get straight to business? Last night, you were told the reason you were under arrest was for suspicion of human trafficking. That's a very serious charge, Mr. Granger."

She hesitated, her gaze never wavering from Granger's.

"My client, as you can see, is injured," the lawyer claimed. "He was shot trying to do a good deed."

Rice scoffed, her gaze shifting to the lawyer's. "Really? That's funny. As we speak, the two girls are telling my men how your client here bought them." She looked back at Granger. "How long have you been in control of Adaline and Blair?"

The lawyer leaned in to whisper something into Granger's ear. Without smiling, he nodded, then regarded Rice.

"Adaline was, uh, sent to me a few months ago. November, I believe. Blair has been with me for almost two years."

Harper was surprised to hear Granger's honesty. She wondered if he was going to ask for a deal to get out of the charges against him.

Rice wrote something in her notebook before continuing.

"Who brought them to you?"

Granger leaned to his lawyer's ear, who shook his head, whispering something back.

"If he tells you, he's going to need to get something back," the lawyer said.

"How about the satisfaction that he's protecting more girls from being kidnapped and trafficked?"

The lawyer scoffed. "Nice try, Lieutenant. But I was thinking more along the lines of making a deal. Five years in jail, one-year probation."

It was Rice's turn to scoff. "Five years? You can't be serious. Mr. Van Buren, your client held three victims against their will to perform as sex slaves. Two of them are under the age of eighteen. That's child abuse, rape, negligence…the list goes on and on. That's not even including Miss Matthews. You're going to be in prison for the remainder of your life, Mr. Granger."

Granger leaned across the table with a smile. "Maybe so, but without me, you can't find the answers. So, let me ask you this, Lieutenant Rice…how badly do you want to find my associates?"

Harper's heart clutched in her chest.

Could he really force them to make a deal? Five years out of life imprisonment?

"I'm going to have to discuss this with the district attorney," Rice told him.

"Then you best hurry," Granger said. "Every day, things change. They rarely stay the same. Tick tock, tick tock."

He leaned back again, a smile spreading across his face.

"How is…Miss Matthews? I'd like to talk to her."

"Forget it," Rice said. She began to gather her files. "I'll speak to the district attorney about making a deal."

"You get me the deal, I tell everything…to her."

Rice gazed at him before speaking.

"Forget it," she replied. "You are not to speak to her."

"But I will…if you want me to tell you everything I know." He shrugged, then sighed. "But, if not, then I take it to my grave."

After a moment of silence, Rice left the interview room, her heels clunking against the floor.

"Can he do that?" Harper asked her as she watched the lawyer and

Granger talk softly.

"Criminals make deals all the time," Rice said. "Depending on the situation, they sometimes get it."

"So, you're telling me I'm probably going to have to talk to Granger? Get him to confess everything to me?"

"It's highly unusual, but it does happen. I'll talk to the DA about making him a deal. But, if you don't want to speak to him, I understand. I'll let you make that decision yourself."

"If the DA agrees to the five years and I don't want to talk to him, then what?"

"The deal will be off the table. We'll hold Granger and the three we arrested along with him until arraignment. Based on their charges, it's likely they'll be remanded until trial. Then it'll be up to the jury to decide. If found guilty, they'll go to jail for a long time, possibly life."

"But you won't be able to arrest anyone else? Including The Ghost?"

Rice let out a despondent sigh as she regarded Granger.

"Let's not jump to conclusions, Harper," Rice said. "You still have to talk to Lieutenant Quintos. We hope to raid the first house you stayed at. We may find someone there to give us answers without allowing Granger to have any deals."

"But, if that doesn't happen…"

"If that doesn't happen, we'll go on from there." Rice shook her head. "I'm sorry, but it's rarely cut and dry, especially dealing with high profile cases like this."

"When am I going back to Atlanta?" Harper asked.

"Whenever you're ready. How about after lunch?"

"That's fine," Harper agreed. "What about Liv and the girls? Will they be staying here?"

"Yes. The girls' job is finished for now. That is, after their statements have been made. Granger threatened your friend, so it's best she remains in protective custody as well. Even though Granger is in jail, he still has plenty of friends. And it's probable someone deeper within told Granger about Olivia. I get the feeling he's only one of the many pawns. Whoever The Ghost is, is who we need to go after."

"I agree," Harper told her. "That's why I'm willing to talk to Granger whenever it's needed. The Ghost ordered Daniel to be killed. He…or she…ordered Adaline to be taken from her family. Adaline even told me it was The Ghost who removed her from the house before I showed up."

"She did?" Rice asked. "Did she see him?"

Harper shook her head. "She was drugged up. Her vision wasn't clear. She said the voice she heard sounded funny. It was probably the effect of the drug."

"Maybe with time, she'll be able to remember more," Rice said as they walked away from the interview room. "It's common for people to remember details later. They begin to feel safe, and can't help but to remember specifics weeks, even days later."

When they reached Rice's office, she opened the door and they stepped in. Adaline and Blair were waiting with Olivia.

"We're all done for now. Why don't we get you girls fresh clothes? Have you had breakfast?"

"No," Harper said. "We came straight here."

"The police officer gave us some donuts," Blair said. "But I'm still hungry."

"Me too," Adaline piped.

"That's not fair," Harper said, faking a frown. "I didn't get a donut."

"How about I pay for your breakfast?" Rice replied. "As a thank you for everything you've done."

"I haven't done anything except make matters worse," Harper insisted. "But, since I don't have money on me, and I'd hate to keep taking advantage of Liv, I accept your invitation."

"Great," Rice said, grabbing her handbag. "We'll eat, then go clothes shopping. Is that all right with you ladies?"

Blair and Adaline nodded with amusement.

"Can we have pancakes?"

"Of course. We'll go to a place where you can have anything and everything you want. As long as it's on the menu."

Twenty-six

After they had their breakfast, Harper and Olivia took the girls shopping for new clothes. Two men in plain clothes trailed behind them.

Lieutenant Rice said they would contact the girls' families after they returned to the station. Blair seemed dejected about reuniting with her parents. Harper made a mental note to talk to her about it before she left for Atlanta. Adaline, on the other hand, continued to talk about her family and Daniel, making Harper saddened that he died trying to bring to light of what was happening.

Could Harper have prevented his death? If she never went to him, would he still be alive? Would he have been able to find Adaline and Blair and save them? Or would he still have been killed?

Did Daniel really talk to Craig?

Was Craig even still alive? Or did Granger tell her he was dead so she wouldn't realize Craig tricked her into going undercover?

Why did she allow herself to be so gullible? The more Harper worked through her issues with her dad and failure of men relationship, the more she'd have trouble in trusting anybody. And when she allowed herself to open a little bit of trust, she'd realized she'd again find herself in a sinking ship.

"Harper?"

Feeling a hand on her shoulder, Harper blinked at Olivia.

"You okay? I've been talking to you."

"Oh, yeah," Harper said, waving her hand as if to erase the memory. "Sorry, I was just thinking."

"Anything you want to clue me in about?"

Harper cocked her head. "You know, when I called you the other day, I thought I heard someone in the background. Was someone with you?"

"We're talking about you, remember?"

Harper laughed as she nudged her friend. "And now, we're talking about you. So, who is this mystery guy? Someone new, or have you kept him hidden in the shadows for a while."

Olivia arched her eyebrow. "What makes you so sure it was a man?"

Harper allowed her shoulders to rise and fall. “Sounded like a man. But, honestly, I wasn’t in the state of mind when I called you. I just thought I heard someone.”

Olivia hesitated before speaking, watching as the girls pulled a few outfits off the rack and entered the dressing room.

“It was nobody,” she said. “Don’t worry about it.”

“I wouldn’t say I’m worried. I just want to know what life on the outside has been life.”

“‘Life on the outside?’” Olivia echoed. “It’s not like you were in jail, Harper.”

“No, I wasn’t,” Harper snapped. “Where I was was a whole lot worse. You have no idea what I’ve been through. What they’ve been through.”

“I didn’t mean anything by that,” Olivia said.

Harper pinched the bridge of her nose, closing her eyes.

“I know,” Harper told her. “But I’m just trying to get back to normal life. You and I always told each other everything.”

“Not everything. You never told me you were sleeping with Jonathan Parker.”

Harper cleared her throat. “Jonathan was a mistake. I think a part of me knew it even when he coaxed me into bed.”

“Why didn’t you tell me?”

“I don’t know,” Harper said. “I guess a part of me knew it wouldn’t last. Either he would mess it up, or I would.”

“He just wasn’t the one for you,” Olivia said. “I’m sorry he treated you the way he did. You don’t deserve it.”

“What about now?” Harper asked. She turned to face her friend. “What about now? For the last couple weeks, I’ve had to sleep with…at lost count at seventy-five different men.”

“That’s not your fault,” Olivia protested, shaking her head.

“Really?” Harper’s voice cracked as she spoke. “Because I see the way you look at me now. I haven’t even gone into all the gory details with you and you’re looking at me like I’m a prostitute.”

“How can you say that?” Olivia said, her mouth hanging open. “I’m your best friend. Don’t start thinking I don’t want to help you through this, Harp."

Harper frowned. "I'm sorry, Liv. It's just the vibe I keep feeling from you."

"Well, it's in your head," Olivia insisted. "I won't ever turn from you, no matter what happened. I just…to be honest, I'm only trying to figure out what I need to say or do."

"I'm still trying to figure out how I got myself into it," Harper said under her breath. "I…I really thought Craig was genuine in wanting to help."

"Maybe he was," Olivia told her. "Maybe he really was killed."

"I don't think so," Harper admitted. "These guys are smart. Craig told me just enough of the truth. And I fell right into his trap, hook, line, and sinker."

She hesitated as the girls exited the dressing rooms, handing their unwanted items to the attendant.

"They wanted to kill Daniel because he was getting close. They wanted to get me out of the way in case I knew more than I did. But, killing me may have been too coincidental. Especially since I didn't die in that shootout at the hotel."

"Unfortunately, that does make sense." Oliva put a hand on Harper's shoulder as Blair and Adaline approached. "I want you to know I'm here for you. Always. Whenever you're ready."

Harper reached her arms out to give Olivia a tight hug.

"Thank you."

She turned to the girls.

"Did you decide on something?"

They nodded.

"All right," Harper said. "Let's get going, then. We're going to contact your parents once we get back to Lieutenant Rice's office."

"Are we going to see them soon?" Adaline asked.

"Yes," Harper told her. "Lieutenant Rice is flying them to Atlanta. We'll meet them at the airport."

"Do they know about Daniel?"

"I don't know," Harper admitted. "They probably were informed shortly after his death."

Olivia looked down at Blair.

"Are you excited to see your parents, Blair? You've hardly said anything about them."

The girls set their clothes on the counter for the cashier to scan.

Blair shrugged.

Harper knelt next to her. She moved a strand of hair that had found its way into her mouth.

"It's okay to be nervous, honey," she told her.

"Is Lieutenant Rice going to tell them what I was, and what I did?"

"Yes, I think they'll know. But they know it wasn't your fault. Your mom and dad will be so happy to see you, no matter what happened. They love you."

"It's my fault," Blair said.

"No, it's not," Olivia interjected. "It's Granger's fault. And the others he associates with."

"That's right," Harper agreed. "No matter what happened to you or how it happened, your parents will always love you. And I'm sure once they see you again, they'll shower you with their love."

"Don't be so sentimental," Blair said with a giggle.

Harper laughed as she pushed to her feet. "I'm being factual."

Harper grabbed Olivia's arm to look at her watch. It was almost eleven o'clock. In two hours, she and Lieutenant Rice would be on the hour drive back to Atlanta.

She wanted it to be over. She couldn't wait to be able to stop thinking about what she went through.

As they left the store, Harper tried to think about something other than her upcoming meeting with Lieutenant Quintos. In a few hours, she knew she'd be back in Atlanta.

Back where it all started.

Twenty-seven

Lieutenant Rice pulled in the parking lot of the police station in Atlanta. During the drive, Harper didn't speak. To fill the silence, Rice had turned on the radio, the speakers blaring a Bon Jovi CD.

After she removed the key from the ignition, Rice turned to Harper.

"Just tell Lieutenant Quintos everything you told me," she reminded Harper. "It'll be fine."

Harper lifted the corners of her lips to a smile, hoping to hide her trepidation. "I know."

"It'll be over soon," Rice said. "I promise."

"I appreciate you saying that, Lieutenant," Harper told her. "But, it won't be over anytime soon. First, we've got to put these people, including The Ghost, in prison. Then I'm going to have to live with everything they did and everything I did for the rest of my life. I knew the majority of what I'd need to do going in, but the more I think about it, the sicker it makes me."

Rice glanced over, her eyes reflecting her understanding.

"It's funny, you know?" Harper said, looking out the windshield at the large building. "When I was younger, I thought the worst thing that could happen would be going home to my dad. There were rare times when he didn't shove me inside a closet. Sometimes I'd purposefully get detention at school because I was afraid to go home. I never could tell anyone what he was doing to me, or to my mother. I was ashamed."

"Do you have any good memories of him?"

Harper nodded. "He took me to the Braves games sometimes. I was always excited when he told me he ordered tickets."

"That's nice."

"It was," Harper told me. "But, very often, the feeling didn't last for long. If the Braves lost, he'd take it out on me. Still, as a little girl, I liked going to the games because for a few hours, I could hang out with him. Silly, huh?"

"No," Rice told her. "Not at all."

Harper looked sideways, putting her hand on the door handle. "Let's get this over with."

Without saying anything more, they walked into the building. Rice flashed her credentials and let the desk sergeant know Lieutenant Quintos was expecting them. They were instructed to take a seat and Lieutenant Quintos would be out momentarily.

Rice and Harper sat in a chair to wait. Rice began to read something on her cell.

"Do you think someone can get my dog?" Harper asked after a moment. "Olivia was keeping him for me. Since we don't know when we'll get to go home, I'd like to have him with me."

"What's your dog's name?" Rice asked, looking at her.

"Collier," Harper said. "He's a Sheltie. Probably made a mess of Liv's apartment."

Rice smiled. "A miniature collie. How sweet. I don't think you'll be able to have him at the hotel, though."

"Oh. Right."

Rice slipped her phone in its holster. "But I suppose I can take him for a few days."

"You'd do that? Are you sure it's not much trouble?" Harper asked. "I had a friend who usually takes him. My neighbor. But he didn't have any idea about what's been going on. Even if he could take Collier, though, I'm not so sure he would. He probably wouldn't be speaking to me."

"It's best not to have your friend involved in any way, even to pick Collier up," Rice told her. "As long as he doesn't know anything, he'll be safe."

Harper shook her head. "He's dead."

"Oh," Rice said. "I'm so sorry. I didn't realize."

"It's okay," Harper said, her voice soft. "I'm still trying to wrap my head around it. It was sudden."

"How did he die, if you don't mind me asking?"

"Car accident," Harper answered. "A few days after I left with Craig. I didn't know until the night I met up with Liv."

"That's terrible," Rice said. They fell into silence before the lieutenant spoke again. "It's no problem for me to take your dog. My daughter would even love it. I'll arrange it when you're with Lieutenant

Quintos."

"Thank you so much. You have no idea how much that means to me."

Rice reached over to squeeze Harper's arm. "It's my pleasure. Why wouldn't your friend be speaking to you? If you don't mind me asking?"

Harper frowned. "We didn't part on the best terms."

"I'm sorry," Rice said. "I know it's none of my business."

"It's okay," Harper told her. "I've known Ollie since high school. We were good friends ever since. I've always known he had a crush on me. Even in love with me."

"Did he ever ask you out?"

Harper wavered her head to say he didn't.

"I don't know why he didn't. I never had a boyfriend. But, with everything I was going through with my dad, boys were the last thing I wanted to think about."

"I understand."

"After graduation, I went to school out of state," Harper continued. "Thankfully, I had a full music scholarship at Juilliard."

"Very impressive. I didn't realize you played an instrument."

"Yes. Violin," Harper told her. "Of course, going to Juilliard meant leaving Ollie behind. He was the one part of my past that made me feel safe. I left for Juilliard and stayed away for about ten years. In between time, Ollie met a woman at college. I even met someone. Ollie married her and was very happy for several years. They had two beautiful daughters together. Twins."

"What happened?"

"Alyssa was killed in a car wreck. She had the girls with her. Thankfully, they escaped with hardly a scratch. But, Alyssa was pinned in the car. They had to cut her out. She died on the way to the hospital from a punctured lung."

"That's so horrible," Rice said.

"Yes, Ollie was a mess. Nothing was going for me in New York, and the guy I was with wasn't a very good guy, so I came home. When the apartment across from him became available, I snatched it up."

"That's—"

"Lieutenant Rice?"

The man interrupting her approached, extending his hand. He wore a large tanned cowboy hat with a shirt to match. When Harper and Rice rose to greet him, Harper guessed him to be close to six feet, two inches taller than herself.

"I'm Lieutenant Quintos, thank you for coming.

As he shook Rice's hand, he studied Harper.

"You must be Miss Matthews," Quintos acknowledged. He moved his hand in her direction. She accepted.

"Why don't we go into my office?" Quintos suggested. "Would you like something to eat or drink?"

"Water would be nice," Harper said.

"I'll be right here," Rice told Harper.

With a nod, Harper followed Lieutenant Quintos.

After the reached his office, he motioned for her to have a seat. He used his desk phone to request for someone to bring her a bottled water.

"How are you doing today, Miss Matthews?"

"I'm okay. And call me Harper."

"Do you mind if I record our conversation?"

Harper shook her head as someone knocked and opened the door. She was handed a bottled water. Harper thanked the young boy and unscrewed the cap.

"Okay, then, let's go ahead and get started."

As Harper listened to Quintos speak into the recorder, she took a long swig of water to wet her throat.

"Miss Matthews," Quintos began. "Over the telephone, I spoke with Lieutenant Charlotte Rice from the Conyers PD. According to her, you escaped with two young girls from a man named Granger. Is that correct?"

"Uh, yes, it is."

"Tell me what happened until then."

Harper explained to Quintos about meeting Daniel Clark on the airplane, then her search for Daniel. She mentioned being at the Hilton Atlanta talking to Daniel when someone opened fire, killing him. She told Quintos about meeting Craig and going undercover to finish what

Daniel started.

"After I was transferred to the second house," Harper concluded, "I knew I needed to escape. I couldn't go without the girls, so I waited until I had the opportunity and, I guess the nerves, to leave."

"What happened while you were in these houses?"

Harper didn't respond immediately.

Noting her hesitation, Quintos paused the recording and leaned over his desk. His green eyes bore into hers, forcing her to look away.

"I realize this is hard for you, Miss Matthews, but, we need to know what happened to you. It's the only way."

She nodded. He pressed the button to resume the recording.

"Tell me what happened."

"I…I didn't have to do anything until I was sent to the other house," Harper evaded, feeling the hot tears lingering on the corner of her eyes. "I don't know how I got there, or why Craig let me go. But, when I arrived, almost immediately, I was sent to, um…work."

"What kind of work?"

"I had to have sex with men. A lot of men. Granger would punish us if we didn't do what was expected. He even threatened a friend of mine."

"Thank you, Miss Matthews. Is there anything else you remember?"

Harper shook her head. "No."

"Okay, then. This concludes our recorded interview." He turned off the recording and began to write on a piece of paper.

Harper took sips of her water as she waited.

"Do you recall where this Craig took you?" Quintos asked without looking up.

"I think so. I don't know the address, though."

"You do realize it's dangerous for a woman to enter a situation like that, willingly?"

Harper thought she detected an accusing tone to his words. She frowned, willing herself not to allow herself to be agitated.

"I only wanted to help. Daniel said he was getting close to who the big people were. And his sister, Adaline, she was with them. I didn't want Daniel to have died in vain. So, when I met Craig, and he gave me a chance, I took it."

"I asked around at other precincts and there's no undercover cop by the name of Craig, Miss Matthews," Quintos informed her in the same accusing tone. "Of course, it's always possible that 'Craig' was a made up name."

"Yes, I realize that," Harper told him.

"And still you accepted his invitation?"

Again, Harper frowned. "I didn't realize it at the time. I know, I was foolish. I fell into his trap. It's something I'm going to have to remember for the rest of my life."

Quintos released a long, heavy sigh, as if he'd just wasted his time.

"Look, Lieutenant," Harper told him. "I realize that, yes, I did get myself into a world of trouble. But, knowing what I know now, I would do the same thing given the chance. There are women and young girls being taken from everything they know. These men use them as objects to satisfy their disgusting needs. And when they have no use for them anymore, they sell them or shoot them in the head."

She narrowed her eyes.

"Judge me if you want, Lieutenant," Harper said. "But this can't keep going on. These girls haven't done anything to deserve it. Their innocent has been stripped away. They'll never get it back. I hear how the police arrest underage prostitutes. What about the men that have sex with them? They get a slap on the wrist and released to do it again? This can't keep happening."

Quintos' unwavering gaze from across the desk made her skin crawl. One thing she remembered Craig saying is that anyone could be involved. People everywhere had second lives. Lives no one knows about.

Even cops.

"You're right," Quintos told her, setting his pen on the desk. "You're quite right. Will you be willing to guide us to the house?"

"Will Lieutenant Rice be coming?"

"I can arrange it."

"If she goes, I'll take you wherever you want."

Twenty-eight

"You okay?" Rice asked. "You haven't said anything since leaving Quintos' office."

Harper sat in Rice's car, arms crossed tight against her chest. Her lips were turned into a frown. The embarrassment and anguish at herself slowly dissolved into infuriation.

"I don't like Quintos," Harper admitted. "I felt like he was accusing me of something. Like it was my fault for getting myself stuck in that situation. I only wanted to help."

"I understand, Harper," Rice said. "Believe me, I do. There are always going to be people who blame others just because it's easier than facing the fact. People blame prostitutes for being raped. Because they make a living out of it, they've got to want it, right? Well, the answer is not always. But there are people who disagree. And if you get yourself into a situation, people say it's your fault because you made the move to do so. But, Harper, there are some people who knows the truth. They aren't blind to it. I'm one of them. Forget what Quintos says or thinks, all right? I think what you did was very brave and heroic."

The corner of Harper's lips curved in a slight smile. "Do you think so?"

"I'm a cop," Rice reminded her. "I carry a gun, I'm trained in self-defense. I won't be modest to say I can take down most of my colleagues. But even I am not sure if I would be brave enough to go undercover the way you did. That takes a special kind of courage."

"That means a lot," Harper said softly.

"I'm being truthful," Rice told her.

"I know," Harper said.

"Let's get going. Hopefully, we can end this soon so you, Olivia, and the girls can return to your lives."

Rice's cell phone rang, and she answered. After a moment, she ended the call and turned the ignition.

"We've got the warrant. Time to get the show started."

Rice took the lead, so Harper could give her directions.

It'd been a lifetime ago since she first arrived at the house. Harper could only hope and pray she remembered the way.

Soon, an hour and a half passed by and they finally reached the familiar stretch of the road leading to the large white house at the end. The cars scattered around the building and the police jumped out.

Harper watched as they crashed through the door with a battering ram.

Gunshots rang in the air.

Harper gripped the handle of her door as she watched, feeling helpless.

She noticed the curtains pulled back in the window, then a man climbed out. He walked along the roof, toward a nearby tree. The man jumped, missing the branch by almost an inch.

Harper left Rice's car and ran to the man's side.

"Are you okay?"

He released a groan as he rose to his feet.

"I'll be fine," he muttered.

"Good." Harper kicked him in the groin, forcing him to grab himself as he fell backward.

"Harper!"

She looked up to see Mai standing in the window.

"Mai! Are you okay?"

"What's happening?"

"The police are here," she explained. "Where are the other girls? Are they with you?"

"Bonita and Jenny in another room. Keiko and Jenny downstairs. I don't know where is Katie and Nghia. They leave when you leave."

"Can you get Bonita and Jenny into your room so you can climb out?"

"They with men. I don't know if they can come."

"All right," Harper said.

"I'll climb up to you, then. Stay where you are."

Seeing the man still hunched in pain, Harper used the awning of the house to pull herself off the ground. She almost lost her footing once, but soon, she'd reached Mai's window. She climbed inside to be greeted with a hug from Mai.

"It is good seeing you," Mai told her.

"It's good to see you too." Harper looked around Mai's room. "Get inside the closet, okay? I'll come to get you soon. I'm going to find Bonita and Jenny."

Mai nodded and slipped inside the closet.

Harper heard the gunshots ringing from downstairs, followed by silence and then more gunshots. She peered outside of Mai's room and saw the coast was clear.

She went to the first closed door and knocked.

No one answered.

"Bonita? Jenny? Are you in there?"

"Harper!" a muffled voice said.

She heard someone hiss something. Harper turned the knob to find it locked.

"Jenny! Are you okay? I'm coming in!"

Harper stepped back, raised her knee and connected the heel of her foot to the door. She had to recoil twice before it finally splintered open.

A man held Jenny's arm behind her back, one hand over her mouth.

"Let her go," Harper said. "Please. It doesn't have to be worse than it is."

"I can't go to jail," the wide-eyed man said. "My wife will leave me."

"You should have thought of that before paying to sleep with a thirteen-year-old," Harper hissed. "Let her go. Now."

"Please," the man whispered. "I'll give her to you if you'll let me leave. I can't go to jail."

"You're going to go to jail no matter what happens," Harper pointed out. "The only difference is for how long. You kill her, it'll be a long time before you get out."

"Please," the man begged, his eyes clouding with tears. "I can't lose my wife."

"Fine. I just want Jenny safe. You can crawl out the window in the other room."

The man hesitated before walking slowly with Jenny toward the door.

Once in the hallway, he pushed Jenny into Harper's arms.

"Are you okay, sweetie?" she asked, lowering herself to eye level.

Jenny nodded. "I think so."

"Mai's in her room in the closet," Harper said. "Go to her. I'm going to get Bonita, then we'll get out of here."

Harper stood by the next door as she spoke. She reached her hand for the knob to double-check that it was unlocked.

"Come in, Harper," a familiar voice said, causing her to freeze.

Her movements slow, Harper turned the knob, pushing the door open.

She saw Bonita in the arms of a man holding a knife to her throat.

Not just any man.

Craig.

Twenty-nine

Harper's heart skipped several beats as she watched Craig grip Bonita's neck with one hand, holding the knife with the other. His eyes burned with an emotion Harper never saw him have. Then again, she hadn't known him for very long.

"Craig," Harper said. "You really are alive. Granger told me you were dead."

"Yeah, well, couldn't have you searching for me, you know?" Craig told her.

"Why?" Harper asked him through her teeth. "Just tell me why you pretended to be an undercover cop. Why did you want to trick me into coming here?"

Craig smiled. "Because we couldn't have you running your mouth about what Daniel knew."

"Daniel didn't tell me much," Harper said. "I didn't know who was behind this. I didn't know where this place was located. He didn't even know. So how could I?"

"I saw you go into his hotel room. After I killed him. I knew you wouldn't stop searching for the truth. Daniel's impression of you was right. You're stubborn. The sort to want to ruin an old thing going."

"Good thing?" Harper scoffed. "If you are wanting to make money, there are other ways. *Legal* ways."

"You should have been dead at the hotel along with Daniel. But since you weren't, we had to silence you somehow."

"You killed Daniel? But…why did you have to shoot up that hotel? Other people died that day! They did nothing."

Craig let his shoulder rise, then fall.

"Collateral damage." He narrowed his eyes. "I never lied to you, you know. I only withheld the whole truth. You came here on your own accord."

"And if I didn't?" Harper asked.

Craig didn't respond, but it was enough for Harper.

Bonita whimpered, speaking in Spanish underneath her breath. From the corner of her eyes, she saw movements move slowly up the stairs. She glanced to her right to see Rice and Quintos approaching with their weapons at the ready.

"Tell them to go back downstairs," Craig said. He held the knife closer to Bonita's neck. "Tell them."

Harper shook her head at the lieutenants. "Don't come any closer. He wants you to go back downstairs."

"Miss Matthews—," Quintos began.

"He's got a hostage."

Rice frowned but acknowledged by touching Quintos's shoulder. Harper motioned with her eyes to the other room, hoping Rice would understand what she was saying. Rice glanced at the door with a nod, entered the room, and a second later quietly carted Mai and Jenny down the stairs, followed by a disgruntled Quintos.

Harper turned back to Craig.

"Okay, they're gone now. Why don't you let Bonita go?"

Craig laughed. "She's the only thing that's making you behave."

"Who is The Ghost, Craig? You said before there are some people high up who knows who he is. I'm guessing you're one of them."

"Forget it. I'll take that to my grave. I start talking about The Ghost's identity, he'll start killing off the people I love. Can't have that. It's all a very vicious cycle, ya know."

"My last night here," Harper started as she considered a plan to free Bonita of his grasp. "I can't remember what happened. Can you tell me? Please? I really want to know."

"Rocco took you into the room, injected you with heroin. He raped you before The Ghost showed up and killed him. The Ghost had you transferred to Granger."

"To get me out of the way?"

Craig nodded. "Consider yourself lucky. Granger was one of the nicer ones."

"How wonderful, I am lucky," Harper derided. "He's in jail now."

"Can't say I'm very surprised. He's not the brightest cookie in the batch."

Harper noticed a red light reflecting off the curtains in the window.

"It's over, Craig," Harper said. "You know it is. You can kill Bonita, you can kill me, but you're not going to walk out of here free. They'll either arrest you or kill you."

She studied his face, hoping to find something that would tell her she was getting through to him. But, his eyes remained cold.

Hardened.

"If you cooperate," Harper said. "I'm sure Lieutenant Quintos would be willing to make you a deal. That's what Lieutenant Rice was going to do for Granger."

Craig scoffed. "They're going to give him a deal?"

Harper had seen enough cop shows to know that sometimes it's effective for the suspect to think if he talked first he'd be the one to land the deal. Harper hoped it would be true in real life.

"Yeah. In fact, before we came here, I overheard Lieutenant Quintos and the district attorney say they were going to give you the same deal. Five years in jail, one year of probation. If you told them everything you knew, they'll give you that deal. Otherwise, it'll go to Granger."

Craig shook his head. "Granger doesn't know anything I know. So, the deal's of no use for him."

"That's not what I heard," Harper said, trying her best to look confused. "Granger said something about The Ghost arriving at the house the night I first arrived."

"Granger is at the bottom of the totem pole," Craig insisted. "The Ghost wouldn't personally deal with the likes of him."

"But do you know for sure? If Granger tells the cops anything, and it turns out valid, that'll earn him a deal and you, life in prison. What'll happen to the ones you love then?"

Craig didn't reply.

Harper kept one eye on him, the other on the movement of the red dot.

"If you help us, I'll personally make sure Quintos protects your family. Too many people have already died, Craig. Don't you see? It shouldn't be like this."

Before Craig could respond, a loud bang erupted in the air. Blood exploded from the back of Craig's head.

Bonita screamed as she fell to the ground, Craig on top of her.

Harper rushed to her side and helped Bonita to climb out from underneath him. She pulled Bonita from the ground and slowly backed out of the room, looking at Craig's stiff body.

"It's okay," she said, knowing Bonita wouldn't understand her. "You're okay."

Harper descended the stairs as the police re-entered the house.

Rice and Quintos walked up to her.

"You okay?" Rice asked.

"Yeah, we're good," Harper said.

"You should have remained by the cars," Quintos scolded.

"I had to make sure the girls were okay," Harper told him. "I couldn't just stand by knowing they were in there with gunfire. How are they, anyway?"

"A squad car took them to the hospital. They're traumatized, but I think they're all right."

"We're you able to get anything from him?"

Harper shook her head. "I don't know if I was getting through to him or not. He was shot before I had the chance. But he did claim Granger doesn't know anything."

"Even if Granger doesn't know anything," Rice said, "he'll know of someone that does know. I'll have the DA offer him the deal. If he accepts and what he says leads to capture, he'll get it."

Rice paused to regard Harper, her eyes studying her face.

"Will you be okay with that?"

Harper didn't reply immediately. She glanced back at the house to see a few of the officers pass by the window where Craig once stood. She looked back at Rice.

"Don't worry about me," Harper told her. "I just want The Ghost found."

"Let's get you to the hospital, okay? I'll leave Quintos to his work."

Rice put a hand on Harper's shoulder as they walked.

"You did good, Harper," Rice told her. "You did very good."

But, Harper wasn't so sure. She was leaving the house without answers and the one man who could give them to her was dead.

Thirty

The next few nights, Harper couldn't sleep. The girls have all been returned to their families, Harper and Olivia to their own normal lives. For the first couple of nights, Harper and Collier remained at Olivia's apartment. She wasn't sure if she'd be able to walk across Ollie's apartment, knowing he wouldn't be inside.

Harper sat at Olivia's kitchen table, a coffee cup in her hand. She stared at the newspaper article with Ollies' obituary.

Oliver (Ollie) Francis Baldridge, Jr., age 34, went to be with the Lord, on Thursday, June 25, 2019.

Ollie was born on September 30, 1985, in Atlanta, Georgia. He worked at the law offices of Baldridge & Son. Ollie was the founder of New Life Outreach, a ministry providing services to the homeless in the area.

Survivors include his daughters Emma and Baylee, his father, Oliver Baldridge, Sr. Ollie was preceded in death by his mother, Eileen.

Services will be held at 2 p.m., Sunday, June 28, at the New Life Outreach. Burial will be held in private.

In lieu of flowers, the family wishes donations to be sent to New Life Outreach.

Harper reread the obit, ignoring the tears that fell from her eyes. She ran her hand against the black and white picture of Ollie, her hands shaking.

"Forgive me, Ollie," she said, her voice hoarse. She set the coffee mug on the table and covered her face with her hands. "I'm so sorry."

"Harp?"

Harper didn't look up when she heard Olivia's voice. Instead, her shoulders shook as the floodgate burst.

"It's my fault, Liv," she forced out. "He's dead because of me."

"No," Olivia protested, her voice soft and soothing. She put a hand and rubbed Harper's back. "You didn't kill him."

Leaning into her, Harper said, "If I hadn't gone undercover at the house, Ollie would still be alive. It's my fault. Everything. I didn't even get to tell him goodbye. The last time we talked, we were so angry at each other. I never got to tell him I was sorry."

"He knew, Harper," Olivia assured her. "He knew."

Harper pulled back and stared at the obituary. "I didn't even get to go to his funeral."

"I know," Olivia whispered. She sat in a chair. "Ollie knew how you felt about him. I don't know if that helps or not, but he did know."

Harper wiped her eyes. "I should go to his dad's. Give him food, or flowers, or something."

"Would you like some company when you go?"

"Would you, Liv? I'm not sure I'd be able to face them alone."

Olivia offered a brief smile. "Of course."

When they fell into another silence, Harper picked up another article.

Ollie's death notice.

She'd read the article so many times, she felt she could recite every word. According to the article, his brakes failed, and he crashed onto a cemented divider. The impact of his car forced him through the windshield. He was dead on the scene.

"It doesn't make sense, Liv," Harper said.

"I know. Ollie was a good man. And a good friend. He will be missed."

Harper shook her head, still staring at the news article.

"No, Liv," she said. The article clutched tight in her hand, she rose and paced the small kitchen. Collier rested by the door, his head on the floor, eyes on her every move. "The way he died doesn't make sense. Ollie always…always…wore a seatbelt. And the airbag? How could he fly through the windshield?"

"I'm sure it happens, Harper. Maybe he was in a hurry and he didn't have time to put on the seatbelt. Maybe the airbag failed."

"That's quite a coincidence, don't you think? Ollie's brakes fail at the one time he's not wearing his seatbelt and his airbag isn't working?"

Olivia didn't respond.

"I know there's something else to this, Olivia." Harper leaned against the refrigerator, staring at the picture of the crash site. "Ollie could be late for a meeting with the *queen* and he would take the time to put on his seatbelt."

"What are you thinking, Harper? Someone killed him? But who? And why?"

"I'm not sure. What if Craig did? What if The Ghost did? Someone could have seen him with me at the Hilton when we went into Daniel's hotel room. Killing him with a gun or another way would have seemed too fishy, don't you think?"

"But if he were to die in an accident..." Olivia trailed off, covering her mouth with her hands.

"No one would know his death was indirectly connected to trafficking. They've already shown they'll kill at will when they killed Nghia and the bystanders at the hotel."

"I wonder why they didn't kill you? I mean, why keep you alive at all? If they wanted to tie up loose ends...why not just kill you? You said that Rocco guy was attacking you. They could have killed you and put the blame on him. Why send you to Granger? They didn't have to keep up the charade."

"I don't know," Harper said. "But, I bet Granger knows the answer to some of our questions, if not all."

"When does Lieutenant Rice want you to talk to him?"

"They're discussing the situation with the ADA. I'm waiting for her to give me a call." Harper regarded Olivia. "But I'm done waiting. I know someone murdered Ollie and staged it to be an accident. I want to know who. Granger may be able to help with that."

"Be careful, Harper," Olivia warned. "The further you get into this, the more danger you'll get into. Ollie's already lost. I don't want to lose you too."

"I owe it to him, Liv. Especially if Ollie was killed because of me." Harper snatched her phone from the counter. She turned on the screen and frowned, realizing it was two in the morning.

"I guess I better wait until I know Lieutenant Rice is awake."

"You need your sleep anyway," Olivia told her. "Your eyes are bloodshot, and you have dark circles."

"I haven't slept. Not really. If I sleep, I have nightmares," Harper said. "So I don't want to sleep."

"I can't force you," Olivia told her. "But, I don't think I can stay up any longer. Goodnight."

Harper hugged her. "Goodnight. I'll see you in the morning."

As Olivia left the kitchen for her bedroom, Harper reclaimed her seat at the table, thinking about everything she wanted to ask Granger.

Thirty-one

"Granger may not know anything about your friend," Rice reminded her "And if he did, he may not tell you what you want to know. It's very likely Ollie's death was an accident."

"It wasn't."

Harper had spent most of the night rethinking everything she knew. By the time she entered Lieutenant Rice's office the next morning, she had the confidence that Ollie had been murdered. She reminded herself that Rice was right about one thing: Granger may not know who killed Ollie, or even if he was killed. But she was sure Granger could give her some answers, and while answers tend to lead to more questions, they also tend to lead to answers to questions.

"The ADA approved my request to let you talk to Granger. He's been making it pretty clear he'll only tell us what he knows if he talks to you." Rice released a sigh. "I don't want your hopes up, though. People like Granger use the position they're in to their advantage. Make a bad situation seem better. He may only want to see you, so he can look into your eyes and see your desperation."

"I understand," Harper said. "He's going to understand that desperation is not what he's going to get. Not from me. Not this time.

Rice nodded, her lips curved in a smirk. "Good. If you're ready, we can get you started."

"I'm ready."

Rice rose from her chair, opened her door and led the way through the station to the interview room. Before she opened the door, she turned to gaze at Harper.

"I'll be right here, so you don't have to worry about anything. I'll be watching and listening."

Harper forced a tight smile. "I know."

Rice opened the door.

Pulling in a deep breath, then pushing it out, she stepped over the threshold. Harper looked over her shoulder when she heard Rice click the door shut.

It was then she began to feel the small, gray room closing in on her.

She closed her eyes, to try controlling her breathing. It didn't work, but, she knew she couldn't leave.

Not until Granger gave her useful information.

Her blood pulsing in her ears, she turned to study Granger.

He sat in an orange jumpsuit, his hands folded on the surface of the gray table.

"How are you, Harper?" Granger asked as if speaking to a friend.

Harper walked to the table, her movements slow and footsteps echoing against the walls. She sat across from Granger, intent on not breaking eye contact.

"I'm…I'm doing great." To her ears, her voice sounded small, like a child's. She hoped no one else noticed. "How are you, Granger?"

"Glad to see you again."

"Why is that?" Harper asked. "Why did you want to see me?"

Granger cocked his head. "Why not?"

"I saw Craig. I found out the truth about him."

Granger smiled. "I see. How did that make you feel?"

Harper scoffed. "Are you a psychologist or something? Do you moonlight as a human trafficker?"

"No."

"You told Lieutenant Rice you would tell us everything you know if I came to talk to you."

"That's true, I did."

Harper folded her hands on the table, ignoring the thrumming of her heart behind her ribcage. "Well, I'm here. Tell me."

"What is it you want to know?"

Harper frowned before speaking. "Okay, um, who is The Ghost?"

"I don't know. Next question."

"You expect me to believe you don't know who The Ghost is?"

"Yes, because I don't know," Granger said. "He's called The Ghost for a reason. He doesn't come around. Only a few people knew his identity. Word has it The Ghost doesn't like his hands dirty."

"Craig knew who The Ghost was, right?"

"He did. So, you should ask him."

"Can't. He's dead."

"Shame."

"Who else did The Ghost confer with? Surely Craig wasn't his only contact."

"He wasn't, but I'm not sure who knew him. Sorry, can't help you on The Ghost. Next topic."

"All right," Harper said through her teeth. "Let's talk about me, then. Why didn't Craig kill me when he could have?"

"The Ghost ordered him not to."

"Why?"

Granger lifted the corner of his lips to a smile as he raised his shoulder to his chin. "You'll have to ask either The Ghost or Craig."

"Fine." Harper turned to the glass behind her. She saw her reflection and Granger's smiling face. As the moments went by in the interview room, she felt her face grow hot, her palms clammy.

She turned back to him. "The day after I first arrived at the other house, I was taken to you. Craig told me you were supposed to kill me. Why didn't you?"

"I received a call from The Ghost. He told me I could do whatever I wanted but kill you."

"He didn't tell you why he wanted me dead?"

"He told me he had his reasons. When I finally saw you, I realized you'd be good anyway. You're pretty. Pretty gets paid a lot of pennies, you know?"

"What about Ollie? Someone murdered him, didn't they? Do you know who? Was it Craig?"

"I don't know who that is."

"He was my best friend," Harper told him, trying not to let her tears come through her words. "He was killed in a car accident. But I think it was staged."

"Well, if that's true, then he knew something he shouldn't have known, or they believed he knew something he shouldn't have known."

"He didn't know anything," Harper said through her teeth. "He had no idea what was going on."

"Sorry, can't help you with that."

"Is there someone that does most of the dirty work? Like stage an accident?"

"Not necessarily. The Ghost orders the contract."

"Fine," Harper spat. "Then why did you want to speak to me? You realize they're going to take away the deal unless you give them something. Did you just want to look at me?"

Granger leaned across the table. "I may not know who The Ghost is, but I do know who comes and goes in the brothels, the houses. We get a lot of business from a lot…and I do mean a lot…of big names. Governors, Congress, police officers…you name it. The girls get traded every so often. If these men have a favorite, I guarantee they're going to follow them."

"Who?"

"Got some paper?"

"I'll go see if Lieutenant Rice will get me some."

Harper rose, making her way for the door. When she stepped on the other side, Rice handed her a pad and pen.

"You're doing good," she said.

"I don't know," Harper replied. "I was really hoping he would tell me about Ollie."

"It's possible that Granger knows nothing about Ollie's death," Rice reminded her.

Harper noted the hesitation in her words and could tell what Rice was thinking: It may have been an accident after all.

But, Harper didn't believe that. She couldn't shake the feeling Ollie was murdered because of her involvement with Granger and the other men. She had to find out the truth.

She took a deep breath, counted to ten, then returned to the interview room and slid the pad across the table.

She watched as Granger wrote names across the sheet, some names she recognized, others she didn't. He wrote slow, and Harper wondered if it was intentional. He couldn't torment her with her body anymore, so he wanted to torment her mentally.

When he was finished, he set the pen on the pad and passed it over.

"You tell Rice to be sure the ADA gives me my deal."

Harper snatched the pad from the table and rushed to the door. She put her hand on the doorknob, drew in a couple of deep breaths before turning back to him.

"I hope you die before you have the chance to get out," she told him. "I really hope you die, and your death is slow and painful."

Letting her final words linger in the air, Harper left Granger to sit in the small, gray room.

Thirty-two

"Are you okay?"

Harper turned to see Lieutenant Rice walking toward her. She turned back to look across the parking lot. The sun was warm against her skin.

"I'm fine," she said. "I just needed to get some air."

"Understandable," Rice told her.

Harper regarded the lieutenant. "What happens next?"

"Now it's time to notify the feds. We'll be forced to work with them because not only are some of these men out of my jurisdiction, I should have contacted them from the moment I heard about you and the other girls."

"So, it's true…cops really don't like the FBI?"

Rice snickered. "I don't think it's that we don't like them. We tend to be territorial. We don't want to rely on someone else to do the work on our turf."

"Oh."

"I want to thank you for all you've done, Harper," Rice told her. "I realize a lot of people were lost in different ways, and I know it'll take some time before you can heal. But, I do admire your strength."

"I never felt strong," Harper admitted. "I felt scared. Even before I agreed to go with Craig. But I admit that I didn't realize how scared I should have felt. I did things I never would have done otherwise. I kept reminding myself it was for a purpose. I kept telling myself there had to be a way for me to get out and finish what I set out to do."

"And you did," Rice said. "We'll find The Ghost, Harper. I know it. One of the men on the list is bound to know his identity. But, I will be bluntly honest. Once we put The Ghost behind bars, there are still hundreds of operations around the world, including here, where people are being trafficked. I have to remind myself even if we can save one victim, we're working on making a difference. You, Harper, saved several."

"Thank you for saying that," Harper told her. "It means a lot."

"What are you going to do now?"

Harper focused her gaze on the ground before stealing another glance at Rice.

"I'm going to find out the truth behind Ollie's death. Something doesn't sit right with me and I have to find out what that is."

"Just don't do anything that requires the police," Rice warned.

"I won't."

"If you need help, let me know. I probably won't be able to do a great deal since he didn't die on my jurisdiction, but I can, and will, give you direction. As long as it's safe. Otherwise, I'll be suggesting you speak with the Atlanta PD."

Harper nodded in answer.

"Where should I start looking?"

"If it were me, I'd find out where he was headed. Building a timeline helps to find opportunities. Next, if the coroner will talk to you, ask him questions about the autopsy. Find out why he thinks what he thinks. Some coroners won't talk to civilians, so if that's what happens, you'll have to find another legal way to prove Ollie was murdered. Once you get that proof, the police can take over."

Harper let Rice's words sink in before extending her hand. "Thank you, Lieutenant."

Rice gripped her hand with a smile. "Good luck to you, Harper. I hope you find the answers you're looking for."

Harper watched as the lieutenant walked away, then made her way for her car.

When she slid in, she texted Olivia, asking whether she still wanted to join her in visiting Ollie's dad.

Replying immediately, Olivia told her she did want to go, and then she asked how things went with Granger. Harper didn't reply to the text. She wanted to reflect on the conversation for a little while before she told Olivia more what had transpired.

She set her cell phone in the seat next to her, turned on the car, and steered toward Atlanta.

Thirty-three

Harper and Olivia accepted their coffees from Ollie's father and sipped before breaking the silence.

With his deep blue eyes and curly hair, Oliver Baldridge, Sr. was a spitting image of his son. The only difference was Oliver had more wrinkles, and his blonde hair had begun to gray. He was a family attorney, building his own practice four years ago. After taking a long break from his school studies due to his marriage and raising his daughters, Ollie had decided to finally follow in his father's footsteps. Harper knew by the end of the year, he would have finished earning his online law degree.

Only now, the plans died along with Ollie.

"I'm so sorry about Ollie, Mr. Baldridge," Harper said. "When I found out, I couldn't believe it. I'm also very sorry I missed his funeral."

"Thank you, Harper," Oliver said. "Ollie had always been very fond of you."

Harper allowed a weak smile. "Me too. He is—was—a very good friend of mine. The best." She glanced at Olivia. "Present company excluded, of course."

The kitchen filled with a soft giggle before quite befell them.

"How are the girls?" Harper asked.

"Hmm…well, Baylee hasn't left her room since the funeral. She hasn't said much at all. Emma pretty much stays with her, but she's been so angry. I had to force her to go to the funeral. I shouldn't have forced it. She should have gone only if she wanted."

"She'll be glad eventually," Olivia assured him. "It'll take some time, of course. But, if she didn't go, she will have eventually wished she had."

"It's tough on them," Oliver said with a heavy sigh. "It really is. Both of their parents dying in a car accident. I'm just glad they weren't with him."

"Where were they?" Harper asked.

"With me. He dropped them off almost two hours before the police showed up at my doorstep."

"Where was he headed? Did he tell you by any chance?"

Oliver shook his head. "I don't know. I guess he had a meeting or something. He said he was going to meet someone."

"He didn't say who?"

Again, Oliver wavered his head.

"Do you know if he was worried about anything lately? Has he been receiving threats?"

"Not that I know of."

He narrowed his eyes at Harper.

"Why all these questions?"

Harper exchanged quick glances with Olivia before taking another sip of her coffee.

"I was just wondering," she said. "He wasn't wearing a seatbelt, so I was curious. It's not like him. He always wore a seatbelt."

"I know," Oliver agreed. "When he was younger, we used to play the game of the last one buckling their seatbelt was a rotten egg. I've always been bad at not putting it on. He'd tell me it may one day save my life."

"Right," Harper said. "That's why I'm wondering about it. It doesn't make sense. He never even moved the car without buckling."

"I suppose he may have been in a hurry getting where he was going," Oliver suggested.

"Had he said anything about the airbag in his car not working?" Olivia asked.

"No, come to think of it. His car would let him know if there was a malfunction. He never mentioned it."

"Mr. Baldridge," Harper said. She hesitated, staring into her coffee while considering carefully what she wanted to say next. "I really hate to say this, but I'm afraid there's something fishy about the way Ollie died. His airbag suddenly not working and he wasn't wearing a seatbelt? Especially on the interstate."

"What are you saying, Harper?"

"I'm saying I think Ollie's accident might have somehow been staged. I think he was murdered."

Oliver frowned. "Who would want to kill my son? He didn't have any enemies that I knew of."

"I'm going to find out," Harper assured him. "I'm at least going to prove that it's something worth looking into so the police can find out."

"You were close to him, Harper. Do you know who would want him dead?"

Harper swallowed, avoiding Oliver's eyes.

"I can't think of names right now," Harper said. "If I do, I'll let you know. I'm going to try talking to the coroner. I want his death to be investigated. The more I think about it, the more I believe his death was not an accident."

The kitchen fell into another silence. She heard Oliver sniff, and he wiped his red eyes.

Again, she finally broke through the silence.

"Do you mind if I talk to the girls?"

Oliver nodded. "I think they'd like that."

Harper smiled, reaching across the table for Oliver's hand. "I know it's hard. I miss Ollie more than I can say. If you need anything, let me know. I'll be here if I can."

"Thank you," Oliver said, his voice coarse. "I know you will."

Harper rose and walked through the house until she found the closed door she knew belonged to the twins.

She knocked.

"Baylee? Emma?" she said. "It's Harper."

The door opened slowly, revealing Emma, her eyes tired and red.

"Honey," Harper said.

She gathered Emma into a tight hug, letting her sob into her chest. Baylee lay on the bed, her back facing them.

"Bay?"

After Emma pulled away, Harper crossed the room to sit on Baylee's bed. She put a hand on her shoulder.

"Baylee, honey, how are you?"

Slowly, Baylee turned to her back. Her face mirrored her sister's.

"Hey, you," Harper said, her voice soft.

Baylee mouthed a response and closed her eyes.

"I just wanted to see you guys before I headed out."

"Why didn't you go to the funeral?" Emma asked. "I looked for you, but you weren't there."

"I know," Harper said. "I'm very, very sorry I had to miss it. I would have given anything to have been there. I hope you realize that."

"Were you mad at him?" Emma asked.

"No, of course not."

"Then where were you?" Emma's eyes flashed with anger.

"I had an emergency," Harper told her. "It was unavoidable. I didn't hear about your dad until I came back home and Liv told me. I was sickened. I would have been there for you if I could. Can you girls forgive me? I don't think I can take you being upset with me."

"It's okay," Baylee said from the bed.

Harper eyed the older twin. "Em? Can you forgive me?"

With hesitation, she nodded.

"Good," Harper said, taking their hands in hers. "I want you girls to do me a favor, okay? Be good to your grandfather. He's hurting too."

They nodded. Harper kissed the top of their heads and made her way out of the room. When she heard Emma speak again, she turned to face her.

"He was going to you," she said.

Harper narrowed her eyes. "What do you mean?"

"I heard him on his phone. Someone called him. Dad asked if you were okay. Then he said he'd have to drop Baylee and me off, but he'd be there soon."

"Are you sure?" Harper asked. "You're absolutely sure he told whoever he was speaking to he was going to meet me?"

Emma nodded.

"Thank you for telling me, Em. I'll check in on you and your sister soon. Let me know if you need anything. I'm here."

She closed the door behind her.

Before walking off, she considered what Emily had told her.

He was going to you.

But why?

Her mind whirling, she found Olivia and Oliver sitting in the living room.

"Mr. Baldridge, you don't by any chance have Ollie's cell phone?"

"No, Harper, I don't. It wasn't found at the scene. Why do you ask?"

"Emma told me Ollie had received a phone call that day. I was just wondering who the last person he was talking to was."

"You really think someone murdered him?"

"Honestly, I'm not sure what to think. Like I said, his death doesn't make sense at all. I just want to explore the possibility. If I find out there's a slight chance, I'll be going to the police to let them sort it out."

Mr. Baldridge frowned. "Will you let me know what you find?"

"Of course I will. Thank you for letting us come by, Mr. Baldridge. Again, I'm so sorry."

"You're welcome anytime," Oliver said as he rose. He reached his arms out to hug her tight. "Thank you for being such a good friend to my son. And to the girls."

"I'll be here if you need me," Harper said, pulling away. "You have my number."

She regarded Olivia.

"Ready?"

Olivia responded by grabbing their handbags as she rose. She handed Harper hers before offering a hug to Oliver.

Oliver walked them to the door.

When the door closed behind them and Harper and Olivia walked to their car, Harper said, "Emma said someone called Ollie on the day of his accident. Supposedly Ollie asked if I was okay. Soon after, he dropped the girls off to meet this person."

Olivia opened the passenger door, her eyebrow arched. "That can't be a coincidence."

"I agree. Do you want to go with me to talk to the coroner? Or do you want to go home?"

"I'll go with you," Olivia said. "Not only do I want to watch your back, but I also need answers myself."

Thirty-four

Harper and Olivia found the Fulton County Medical Examiner's Office and entered the building. They walked up to the reception desk where an older woman was chewing on a granola bar, squinting at the computer screen.

"Hi," Harper said. "I have a question for one of your coroners. It's about an autopsy he performed. Oliver Baldridge."

"What questions do you have?" the woman asked.

"Well, I really would like to speak to the coroner, if possible."

With a sigh, the woman grabbed the phone and punched four numbers into the keypad.

"Doctor," she said a few seconds later, bothering with masking her irritation, "there are two women here to see you. They want to ask you about an autopsy performed…Olivier Baldrige?" She glanced up at Harper for confirmation.

Harper nodded.

Silence. "Okay, I'll tell them."

She replaced the phone on the cradle.

"Dr. Bloom will be with you as soon as he can."

"Thank you," Harper said.

She and Olivia remained standing as they waited for Dr. Bloom.

"What are you going to ask him?" Olivia asked.

"I have no idea," Harper admitted. "I haven't gotten that far yet. Lieutenant Rice warned me that some coroners may not want to talk to me, so I've been too focused on hoping he will, rather than coming up with a list of questions."

Olivia pushed out a breath as she studied a sculpture of a heart.

"It's a little creepy here, isn't it?" Olivia said. "Or is it just me?"

Harper shrugged but didn't respond. She began to wonder who had called Ollie on the day he died. Whoever it was knew her. They knew Ollie would come running at the suggestion of her being in trouble. Craig had seen him at the hotel with her, so could he have ordered the hit on Ollie? Or was it The Ghost wanting to tie up every loose end?

"Ma'am, I'm Dr. Bloom. How can I help you?"

Harper blinked at the interruption of her thoughts and stared into the face of a man. She reached her hand out, afraid to get to her feet. She would be made to feel like a giant compared to his short stature.

"I'm Harper Matthews, Doctor. This is my friend, Olivia. I realize coming to see you is a long shot. We just want to ask you a few questions about a recent autopsy you performed."

The doctor fitted his glasses on his nose. "Oliver Baldridge, Junior, correct?"

"Yes, sir."

"Are you the police?"

"No, sir," Harper said. "We're close friends with the family. There are some things about Ollie's death that I need to clear up before I can let it go."

Dr. Bloom offered a smile. "Why don't you ladies follow me to my office? I'll see if I can't help you with your questions."

"Thank you," Harper said. She rose, Olivia following suit, and followed the man to his office.

"Have a seat, ladies."

When they obliged, Dr. Bloom folded his hands across the desk. "Fire away."

"Okay, well, do you have any evidence that Ollie wasn't wearing his seatbelt?" Harper began. "That was the first thing that struck me odd."

Dr. Bloom turned to his computer and tapped against his keys. "Well, it's likely if he were wearing a seatbelt, Miss Matthews, he wouldn't have gone through the windshield in the first place."

"The airbag didn't deploy," Olivia pointed out.

Dr. Bloom shook his head. "Doesn't matter. It's extremely rare for someone to fly through the windshield while wearing their seatbelt. Even then, the car had to be going very fast. As I understood it, his brakes failed, so it's possible for the car to lose control. That said, no matter what the case was, he would have had marks where the seatbelt would have held him. He didn't."

"Okay, so the seatbelt definitely wasn't on him when he crashed. Was there anything in the autopsy that stood out? Did he have a heart attack? Stroke?"

Dr. Bloom shook his head, glanced at his computer screen, then released a breath he was holding.

"There was something I noticed," Dr. Bloom admitted. He cleared his throat and leaned back in his chair. "I had included it in the autopsy report, but strangely enough, there was no trace of it when I turned it in to the police."

Harper exchanged glances with Olivia. "What was it, Doctor?"

Dr. Bloom hesitated before speaking and Harper returned her attention to him. She assumed he may have reservations about telling her confidential information.

"Doctor, I need to know," Harper told him. "Ollie Baldridge never hurt anyone in his life. He was a good man. If you have thoughts that he may have been murdered, we need to take steps in finding out.

Dr. Bloom turned his lips to a frown. "Whether he was murdered, I can't comment on that. However." He removed his eyeglasses and Leander forward, folding his hands on his desk. "The cause of death was listed as accidental rather than suspicious."

"Suspicious? What did you see?" Olivia asked, leaning forward in her seat.

"I saw traces of aconite in his system."

"Aconite?" Olivia echoed.

"That's poison," Harper said. "It means he was murdered. Who would want to take it out of the autopsy?"

"I'm not sure," Dr. Bloom said. "I was going to inform the police, then this was on my desk after I returned from lunch one day. I haven't a clue who sent it."

Dr. Bloom opened his drawer and pulled out a brown envelope. He glanced up at Harper before passing it over. "I probably shouldn't be sharing any of this with you."

After another short pause, he handed her the envelope.

She accepted it, studying the item. There was nothing written on the package. At first guess, someone must have hand-delivered it. Harper opened the envelope and read the note.

Do not make changes to your autopsy report. If you do, we'll pay a visit to Joyce Winter's home and have a discussion with her and her son.

Besides Joyce Winter's name was an address and telephone number.

"Who is Joyce Winter?" Harper asked, glancing at him through her eyelashes.

"My sister," Dr. Bloom replied. "That's her address and phone number."

"So, whoever called Ollie had used me as an excuse to get near him," Harper muttered. "They messed with his car and poisoned him. He loses control of his car, flies through the windshield and is killed. They covered the poison to make his death look like an accident."

She replaced the note and looked up at the doctor.

"And they threatened your family to make sure no one ever knows."

"Forgive my silence," Dr. Bloom said with a despondent sigh. He crossed himself.

"You did the right thing," Harper assured him. "Whoever killed Daniel killed Ollie because he was close to me. They killed him in case Ollie found something out along the way. If you had brought it to the police's attention, your sister and her son would be next. Too many people have died already."

"What do you want to do?" Olivia asked Harper. "With his testimony, Ollie's accident will have to be reopened. But if he testifies, his family will be in danger. We can't let that happen."

"I know," Harper told her, her voice low. She regarded Dr. Bloom. "Is there somewhere your sister and her son can stay for a few days?"

Dr. Bloom frowned. "Yes, but I still don't know about this. I'm sorry about your friend, I truly am. But the note rattled me and I don't want them to come after me next. Surely, you understand? I have to think about what's best for me and my family."

Harper wanted to protest but realized changing his mind would prove to be fruitless. She would have to come up with another way to make the police reopen their investigation.

"I understand, Dr. Bloom," she said with a nod. Harper stood and extended her hand. "We appreciate you talking to us. Now that we know we're in the right direction, I'm hopeful we'll find a way to prove Ollie was murdered."

"Good luck to you," Dr. Bloom said. "I'm sorry I couldn't be of more help."

"You've given us a lot," Harper assured him. "I wasn't expecting you to talk to us."

"I think a part of me wanted to come clean. Truth be told, I haven't been able to think of anything else. Maybe now, my conscience can be cleared."

"Thanks again," Harper said.

She and Olivia left Dr. Bloom's office and walked in silence to the car. When they climbed in, Harper set the keys in her lap. She couldn't tell if she was happy or angry about learning Ollie was poisoned. Whoever was behind his death went through a lot of trouble to cover their tracks. Watching the news, they've referred to the hotel shooting as a "senseless massacre," one of the many the nation has had. The reality behind Daniel's death was swallowed in the shooting.

And then, there was Ollie. Another unwitting victim.

He was poisoned for his connection to Harper, and the car accident staged to cover up the poison. They even went so far as to make sure the doctor never allowed the poison to be listed as the cause of death.

"Harper?"

It took a few minutes for her to realize Olivia was trying to get her attention.

"Sorry, Liv," she said. "What did you say?"

"What did you want to do next?"

"Maybe talk to Lieutenant Quintos. I want him to be aware that Ollie's death wasn't a simple accident. Hopefully, we can convince him to start asking questions. Maybe they can exhume his body and have another pathologist to perform the autopsy."

"Are you sure you want to do that?" Olivia asked. "I mean, Mr. Baldridge already buried his son once. Should we ask him to do it a second time?"

"If you have another option," Harper said, "then I'm all ears because this is the only one I've got. I'm the only one that sees the connection."

"I see it too, Harper," Olivia told her. "I'm just worried about Mr. Baldridge and Ollie's daughters."

"I can't just let this slide, Liv. If you don't want to be a part of this anymore, then I'll take you home. I'll go myself."

Olivia pushed out a breath. "I'm already too much invested in this. I might as well see it through. Whatever you want to do, we'll do. I want justice for Ollie too."

Harper hesitated for a moment more, then inserted the key in the ignition.

"Then let's go get it."

Thirty-five

After Harper went into details on what she believed to be true about Ollie's death, she stared across the desk, waiting for Lieutenant Quintos to respond.

"I admit it is curious," Quintos agreed after a few minutes of consideration. "But I'm afraid my curiosity isn't enough to reopen the investigation. I'm sorry, ladies."

"But what about what Dr. Bloom found in his original autopsy?" Olivia protested.

"From what you've told me, Dr. Bloom isn't willing to come forward. Unless you have solid proof of the original autopsy revealing signs of aconite poisoning, my hands are tied. Either Dr. Bloom needs to come forward or I need something else that's concrete."

"What if you exhumed his body and have another autopsy performed?" Harper pressed.

"Miss Matthews, I can't just go dig up a body unless I have cause to do so. I don't at the moment. Not without Dr. Bloom's testimony about the change in his report. The final autopsy report reveals your friend died in an automobile accident. I'm sorry for your loss and I'm sorry I can't do more."

Harper felt the tears threatening to fall.

"Don't you think it's strange? A friend of mine who was present during the hotel shooting? The same hotel Daniel Clark was killed at? Don't you think it's possible they killed him to keep him in case he knew something?"

Quintos hesitated, before shaking his head. "I'm sorry."

"What if his dad asks?" She ignored Olivia's glare. "Will he be able to request it?"

"He knows some big names in town," Quintos muttered, "He can petition the exhumation. Of course, it'll depend on the judge. No matter what, they always have the final say in these matters."

"Okay, then I'll call him," Harper said. "Thank you, Lieutenant."

Harper rose and left Quintos' office, fishing her cell phone from her back pocket as she walked. She searched her contacts for Oliver

Baldridge's number.

"I'm not sure this is a good idea," Olivia insisted, keeping in pace with her friend.

"What choice do I have, Liv?" Harper said, putting the phone to her ear. "You heard what Dr. Bloom said. Ollie was murdered. Plain and simple. If something's not—"

"Hello?"

"Mr. Baldridge, it's Harper."

"Hey," he said. "Have you found out anything about Ollie from the coroner?"

Harper pulled in a breath and pushed it out. She scratched her head, biting her lip.

"I think so," Harper told him. "The only problem is we need to perform another autopsy."

"Another one? Why?"

"Dr. Bloom, the original pathologist, saw something in his original autopsy. But someone went behind him and changed the method of death."

"Okay," Mr. Baldridge said slowly. "Go on."

"He found that Ollie was poisoned. With aconite."

A long silence filled the phone line.

"Mr. Baldridge? Are you still there?"

"Yes. What are you asking me to do?"

"I know it'll be hard on you, Mr. Baldridge," Harper began, "But Lieutenant Quintos says he won't exhume Ollie's body unless you ask him to. I really think we need another autopsy done by a different pathologist."

Another long silence.

"I don't know about this," Mr. Baldridge replied. "An exhumation is extremely expensive. Unless the police have something—I'm afraid a judge won't approve." Harper detected an edge in his voice. "If what you're saying is true, why won't this coroner come forward with the real report?"

"Whoever doctored the original report threatened to kill his family. I don't want to put them at risk."

"But you want me to dig up my only child?" Mr. Baldridge said, his voice laced with anguish.

"I hate to ask this of you," Harper said. "And I wouldn't if I saw another way. But, Mr. Baldridge, Ollie's death is a result of something bigger. I know it."

Oliver fell into another silence before he finally answered.

"I'm going to have to consider the consequences, Harper. I agree Ollie's death is suspicious. However, we have to follow the law. Give me some time. I'll see what I can do."

"Thank you, Mr. Baldridge," Harper said.

"Do you have any idea who would poison my son?" Mr. Baldridge asked. "And why they would cover it up in an accident?"

Harper wavered her head to say she didn't know, then realized he couldn't see her. "Whoever it was is trying to conceal the truth. I think either Ollie found something out or they thought he knew something."

"But do you know what it could have been? Ollie has done nothing but help others. You know that. He never fell with the wrong crowd, and he cared more about Baylee and Emma than anything."

Harper paused before shaking her head. She couldn't bring herself to tell the older man what had happened to her in recent days. She didn't want to tell him Ollie's death was likely her fault.

"I'm sorry, I don't," Harper replied. "Maybe…maybe he came onto something by accident or something."

"I do appreciate your dedication to him."

"He was my best friend," Harper said, her bottom lip quivering.

"I know."

After the phone call ended, she regarded Olivia, blinking back tears. "He's going to think about it. I hope I'm doing the right thing."

Olivia put a hand on Harper's shoulder. "If it helps find who murdered him, then it is the right thing to do. How are you handling things, Harp? I don't think I ask enough."

"I'll be fine," Harper said. "I'm trying not to think about it. But it's hard. Especially when I think Ollie's death is connected."

"I want you to know I'm here for you if you need me," Olivia said. "Remember that."

"I know," Harper told her. "And I'm grateful for it. I'm also grateful you took time off work to help me through this. It means a lot."

"Jonathan Parker wasn't too pleased I cashed in vacation time," Olivia said with a roll of her eyes.

"Why would he care?" Harper asked.

"Oh, I think he just wanted another vacation. Jealous, I guess."

"Oh."

"Let's get something to eat," Olivia suggested. "I don't think you've had much of anything in the last few days."

Harper waved her hand. "I'm fine. I haven't had the stomach to eat."

"I don't want you to get sick," Olivia told her. "You need to eat something."

"Thanks, Mom, I'll keep that in mind."

"I'm not trying to mother you. I'm just—"

"Worried. Yeah, I get that. I'm a grown woman, Olivia. Let me decide when I should eat."

"Fair enough."

Thirty-six

After Harper forced herself to eat food she wasn't in the mood for, they returned to Olivia's apartment. She decided it was time to return to her own home, so Harper grabbed Collier and their things, said goodbye to Olivia, and left.

Collier's head hung out the window, his tongue rolling out of his mouth. He turned to gaze at Harper, barked once, then returned to watch as the city of Atlanta blurred by.

Recognizing they were nearing the apartment, Collier became more excited, moving from passenger window to driver's side window and back again. His barking became more infrequent.

Harper didn't have the energy to tell him to settle down.

After she pulled into the parking space, she opened her door, unbuckled and waited for Collier to hop out. He went to the nearby bushes and lifted his leg as if he'd been holding his bladder for weeks.

Harper gathered her things, waiting for Collier to finish relieving himself.

When he did, she opened the building and stepped inside, aiming for the elevator.

Harper pressed the button and waited for the door to open.

When it did, she let out a gasp as she looked into the face of a tall man in a pilot's uniform.

"Jonathan. What are you doing here?"

"Hey, Harp," Jonathan said with a slight smile. "I just came back to town. I wanted to see how you were doing, but you weren't home...."

"Yes, I've...been out of town for the last few weeks. I had an emergency."

"I see," Jonathan said. "I hope everything is well."

She nodded. "As can be, thank you."

Jonathan removed his cap. "I was sorry to hear about your friend."

Harper forced a smile. "Thanks, John."

His face remained clear of expression. "It's good to see you, Harper. Would you like to go grab a cup of coffee? Dinner? My treat."

She shook her head. "Thanks for the offer, but I really want to get home and spend some time by myself."

Jonathan nodded. "I understand. Maybe next time."

"Maybe. Thanks for stopping by, John."

He leaned in to kiss her cheek, then walked away. Harper stepped into the elevator, pressed the button to her floor, and fell against the wall.

"I feel like I haven't slept in a week," she muttered to herself, closing her eyes.

When the door slid open, Collier darted out, and when he reached her apartment, he laid on the floor.

She followed him. Before unlocking her door, she glanced at Ollie's apartment, feeling the squeeze in her chest.

Harper let Collier in, put their belonging by the counter, then found herself a few seconds later standing in front of Ollie's apartment. She raised her hand to knock, hovering a few inches from the door. Instead, she used her keys, opened the door and walked inside.

It felt cold and eerily quiet. She seemed to be a stranger in a strange place although she'd been in Ollie's apartment many times in the past, even when he wasn't home.

There were many pictures scattered on the tables and along the walls of his late wife and their daughters.

Harper picked up a black and white striped photo from the television stand. In each photo, she and Ollie made funny faces at the camera.

They were of high school age. If Harper remembered correctly, the photo was taken during a carnival the school was hosting.

She set the picture down and walked into his bedroom. The bed was unmade, his boxers draped on the corner.

Harper frowned.

She presumed he must have been in bed when he got the call from the man who killed her.

Harper climbed in the bed and pulled the covers to her chin. She still smelled Ollie in the sheets. She closed her eyes to breathe him in, imagining he was nearby.

"I'm sorry, Ollie," she whispered to the empty room. "It's my fault. If you weren't associated with me, you'd probably still be here. If I could change things, I would."

Harper continued to lay there until fell asleep.

When Harper woke up, she scanned her surroundings, realizing she was still in Ollie's apartment. She climbed out of the bed and search for possible clues which may explain his sudden death. She found nothing. With reluctant, Harper left the apartment, locking the door behind her.

Feeling as if her knees would buckle underneath her, she held onto the walls for support as she entered her home.

In the kitchen, she grabbed a granola bar from the cupboard, suddenly feeling hungry. When she and Olivia had their early supper, she didn't each much more than a side salad. She realized she had to have lost a good bit of weight. When she was at Granger's house, they only ate enough food to survive, but a good bit of it, she was too sickened about the situation to eat.

Harper scanned her apartment, realizing she hadn't been home in almost a month. She'd only spent one night during her week of vacation, then the next night, she'd been attacked by an intruder searching for the photos of the girls Daniel had given her.

Another bout of guilt surged through her as she remembered accusing Ollie of attacking her when he hadn't done a thing. It was Craig who had instilled the notion in her when he warned her anyone could be associated with trafficking. She hadn't even realized her paranoia was sitting in by that time.

"It's over, Harper," she reminded herself.

But it wasn't over. Not by a long shot. As much as she wanted to keep searching for Ollie's killer and The Ghost, her hands were tied. The Ghost investigation was in the hands of the feds, and it wasn't a given a second autopsy would be performed.

When she finished her granola bar, she tossed the wrapper in the trashcan and walked to her violin corner. She set the chair, which had been knocked over during her struggle with the intruder upright and gripped her violin. After inspecting for damage, Harper lowered herself to the chair.

She placed the violin underneath her chin and began playing. She cringed when she hit a sour note, then tried again. Again, hitting the sour note, Harper tossed the instrument onto the ground with frustration. She set her head in her hands.

Collier released a soft whimper. She glanced behind her to see the Sheltie laying on the couch, staring at her, his head tilted in wonder.

"Guess I'm a little rusty," she told him.

Collier barked once, his tongue rolling out of his mouth.

Giving up on the violin, she left the corner to sit on the couch next to Collier. He propped his paws in her lap and rested his head. She retrieved the television remote from the end table and turned it on for sound.

After surfing the channels, she finally settled on the news, where they were talking about busting the trafficking ring. There was no mention of The Ghost. Harper wondered why. Maybe they felt they didn't have enough information to mention him at the time. Or maybe they were afraid The Ghost would think the police were zeroing in on him.

She watched the news report for a few minutes longer before deciding she'd had enough.

Harper flicked the TV off and walked to her medicine cabinet for a sleeping pill. She stared at the white prescription bottle for several long minutes before replacing it and returning to the kitchen.

She grabbed a wine glass, poured some cabernet, and with three gulps, emptied the glass. She poured herself another glass, this time taking her drink and the bottle to the bedroom.

She set the wine on the bedside table, undressed and climbed under the covers.

Collier jumped onto the mattress and curled up at the foot of her bed. She sipped her wine in silence, trying hard not to think.

By her fourth or fifth glass—she lost count—Harper slunk deeper underneath her covers and closed her eyes. Within minutes, she'd fallen in a deep sleep.

Thirty-seven

Harper woke up to a wet, sticky pink tongue attacking her face. She pushed Collier's head away and rubbed her eyes. Looking at the clock, she saw it was almost noon.

There was still some wine left in her glass and the bottle almost empty. Without much consideration, Harper drank the remainder of the wine before noticing Collier's eager circling.

He was aching to go outside.

"I'm coming," she muttered within her yawn.

Harper climbed out of bed, pulled on a robe and walked to the kitchen. She checked her cell phone in case she had a message. She didn't.

Collier barked twice. Obliging, she slipped on the leash and opened the door. She followed the Sheltie to the elevator and they took it to the ground floor.

Harper waited in patience for Collier to finally relieve himself.

After he was through, they returned to the apartment. As Harper fumbled with the key, she heard the phone ringing. When she managed to get the door open, she fell in, snatching the cell from the table.

Jonathan Parker.

Her finger lingered above the screen as she considered whether or not to answer. Instead, she tapped *end call* and went to her room to grab the wine glass. Instead of washing the glass, she opened a new bottle of cabernet. She poured it into the glass, watching Collier watch her.

"What? It's almost noon," she told the sheltie. She sipped the wine as she scrolled through her phone's contact list for Lieutenant Rice's personal cell number.

"Rice."

"Lieutenant, this is Harper Matthews." She took a sip of wine and leaned against the counter.

"Oh, yes, how are you doing, Miss Matthews?"

Harper scoffed, then cleared her throat in an attempt to cover it.

"What do I have to do in order to have an exhumation done?"

"Exhumation?" Rice echoed. "Uh, well, there's a lot of steps. The first is to find concrete reasoning about why this exhumation needs to be completed."

"No loopholes, huh?"

"It's rare," Rice admitted. "Why do you ask?"

Harper hesitated before responding. Lieutenant Rice was out of jurisdiction, so she wouldn't be able to push for the exhumation. However, it was possible Rice would be willing to point Harper in the direction of what she needed to do in order to find answers. At the same time, being a cop, Rice would likely tell her she needed to let the investigation alone.

"Well," she began, taking another sip. "Olivia and I went to visit the coroner. Dr. Bloom claimed my friend, Ollie was poisoned."

"Poisoned? Did he not include it in the official report?"

"He did," Harper confirmed. "The problem is someone changed the report, then threatened to hurt his family if he didn't keep the change."

"I see."

Harper refilled her wine glass.

"I'm assuming Dr. Bloom refuses to admit such occurrence happening?"

"Unfortunately. I talked to Lieutenant Quintos and he won't do anything."

"I'm afraid there really isn't anything to be done, Miss Matthews. Not without Bloom's testimony."

"So I've been told," Harper replied gloomily.

"I'm sorry, I know it's not what you're wanting me to tell you."

"So, whoever killed my best friend is going to get off scot-free." Harper cursed underneath her breath, then closed her eyes.

"I wish I can help you."

"How can I get the proof that I need?" Harper asked. "Where would I start looking?"

"I'd advise against that, Miss Matthews. It's not your place and you could likely end up in danger."

Harper pushed out a breath of disappointment although she knew Lieutenant Rice's response beforehand.

"Unofficially," Rice began again.

Harper heard the sound of a door closing.

"You're quite sure, aren't you that your friend was murdered because of the trafficking ring?"

"I can't think of any other reason," Harper said. "Ollie was never dealt with shady business."

"Regardless of whether an autopsy was performed and revealed aconite poisoning, you'll have a hard time proving his death was connected."

Sensing the lieutenant wasn't finished speaking, Harper sipped her wine in silence.

"So...*unofficially*, I would advise you to find out everything Daniel Clark learned. That may give you a general start."

"Thank you, Lieutenant," Harper replied.

He heard the door opening and soft murmurs.

"I'm sorry I can't help you anymore, Miss Matthews."

Without saying goodbye, they ended the call. Harper swished her wine in the glass, watching the tornado rise in the center.

She knew if he was going to find answers, if he would find justice for Ollie, then she would have to start digging.

And, the more she considered it, the more Harper knew she'd have to start from the beginning.

Thirty-eight

The best way Harper knew to find information on Daniel Clark was to go through his laptop, but she didn't have that. The police likely had confiscated it after the hotel shooting, but she wondered if Daniel kept all of his vital information on the laptop.

He was smart. That much she knew.

Any information he had would likely be put somewhere he knew was safe. A safe deposit box, maybe?

Harper locked up her apartment and drove to where Daniel had stayed after getting off the plane.

She watched people enter and leave Hilton Atlanta as if nothing out of the ordinary had happened a month before.

As if several people were injured and one man wasn't brutally murdered.

Harper climbed out of the car and took the elevator to Daniel's floor and was disappointed—though not surprised—to see it had been rented out to a family.

As she turned to leave, Harper used her cell phone to book a flight to New York.

She decided to see how Adaline was doing, and maybe after talking with her, Harper would know her next move.

The next flight won't leave until an hour, so Harper called Olivia to tell her of her plans.

"I'm going to visit Adaline, then go into Daniel's apartment. I'm hoping he might have some information hidden in a safe or something. I'm pretty sure he knew who The Ghost was, but was afraid to tell."

"Are you sure this is a good idea?" Olivia asked.

Harper frowned. "I'm not sure of anything, Liv. I just can't sit around and do nothing."

"Are you looking into this because you really think you'll find something the cops won't be able to? Or are you doing it so you won't have to think about everything that has happened?"

Harper remained silent, chewing her lower lip.

"That's what I thought."

"No," Harper affirmed. "It's not what you're thinking. What if you were in my position? Would you want to wait around, knowing without a doubt you caused your best friend's death?"

"That's just it," Olivia said. "You don't know."

Harper pulled in a sharp, shaky breath, then released it. "That's why I have to find out. That's why I need to go to New York. Somebody there has to know what Daniel knew. Or at least they can give me some direction as to where I need to go."

"Okay, Harp," Olivia replied. "Do you want me to go with you?"

Harper considered the offer before shaking her head. "No. This is something I need to do myself. I'll call you when I get there."

"Be careful," Olivia warned. "Please."

"I will. Will you—"

"Don't worry about Collier. He'll be fine," Olivia interrupted.

Harper lifted the corner of her lips to a smile, thanked her friend, then ended the call.

She had forty-five minutes to pack and make it to the airport, so she hurried to take care of her tasks before taking off.

Harper pushed through the bustling airport and waved a cab down. Because of a confrontation with an older woman, she had to take the second cab she found. When she did, she told the driver to take her to the Four Points hotel, where she had already reserved a room.

It'd taken her almost two and a half hours to make it from the airport to her room. When there, she dropped her bag and opened the curtains to take in the sights. New York during the day wasn't as magnificent as it would be during the nighttime, however, it still appealed to Harper every time she looked down.

"First thing I need to do is find out where Daniel Clark lived," Harper said to the empty room.

She used her phone to look through the white pages for an address on Daniel, but she was shown more results than she wanted.

Finally, she decided to try the Adaline approach.

Harper called the number her parents have given her.

"Clark residence," a male voice said after the third ring. Harper recognized it as Adaline's father.

"Mr. Clark, this is Harper Matthews. I'm Adaline's—"

"Yes, Miss Matthews! How are you?"

"I'm good," she told him. "I'm actually in New York. I was wondering if there's any way I can stop by and see your family for a bit."

"Of course," he replied. "You're a part of the family," Mr. Clark said. "We'd love to have you over for dinner tonight if you don't already have plans. We'd like to thank you properly for saving our Adaline."

"That's kind of you," Harper said. "But you don't have to thank me."

"When we heard Adaline went missing," Mr. Clark began, his voice growing dark, "it was as if our whole world was shattered. And soon after, our son was killed."

Harper said nothing as she remembered the sound of gunfire exploding. She remembered vividly people screaming and Daniel telling her to run. During the long stretch of a minute, the chaos ended, and Daniel had been shot.

"You saved Adaline, Miss Harper," Mr. Clark continued. "You gave hope back to us. Won't you please allow us to show you our gratitude?"

"Of course," she told him. "What's your address?"

After Harper ended the call, she turned to the mini-fridge and pulled out a bottle of wine. She had a couple of hours to meet the Clarks for dinner, so she may as well relax.

Thirty-nine

"Harper!"

Adaline nearly knocked Harper off her feet as she wrapped her arms around her waist in a tight bear hug.

"Hey, honey, how are you?"

Adaline looked up and smiled, but Harper noticed her eyes glassy. She knelt to be at eye level.

"You're not sleeping, are you?"

Adaline raised her shoulders, then let it fall.

"You know it'll be okay, right?" Harper asked. "Your nightmare…it's over now. You're safe."

"I-I keep seeing The Ghost at night."

"Why don't we move into the den," Mrs. Clark said.

Her face mirrored her daughter's, showing she hadn't been sleeping, or at the least have been having trouble sleeping. Her white top and dress pants were wrinkled like she had been sleeping in them.

"Sure," Harper answered. She pushed to her feet and Adaline to her hand.

Mrs. Clark led the way to the dining room where her husband sat in a leather chair by the fireplace, reading the paper.

"Miss Matthews is here, dear," Mrs. Clark announced.

"Call me Harper."

"I'm glad you could join us, Harper," Mr. Clark said. "Have a seat."

As she obliged, Harper glanced around the cream-colored walls, at the photos of Daniel and Adaline, as well as plaques for achievement for Daniel's reporting success.

"Thank you for having me. You have a beautiful place."

"Thank you, dear," Mrs. Clark replied.

"What brings you to New York?" Mr. Clark wondered. "Do you have a layover?"

"No, sir, I'm still taking time off. I'm…" Harper cleared her throat. Although she wanted to talk about Daniel and what he was looking into, she didn't necessarily want to start the conversation as soon as she walked into the door. "I'm looking into something."

"Oh? Flight attendant by day, investigator by night?" Mr. Clark winked.

"Hardly," Harper replied. She hesitated, then shifted in her seat. "Since you're asking, I might as well tell you. I wanted to mention it after dinner."

"Is something wrong?" Mrs. Clark asked.

"Oh, not at all," Harper said quickly. "When I—when *we*—got away, I found out my friend, Ollie was killed."

"I'm so sorry," Mrs. Clark exclaimed. "That must have been terrible for you."

"It was. It is," Harper replied. "What makes matters worse is I'm afraid Ollie was killed because of the trafficking ring."

Mr. Clark leaned forward, his eyes narrowed. "Was he involved?"

"Oh, nothing of the sort," Harper replied, raising her hand in front of her. "Ollie was one of the kindest, most gentle men on earth."

"How did he die?"

Harper swallowed hard. "Officially, by car accident. However, I spoke to the coroner who performed the autopsy. He claims in the original report, he included that Ollie was poisoned by arsenic."

"Arsenic?" Mr. Clark echoed.

"Yes," Harper confirmed. "The problem is, the original report is gone and the coroner was threatened if he came forward with his findings."

"What are the police saying?" Mrs. Clark asked.

"Well…Ollie's death has been ruled an accident. He was already buried by the time I learned all this. His dad is a lawyer and knows a lot of people. I asked him to exhume Ollie and find another coroner who can come to the same conclusion. Mr. Baldridge, understandably, isn't sure about it. If he does request the exhumation, he's not positive it'll happen. So I decided to find answers on my own."

"You think New York will provide it to you?"

Harper wavered her head. "I don't know, to be honest. Actually, I wanted to start at the beginning. When I first met Daniel, he was on a plane to Atlanta. Whatever he found out here in New York…it led him to Atlanta."

The Clarks remained silent. Adaline sat next to Harper, chewing on her hair.

"What can we do to help you?" Mr. Clark asked.

"Well, I'm hoping you would be willing to let me search Daniel's home. And also tell me if he has somewhere else he may keep important things."

"I don't know about this," Mr. Clark replied. He exchanged glances with his wife. "Don't get me wrong. We're thankful for everything you've done, even though it was by chance. But you're asking us to invade our son's privacy. I don't feel right about this."

"Mr. Clark," Harper pleaded. "I just want to help."

"But the police already searched Daniel's apartment," Mrs. Clark replied, tears in her eyes. "When they learned he was Adaline's sister. There wasn't anything to be found."

"It's possible they missed something," Harper replied. "It's also possible they didn't. I'll admit that. May I have your permission to just look? For my own peace of mind?"

Mr. Clark leaned back in his chair and considered the question.

"I appreciate your eagerness, Harper, but my family and I only want to put this behind us. I'm afraid I can't let you go through his things."

Harper turned her lips to a frown but nodded.

"I understand. I'm sorry to have asked."

Mr. Clark's smile was warm and saddened. "Thank you."

Harper chatted with Adaline while Mrs. Clark checked on supper, then when it was time to eat, they sat down at the table.

Feeling as if she'd come to New York only to be forced to return home with nothing, Harper wasn't hungry. She forced the food down and made polite conversation.

After they ate, it was Adaline's bedtime.

She'd asked Harper if she would tuck her in, and with Mr. and Mrs. Clark's approval, she followed her to her bedroom.

"I'm glad you came," Adaline said as she gathered her nightclothes. She changed in the adjoining bathroom, then climbed into her bed. "I've missed you."

Adaline climbed underneath the covers and Harper sat next to her.

"I've missed you too, Adaline. I hope your parents aren't angry at me for asking to see your brother's house."

"No," Adaline said. "They're just sad."

Harper nodded. "I know. I wish there were some magic words to make all the pain go away. But there are none."

"Life's funny," Adaline muttered.

"Yes, it is," Harper agreed. She smiled down at her, feeling her heart tug at the thought of Adaline being forced to grow up before her time. "When I first got here, you told me you still see The Ghost."

Adaline nodded. "I dream of him. I want him to leave me alone, but he always comes back. Then I wake up and can't go to sleep again. Mom is always sleeping on that chair." She pointed to a wooden chair in the corner by a toybox.

"If you remember what The Ghost looks like, will you tell me?"

Adaline raised her shoulder to her chin. "He's a blur. They all are."

"Maybe they're finally going away," Harper suggested.

"I hope so," Adaline replied, her eyes closing. She opened them again, then closed them.

Harper stayed next to her for a few minutes longer before leaning down to kiss her forehead.

She left the room, leaving the door ajar.

"Thank you again for inviting me over," Harper said to Mr. and Mrs. Clark.

"You're very welcome, Harper," Mrs. Clark replied. "I'll walk you out."

In silence, they went to the door, and as they stepped out, Mrs. Clark placed a hand on Harper's shoulder.

"Here."

She held out her palm, revealing a key.

"I don't know if you'll find anything, but if you want to search Daniel's apartment, here's his key."

With hesitation, Harper accepted it. "Thank you."

"Daniel also had a girlfriend," Mrs. Clark said. "Her name is Jenny Bluford. I've only met her at the funeral. I didn't even know he was seeing anyone. But from what I gathered, Daniel and Jenny were very close. Maybe if you can find her information, she would be willing to help."

Harper slipped the key in her pocket, then leaned in for a hug.

Mrs. Clark's body quivered and when they pulled apart, Harper saw the tears falling from her eyes.

"Please be careful," Mrs. Clark instructed. "I don't want anything to happen to you. These are obviously some powerful people who will stop at nothing to get what they want."

Harper nodded in agreement. "Neither will I, Mrs. Clark. They've destroyed lives. Adaline, Daniel, Ollie…mine. But I think I have enough of my mother in me to fight back."

"You're quite a woman, Harper Matthews," Mrs. Clark acknowledged. "I'm thankful you've come into our lives. I hope you'll stay."

"Of course," Harper replied. "Adaline and I are now connected. "I think we need each other. I'm not going anywhere."

Forty

It was getting late and she was feeling jetlagged, so Harper decided to go to Daniel's apartment in the morning.

She returned to the hotel, poured herself a glass of wine, then settled on the couch.

She hadn't called Olivia yet, so she used the time to do so.

"How's my boy?" Harper asked when her friend answered the phone.

"Oh, you know how it is," Olivia said nonchalantly. "The poor thing is too used to not seeing his owner. But don't worry! He still misses you. A little. I guess."

Harper giggled. "I miss him too."

"How are things in the Big Apple?"

Taking a sip of wine, Harper filled Olivia in on her dinner date with the Clark family.

"At least you've got something going on there," Olivia replied.

"I just hope it'll pan out. I hope Daniel spilled his enough thoughts and fears with this Jenny Buford."

"Are you doing okay, Harp?"

"Yeah, I'm fine." Harper scoffed. "Don't worry about me."

"You have a tendency to keep things inside. It'll drive you crazy if you don't let it out every once in a while. Are you…seeing a psychologist?"

Again, Harper scoffed, taking another drink. "I don't need a head shrink, Liv. I'm fine. All right?"

"I just wanted to be sure, honey," Olivia replied, her voice still concerned. "You've been through a lot."

"You have no clue what I've been through," Harper snapped. Realizing what she said, she closed her eyes. "I'm sorry, Liv. I didn't mean it."

Olivia paused. "I know."

"I should get some rest. I need to prepare myself for tomorrow."

"Okay."

After Harper said bye, she set the phone on the coffee table and leaned back on the couch. She tried to focus on the television show, but her mind continued to wander until she finally switched it off. She sat in the darkened hotel room, staring at the blank set, hoping, praying the images of the men she was forced to pleasure would escape her.

But, ever since that first time, it was all she could think about.

Harper woke to the sun shining brightly through the windows. She released a groan, rubbing her neck to work out the kinks she created from falling asleep upright.

Deciding a shower was in order, she turned on the faucet, set the temperature to hot and removed her clothing. She stepped into the tub, letting the water scold her back as she washed her body and hair.

After almost fifteen minutes passed, Harper stepped out, dried her body and, with the towel wrapped around her body, went into the living room where she left her suitcase.

After she changed clothes, she left the hotel room to grab a muffin from the café downstairs and left for Daniel's apartment.

She had no trouble hailing a cab, but the New York traffic still made her spend almost an hour in the backseat, smelling old leather and hearing muted rap.

Once at Daniel's apartment, she paid the cab driver and made her way inside.

In contrast to Daniel's parents' house, the apartment didn't show off his money but didn't make him out to be near penniless.

She walked to the stairs, smelling lemon Pinesol, a welcome sensation to the cab's old leather.

Harper walked for the second floor and found Daniel's apartment with ease.

She stood in front of the doorknob, ready to knock, but then remembered there was no need. Instead, she fished the key from her messenger bag and slide it into the lock.

Twisting the knob, she stepped inside, feeling the coldness. Growing up, her father used to leave the thermostat to a cold temperature in order to keep the bill low. She assumed Daniel must do the same when he knew he wouldn't come home.

Harper pushed the door shut and made her way to the kitchen.

Daniel had left pots and pans in the sink. A dishrag had fallen to the corner. The faucet dripped water.

He had left in a hurry.

She entered the living room and saw a table next to a printer, where she assumed he kept his laptop. The television was on, but the sound low.

Background noise.

Noticing printed pages on the printer, she skimmed through but found nothing of importance.

Harper thumbed through the *Writer's Digest* magazines and old newspapers of *The Times*, but still, nothing.

In his bedroom, the bed was made, but his closet was askew. She opened the door and began searching.

Now feeling frustrated, she opened the bedside drawer and found a scrap piece of paper.

Her heart leaped with joy after finding Jenny Buford's name. She immediately called the number.

"Hello?"

"Uh, yes, is this Jenny Buford?"

"Who's asking?"

"I'm a friend of Daniel Clark. I was hoping you can help me find out some information."

Silence.

"Hello?" Harper asked. "Are you still there?"

"I can't talk to you," the woman claimed.

"Please. I just want answers. I knew Daniel only for a short time. I-I saw him get killed."

Harper closed her eyes with a sigh. The words never seemed to get easier coming from her mouth.

"Who is this again?"

"My name's Harper Matthews," she answered. "I met with Daniel's parents yesterday and his mother mentioned your name. She said you seemed very close to him."

"What do you want from me?"

"I just want to talk. Daniel was looking into something and I want to finish what he was doing. Please. I'll be so grateful if you can help me."

"Do you know Café Boulud by Central Park?"

"I do."

Silence.

Harper looked at her phone screen to confirm the call was connected, then opened her mouth to speak. Instead, Jenny beat her to it.

"Meet me there in an hour. Don't be late."

"How will I know who you are?"

Harper heard heavy breathing but couldn't decide whether Jenny sounded nervous or afraid.

"I'll find you. Just be there."

Before Harper could respond, Jenny ended the call.

Forty-one

In anticipation, Harper went to Café Boulon early, ordered a drink and waited.

She watched as the clock ticked by, minute after minute until she decided Jenny wouldn't show. Feeling disappointment seeping through her heart, Harper rose and made her way out of the café.

"Harper Matthews?"

She turned to see who called her name.

A young girl wearing a New York Mets cap stood in front of her, thumbs hanging in her belt loops. Her t-shirt was loose-fitting, hanging carelessly off her slim waist. She wore dark sunglasses.

"Jenny?" Harper asked, narrowing her eyes.

Jenny glanced around them before speaking.

"I just had to be sure you're harmless, you know? He has eyes everywhere."

"He?" Harper echoed. "Are you talking about The Ghost?"

Jenny bit her bottom lip and nodded. "He ordered Daniel to be killed."

"I'm sorry for your loss," Harper said. "Truly. Daniel seemed like a good man."

Jenny nodded, and when she spoke, her voice cracked. "He was. Danny cared about others so much. There aren't a lot of men like him."

"Were you his girlfriend?" Harper asked.

Jenny shook her head. "Just friends. We cared for each other deeply. But I guess we were more brother and sister."

"So Daniel trusted you?" Harper pressed.

Again, a nod.

"Did he confide in you about…" Harper glanced around and lowered her voice. "Did he talk to you about what he was investigating?"

"A little, then he started getting weird."

Harper began walking and Jenny fell into step with her.

"How so?"

"He was acting afraid. Paranoid. He thought someone was following him. He started keeping his distance from me, but I begged him to let me help. He told me they threatened to take his sister if he continued his investigation. And when he didn't stop, they took her. They, again, told him he needed to stop or they'd kill her."

"But he didn't," Harper finished. "We met on the red-eye to Atlanta. During the flight, I had a feeling something was bothering him, but he didn't tell me. Not that I blame him. I was a stranger. But he had a package with him on the plane. I could tell it was important to him. When I got home, I found the package in my messenger bag."

They walked in silence for a few minutes until something arose in Harper's memory.

"On the plane, he said something to me that was a bit chilling."

"What?"

"He asked me if I ever had to make a choice, where the choice was always wrong. I'm now realizing what he meant. He was at a crossroad. If he stopped his investigation, they would free his sister, but then hundreds of young girls would suffer. But if he kept on, then his sister would suffer, even if he managed to save most of the girls."

"I can't imagine having to make a choice like that," Jenny muttered.

"Me either," Harper said. "He couldn't bear to be the one to make the choice so he wanted me to do it. The last thing he said to me after our first meeting was the choice was mine."

"What did you do?" Jenny asked.

"At first, I didn't understand what the whole deal was. A friend of mine and I looked through the envelope and started putting two and two together. I found out where he was staying, so I went to the hotel. He took the envelope, said he made a mistake, then slammed the door in my face."

"You said you were with him when he was killed?"

Harper nodded. "After I left the room, he ran after me. He started to tell me a little bit, but before we really got down to details, someone shot up the hotel. The last thing he said to me was to save Adaline."

"Poor Adaline," Jenny said, her voice low. "She must be so scared. I can only imagine what they're doing to her."

"You haven't heard?" Harper said. "Adaline's with her family now. She's safe."

Jenny's eyes grew as she gaped at Harper.

"That's wonderful! When did she get home?"

Harper opened her mouth to answer but closed it again. She didn't want to tell Jenny the things she endured.

"I'm not sure," Harper lied. "But I had dinner with the family last night. She's doing well, although I'm afraid she won't ever be the same."

"How can she be?" Jenny muttered.

"Jenny, do you know if Daniel may have had copies of his research?"

She hesitated, before saying, "Can I trust you?"

"Yes," Harper replied.

"Come with me."

Forty-two

Harper and Jenny returned to Daniel's apartment. She studied Jenny's face through the corner of her eyes while trying to figure out if she missed something the first time she came.

But Harper remained silent as she followed Jenny through the doors of the complex and up the stairs.

Jenny hesitated before using her keys to enter.

When she did, she marched straight to the master bedroom, glanced around as if looking for something, then opened the closet. She tossed the remaining clothes on the floor, then felt along the walls.

"He told me if anything were to ever happen to him, I should get his notes to the police." Jenny looked over her shoulder at Harper. "That was right before he went to Atlanta. He called me from the airport."

"But you didn't give it to the police?" Harper pressed.

Jenny looked back at the back wall of the closet, running her hand along the surface. "No. I-I was afraid. I knew what his investigation was about and I knew he was getting into something dangerous."

A single tear fell from the corner of her eye.

"I should have stopped him!"

Harper placed an assuring hand on Jenny's shoulder.

"I doubt there was anything you could have done, Jenny. Daniel was an investigative journalist. He was only doing his job."

Jenny sniffed. "And it cost him everything."

"Not if we can finish what he started," Harper said.

"He was looking into the disappearances of a group of girls," Jenny explained. "He found out someone had taken them to Atlanta. He didn't know what to expect when he got there, so he put everything he had in a secret place. He called me at the airport and said someone contacted him. The guy didn't say his name. Or at least Danny didn't tell me his name. They had Adaline, and for proof, they made her talk to him. He didn't know what to do. There was so much at stake. The next morning, he called me to say he made a mistake. He'd given an envelope to a flight attendant he met."

"Me," Harper muttered.

She suddenly remembered being attacked at her apartment, before she went under. The memory made her sick to the stomach as she remembered the fight she had with Ollie afterward. Harper shook her head to clear her thoughts and return to the present.

"I was attacked by someone about a month ago," she said. "Whoever attacked me was after the envelope Daniel had given me. They knew I had it."

Jenny blinked with realization. "They must have bugged his phone somehow."

"Which means whoever did was able to get close enough to him."

"You were there," Jenny reminded her. "At the hotel when Danny was killed. Did they take his phone?"

"Probably."

"Wouldn't they realize he was bugged?"

"I don't know about that. They would have to have a reason to think to look into his phone. What did Daniel say next?"

"He was going to try finding you," Jenny replied. "He told me he couldn't live with himself if he didn't finish what he'd set out to do. He said he was having a lot of trouble sleeping because of his decision. He told me where to find his research and to turn it in to the authorities if anything happened to him."

Harper looked at the wall and placed her palm on the surface as if she could tell something lay within.

"He put it in the wall." Harper looked at Jenny. "Didn't he?"

She nodded.

Harper studied the wall closely and found a slight difference between sections. She found herself impressed at how well he'd managed to cover his tracks.

"We'll have to bust it," Harper said. She stepped out of the room and looked around for something to use as a hammer.

In the kitchen, she found a garlic press and decided it would have to do.

Returning to the bedroom, she went to work at breaking down the wall. It was hollow enough, so it didn't take long. Still, the noise was loud enough to wake the dead.

After creating a decent sized hole, Harper began pulling away the plating, but not before a door opened.

Jenny gasped, her eyes growing.

Harper reached her hand out to touch her arm.

"You were close to him, you have every right to be here. But no one can know about this. Try to make whoever it is leave."

Jenny nodded.

"And be calm," Harper finished.

Biting her lip, Jenny turned to leave, shutting the door behind her.

Harper walked to the door and leaned against the wall, straining to listen.

The voices were muted, so she didn't hear what they were saying, but it was definitely two men.

Her heart started beating against her rib cage as the sounds neared the master bedroom.

"What are you doing?" she heard Jenny exclaim.

Harper glanced behind her for a hiding place. Hurrying, she slid under the be and closed her eyes.

Her breath was caught in her throat as she tried to imagine herself being anywhere but underneath the small space of the bed.

"I told you, I'm just gathering some of my friend's things," Jenny protested.

"And you're sure he didn't give you anything?" the man questioned, his voice sounding gruff.

Harper opened her eyes and glanced at the open closet door. She cursed underneath her breath.

"I'm sure," Jenny replied, her words quivering. "Please, just leave me alone. I don't…I don't know anything."

A harsh silence filled the room and Harper was afraid her breath was heaving too loud.

"Fine," the man said finally. "Let's go. The girl doesn't know anything."

"How can we be sure?" the second voice said.

"You have a point, there," the first replied.

"Wh-what are you doing?"

Harper didn't hear anything.

But the world moved slowly as Jenny tumbled to the ground. Her head was facing Harper, eyes open, still shining with fear. Blood gushed from the hole in Jenny's forehead.

Harper covered her mouth in shock, her entire body shaking. She prayed the men wouldn't find her underneath the bed.

Forty-three

Harper lost track of how long she'd remained under the bed after the two men left. She was both unsure she could find the strength to move, and afraid they'd return.

After killing Jenny, they had wrapped her in the comforter from the bed and carried her out.

When Harper did finally slide out from underneath, she had to rush to the toilet and empty her stomach.

She coughed and let the tears fall as she fell to a sitting position by the toilet.

Once she figured she'd know longer throw up, Harper struggled to stand, using anything near to support her weight. She returned to the closet and grabbed a box from within, then hurried to leave.

She kept her head down, trying to act normal in case she ran into one of the men, but all she wanted to do was run as far away as she could. She managed to stuff the box inside her messenger bag, so at least, she'd be able to hide it from prying eyes.

When she hailed a cab, she climbed in and told him to drive, without giving a destination. She wasn't quite sure where she wanted to go as long as it was away from Daniel's apartment complex.

Her hands shook as she retrieved her cell phone.

She called Olivia and waited for her to answer the phone.

When she did after the fifth ring, Olivia was laughing.

"Hey, Harp," she giggled.

"I-I-" Stammering, Harper closed her eyes, trying to gather her thoughts.

"What's wrong?" she heard the concern in her friend's voice.

"Something terrible happened," Harper forced out. "I think I have everything I need. I'm going to come home now. Yeah, I'm going home. I-"

"What happened, Harper? Did someone hurt you? Did they threaten you?"

"No," Harper breathed. "Not exactly. I'm sorry, I don't mean to worry you. I just want you to know I'm coming home."

"Well, I'm worried!" Olivia said. "I knew you shouldn't have gone to New York. This whole thing is too dangerous! You need to stop!"

Harper heard another voice, but she couldn't tell if it was a man or a woman.

"Shh!" Olivia hissed.

"Is someone there with you?" Harper asked. "Who is it?"

"It's no one," Olivia said. "Just a friend. Listen, I want you to come home now and when you do, come straight to my place. I want you to tell me everything that happened. Please, Harp."

Fresh tears spilled from her eyes. She told Olivia she would oblige.

Ending the call, she instructed the cab driver to take her to the hotel.

Sounds were muted to her ears, although she noticed the driver turning up the radio. Outside, the scenery went by in a blur, whether moving or at a traffic light. Harper gripped the door handle, drawing a deep breath. She tried to force herself to calm, but nothing would do.

With a blink, she saw darkness.

When Harper woke up, she found the cab driver patting her cheek.

She released a sharp groan.

"I call ambulance?" the dark-skinned man inquired. "You need doctor?"

Harper blinked a few more times until her sight returned.

"Where am I?"

"You went cold," the driver said. "I pull over. I try waking you. You need doctor?"

"Uh, no," Harper said. "I'm fine. I'm sorry if I scared you."

"You need doctor," the driver said, more of a statement this time.

"I need to go to Four Points," she insisted. "I need to check out and go to the airport.

When she spoke, she was reminding herself of what she was needing to do more than informing the driver.

"Please."

With hesitation, he nodded, then shut the back door. He made his way to the driver's side then pulled into the traffic.

Harper noticed his eyes glancing to and from the rearview mirror.

When he realized she was watching him watch her, he smiled.

"You need a listening ear? I listen good."

Harper lifted the corner of her lips to a smile. "I think I had a panic attack. I've had them before, so it's nothing new."

"What's a pretty lady like yourself have to worry for, eh?"

"Well, a lot of things have been going on in my life," Harper admitted. "I suppose I'm only now realizing the gravity of things."

"You want talk?"

Harper shook her head. "Thank you, but no. It's personal and I don't want to bore you."

They rode the rest of the way in silence.

When he stopped in front of the hotel, Harper paid him, giving a hefty tip,

He placed his hand over hers to prevent her from moving away.

"I pray for you."

Harper smiled. "Thank you. That means a lot. I could really use it. I'm sorry again for scaring you. Have a good rest of the day."

"You too," the driver said. "Go to hospital."

Harper only nodded and walked into the lobby. She entered the elevator, pressed the button for her floor, then leaned against the wall, closing her eyes.

A few seconds later, the doors slid open, allowing her to exit. She strolled to her room, used the key card to open the door and stepped inside.

Harper made sure she bolted the door and closed the curtains.

She set the messenger bag on the coffee table and grabbed another bottle of wine from the mini-fridge.

As she returned to the couch, she poured the wine in her glass, took a sip, then set it down.

She removed the box she'd taken from Daniel's apartment and set it in front of her. Harper stared at it as if preparing to find the answers she'd been seeking for more than a month.

Harper pulled in a sharp breath and removed the lid.

Inside were a thick folder and a thumb drive.

She first picked up the thumb drive and turned it over in her hands.

She'd have to wait until she returned home in order to view the contents.

Next, she grabbed the folder and pulled off the rubber band.

Harper opened it with care only to find several articles and photos of young girls. Some articles were written by him, most weren't.

"Oh, goodness," Harper whispered, taking another sip of Merlot. "So many innocent lives stolen."

The articles ranged from years.

Unfortunately, the articles didn't provide her answers, only more questions as she considered the fates of the girls. She didn't recognize any from either the news or the houses she said at.

As for what was on the flash drive, she'd have to go home.

Without hesitation, Harper replaced the items in the box, shoved it in the messenger bag and began to gather her things to check out.

Forty-four

"I'm so glad you're back," Olivia said, pulling Harper into a hug. "Are you okay? I've been so worried about you since your phone call. "Tell me what happened."

Harper pulled away with a sigh. She spotted Collier trotting to the door, and when he saw Harper, he barked twice, spinning in fast circles.

"Hey, buddy," she smiled, kneeling to give her Sheltie her attention. She hugged him, her breathing ragged. "I've missed you so much."

"Harper!" Olivia said impatiently.

Harper twisted her body to gaze at her friend who had her hands set on her hips.

"I think the best thing is to keep you out completely, Liv," Harper said. "It's too dangerous to involve you. *I* should stay out of it. But I can't. Not unless I can find some way to prove Ollie's death was connected."

Olivia shook her head and knelt to meet Harper's eyes. "I can't let you go through this alone."

"You're a good friend, Liv," Harper acknowledged. "I love you for that."

"What did you find out?"

Harper swallowed in hopes to wet her dry throat. "I met Jenny Buford."

Harper and Olivia went into the kitchen for coffee as she relayed everything that was said.

"After we made the hole in the wall…" Harper trailed off and lifted the mug to her lips. "We heard a noise. Jenny went to see who it was. I never saw their faces. But I know it was two men. I heard them coming to the bedroom so I hid underneath the bed."

Harper paused a beat.

"Whoever they were, they wanted something. They though Jenny had information. I don't know if it was a part of the trafficking ring or something else. But the next thing I knew, Jenny fell to the floor. They'd shot and killed her, Olivia!"

Saying the words out loud forced more tears to come. She leaned forward, holding her head against the table. She felt Olivia drape her arm around her shoulders.

"They killed her, and I didn't do anything to stop them," Harper forced out.

"It's not your fault, honey," Olivia whispered. "You couldn't have done anything. If you had, they might have killed you."

"I know," Harper said. "I just felt so helpless. And scared. Like how it was when I watched that man kill Nghia. So many innocent people have been killed, Olivia. Where does it end?"

"I don't know," Olivia admitted. "It may never end."

"Then what's the point?" Harper wondered. "I feel like it's a losing battle."

"It might be," Olivia said. "But think about those girls you've saved. *You* saved them. Including Daniel's sister. Don't forget about that."

Harper wiped her eyes and sniffed.

"I can't let Daniel's and Ollie's death be in vain," she said softly. "Or Jenny. Without her, I wouldn't have the information Daniel kept hidden."

"What was it?"

"A box containing more photos of young girls and newspaper articles and a flash drive. I didn't have a computer with me, so I couldn't see what's on it."

"Hold on a second," Olivia said. She jumped to her feet and hurried out the room.

Harper rose to pour herself more coffee. She leaned against the counter, deep in thought until Olivia returned, laptop clutched tight in her left hand. She set it on the table and booted it up.

"Where's the drive?"

Harper walked to her messenger bag by her chair and pulled out the box. She set it on the table, removed the lid and retrieved the drive.

As she slipped it into the port, Olivia grabbed the photos and thumbed through the contents.

"Wow, this is a lot of kids," Olivia muttered.

"Yeah," Harper replied in kind.

"Several are Americans," she noted. "And boys."

Harper pulled up the folder, each file a Microsoft Word document.

She clicked on the first file.

"These look like journal entries," Harper said.

Olivia maneuvered to look over her shoulder. "They could be different articles he wrote. Or maybe he was going to write a book. Journalists tend to do that."

Harper skimmed through Daniel's notes, seeing he'd written about things he had learned about human trafficking, in different locations. The one he came closer to finding out who was in charge was the one which was held in Atlanta.

A man named Bruce Perry was a former boxer. He'd been in prison for selling drugs in a school zone. He was also under suspicion fifteen years ago for molesting his niece. He denied it and was released since the child wouldn't point her fingers at him.

Daniel had found Perry in California and followed him, getting familiar with his habits.

Perry stayed in an elaborate hotel, a different woman leaving his room every night. Every morning in the dining room, he would order a breakfast consisting of bacon, eggs, toast, and coffee. A waiter would approach him, slip a sheet of paper to him.

Next, Daniel would follow him out of the hotel. He saw Perry having a conversation with one of the girls Harper recognized from the envelope Daniel had slipped her.

He noted Perry had left her when an elderly man walked up but returned the next day, again speaking to the same girl.

A week later, the news reported the girl had run away.

Perry, too, had vanished.

Toward the end of Daniel's files, his writing and his attitude had changed.

Perry, himself, approached him at a grocery store.

He spoke no words, just watched Daniel until he left the store. Afterward, Daniel received a phone call from a man who had disguised his voice, threatening to hurt his little sister. Although they didn't outright tell him, they implied they were watching him.

It was at that time, Daniel had begun to worry.

Should he continue his investigation, or should he stop? The rest, Harper realized, was history.

Forty-five

"We have to take this to the cops," Olivia said, for what seemed like the thousandth time. "He even has a list of names, Harper. He saw most of the missing girls with these men."

"Who can we trust?" Harper wondered. "Daniel says some of the men are cops. How do we know which cop we speak to is legit?"

"What about....Lieutenant Rice?" Olivia suggested. "She seems nice and caring. Can we trust her?"

Harper chewed her lower lip. "I don't know. She's the one who told me to start at the beginning if I want to find out who killed Ollie. She might help."

"Call her," Olivia urged. "What have we got to lose? You know we need someone on our side who's in a position to do anything."

"Yeah," Harper frowned. On the laptop screen, she still had the names of men and women Daniel had found during his investigation. "I'll wait to call her in the morning. I'm tired, Liv. I just want to go home and sleep in my bed."

"Okay." Olivia rubbed her back. "Thank you for not shutting me out. I just don't want you to go through this alone."

"Neither do I," Harper answered. She rose, reaching in for a hug. "Thanks."

Harper grabbed Collier's leash and woke him as she slipped it on his collar.

She gathered her things, told Olivia bye, then left her apartment.

As she made her way home by cab, she let her mind drift away to her long-time friendship with Ollie, up until the last day she spoke to him. The day they had the fight. Growing up, her mother always told her to never let the sun go down on her anger. Harper never knew the seriousness of that statement. At least, not until she learned of his death. Her heart was heavy, thinking about it.

"I'm sorry, Ollie," she said underneath her breath.

"You say something, miss?" the cab driver said, glancing in the rearview.

Harper forced a smile. "No, I'm just talking to myself. Sorry."

The driver didn't respond as he braked the car in front of the hotel.

After Harper paid, she and Collier returned to their apartment. She let him inside.

Harper didn't bother dressing. She climbed onto her bed and closed her eyes, allowing sleep to come.

Within minutes, fatigue finally won and she slipped into a steep sleep.

But, soon, she woke, springing into a seated position in her bed.

"That's it!"

Collier lifted his head, tilting it to the side with a curious whine.

Harper jumped off the bed, rushed out of her room and grabbed her keys.

She fumbled with the set, searching for the key to Ollie's apartment.

Once inside, she returned to the bedroom and opened the drawer.

Bruce Perry.

The name was underlined twice, then circled. People didn't circle things that weren't important.

Somehow, Ollie had found out about Bruce Perry.

If Perry learned Ollie was noticing him, it stood to reason he was concerned enough to chat with Ollie, even kill him.

It was here all alone.

Maybe, with Rice's support, Harper could convince a judge to exhume Ollie's body for a second autopsy.

She felt her pockets for her phone, then realizing it was in her apartment, she left Ollie's place and reentered hers. Finding it on her bed, she dialed Lieutenant Rice's number.

It went straight to voicemail.

"Lieutenant," she began. "This is Harper Matthews. Please, please call me back as soon as you receive this message. I want to run something by you and maybe enlist your help to get my friend's body exhumed. I may have found something that could prove he was murdered. At least prove there is doubt he died in an accident."

She ended her call and set her phone back on the counter. She tried to calm herself, but her heart drummed in her chest with exhilaration.

She knew it was possible it wasn't good enough, but it gave her hope. Hope that she would find a way to find justice for Ollie. And maybe eventually finish what Daniel Clark started out to do.

Harper poured herself a glass of wine and returned to her bedroom. She sipped her drink, allowing it to slowly drift her to sleep.

Forty-six

In the distance, the ringing of a cell phone had woken Harper from a steep sleep. She opened her eyes, still feeling tired. Collier wasn't on the bed. She could hear him pacing the kitchen, either in anticipation or in need of the bathroom.

Harper sat up, then saw the paper with the name Bruce Perry next to her wine glass.

Then, she remembered, and realized the caller may be Lieutenant Rice.

She'd left the lieutenant a voicemail late last night.

Harper got out of bed and walked to the kitchen. Glancing at her missed call, she saw that it was Rice. As Harper fed Collier, she called her back.

"Good morning, Miss Matthews," Lieutenant Rice answered. "I was just calling you."

"I'd just woken up. My head isn't really in order today."

"I see coffee is needed," Rice replied.

"You have no idea," Harper muttered as she started her coffeemaker.

"In your voicemail, you said you found something and needed my help," Rice prompted.

Clearing her throat, Harper told the lieutenant about her experience in New York, the flash drive, then finally she ended with finding the note in Ollies' bedside table.

"I don't know how he came up with Bruce Perry's name," Harper admitted. "But doesn't it seem too much of a coincidence to you?"

"Indeed, it does," Rice admitted. "I'm looking him up on the database and I see quite a list of offenses. Your friend's father is friends with judges, right?"

"Yes."

"Well, just because your friend has an ex-con's name in his nightstand doesn't mean he was killed for that reason—or any reason. However, it's possible to urge a judge, depending on which judge it is, to go forward with the exhumation."

"What if he doesn't?"

Lieutenant Rice hesitated, then released a disgruntled sigh.

"I understand why you're doing this. Trust me, I do. However, I believe you're in way over your head."

"No kidding," Harper scoffed.

Silence filled the line.

"I'm not kidding, Miss Matthews," Rice said, her words laced with concern. "You were very lucky you're alive now to tell me the story. Had those men heard you or looked under that bed, you'd be dead. I'm sorry to be so blunt, but I need you to understand this. I wear a gun for a reason."

"I do understand," Harper said. "I just want the cops to take me seriously."

"Well, I hope you find what you're searching for."

"Me too," Harper said. "Thank you for your time."

Harper ended her call with the lieutenant and called Mr. Baldridge. When she answered, she explained what she'd found.

"I think we need to go to the police with this."

Harper waited out the long silence for Mr. Baldridge to answer.

"I don't understand what my son would be doing with the name of a possible trafficker," Mr. Baldridge said finally.

Because he was trying to find out what I was getting myself into. Harper's silent thoughts echoed through her mind, accusing her.

"You knew Ollie, Mr. Baldridge," Harper said. "He only wanted to help people."

"Yes, you're quite right about that," Mr. Baldridge agreed. "Very well, Harper. Give me about half an hour. I'll talk to a friend of mine and see if we can't pull any strings."

"Thank you," Harper said with a sigh of relief. "Thank you."

Forty-seven

Harper waited, feeling anxious for two hours before Mr. Baldridge finally returned her call. He had spoken to a golf buddy of his, Judge Amos Torres, who requested to speak to Harper about the evidence she confiscated.

Agreeing on a time, Harper arrived at the courthouse only a few minutes before she saw Oliver Baldridge Jr.'s familiar blue Cadillac. She opened her car door and stepped into the humid heat, watching as the older man unbuckled. He noticed her and acknowledged with a short nod.

"Hey," she said when he pushed open his door.

"Harper," he replied, tugging at his collar. "Are you absolutely sure about all of this? I just want to move on. It's taking such a toll on the girls"

"Do they know what we're suspecting?" she asked.

"No, of course not. I'm trying to make things as normal as possible. Still, they're very smart girls."

"Mr. Baldridge, I do understand how you feel," Harper replied. "But don't you want to find out for sure? If Ollie was really murdered, don't you want the police to find who killed him?"

"Of course, I do," Mr. Baldridge admitted. "I'm sorry, Harper. I suppose it's making me feel anxious just thinking about it."

"I know," she answered quietly.

"Let's get this over with," he suggested. "Amos is waiting."

Keeping silent, Harper walked with him into the courthouse. Mr. Baldridge led the way to Judge Torres' chambers and spoke quietly to the young legal secretary.

"The judge is expecting you," she replied with a smile. "Have a seat and I'll announce you."

Harper obliged and waited until Mr. Baldridge followed suit before speaking, her voice low enough for only him to hear.

"This Judge Torres," she said. "Are you sure we can trust him? There's no doubt in your mind, right?"

With an arched eyebrow, Mr. Baldridge turned to face her, the movement suddenly resembling Ollie. It was rare, but sometimes Harper could see Ollie in the face of his father. The thought made her smile, if only for a second.

"Exactly what are you insinuating, Harper?" he questioned. "What do you think Ollie has been getting himself in that I can't trust a man I've known my entire life?"

Harper tried to keep her face expressionless.

"I'm sure I'm being paranoid," she said.

"I'm quite certain you are," Mr. Baldridge said. "But to answer your question, I'm confident Amos is trustworthy."

She offered him a smile as the judge's chamber's door opened.

"Oliver," a tall, slim man acknowledged, holding out his hand. He had wrinkles around his eyes and mouth but still appeared to be aging well despite the salt and pepper hair. He was handsome, Harper decided as she waited for Mr. Baldridge to introduce her.

"This young lady is Harper Matthews. She was friends with Ollie for a long time."

Harper rose and extended her hand.

"Thank you for agreeing to meet with us, Judge Torres."

"Of course, young lady," the judge said, offering her a smile to show off his white teeth. "Why don't you folks come into my chambers where we can talk freely." He glanced at the legal secretary "Maddison, please hold all calls and visitors."

"Yes, Judge," Maddison replied.

"Come in."

Harper was the last to enter the office and took a seat in the leather chair.

"Now, Miss Matthews," Judge Torres began. "Oliver was telling me about some evidence you found which may prove Ollie was murdered?"

Harper wiped her hands on the front of her jeans.

Clearing her throat, she told the judge everything that had happened from the time she and Olivia visited the coroner up until the time they looked through the flash drive.

Mr. Baldridge kept his head down as she spoke, while the judge listened with intent, every once in a while raising his eyebrow.

She handed the judge the box she found in Daniel's closet.

After she finished speaking, the judge's chambers fell into a harsh silence while he reviewed the evidence.

Not knowing what to do with her hands, Harper patted her hair, the placed them in her lap.

"That's quite an ordeal you've been through, Miss Harper," Judge Torres said finally. "I admit it is suspicious, this Bruce Perry fellow. As you know, Oliver, it's a lot of money, time, and energy, not to mention traumatic for exhuming someone, especially those you knew well. Do you want this to happen?"

Mr. Baldridge nodded without hesitation. "I do, Amos. I can't live with the not knowing."

"Very well, Oliver," the judge replied. "I've known you for a very long time, and Ollie's death, well, it's almost as personal to me. Normally, I'd like to see more evidence than just a name on a note paper in a Bible. I'll have someone contact this Lieutenant Quintos and request they find Bruce Perry. In the meantime, I'll draw the papers for Ollie's body to be exhumed. Give me some time. I'll try and get it taken care of as quickly and painless as possible."

"Thank you, Amos," Mr. Baldridge said. "I appreciate you doing this."

"Of course," Judge Torres said. "I'll give you a call and let you know the progress."

The judge and Mr. Baldridge rose simultaneously and shook hands. Harper followed Mr. Baldridge's lead, then followed him out of the judge's chambers.

Forty-eight

A week and a half went by before Harper heard anything from Oliver Baldridge. She'd tried to maintain her distance, but it wasn't easy.

Her supervisor had called to find out when she'd return to work, but she wasn't sure she was ready. If Harper was completely honest with herself, she wasn't sure if she would ever be ready. Being on the plane would make her think of Daniel and she'd feel guilty she couldn't save him.

Olivia continuously urged her to go for counseling, but little did she know, Harper had taken it upon herself to talk to a licensed professional.

But, finally, the day Harper had been waiting for arrived.

Mr. Baldridge had called to inform her the exhumation was now complete, and a new coroner was performing a second autopsy.

Her heart went out to the older man as he seemed discouraged and tired.

And then, the phone rang a few hours later on the same day.

Harper set the wine glass she held on the coffee table and snatched the phone up to glance at the caller ID.

Oliver Baldridge.

"Hello?"

"Hey, Harper." A pause. "I wanted to let you know the coroner finished the autopsy." Another pause. "You were right. She found traces of aconite in his system."

"Oh, my goodness." Harper covered her mouth with her hand. Although she figured what the outcome would be like, she still found herself unsure of how to react.

One of her closest friends was murdered.

"So, they're going to reopen the investigation?" Harper wondered.

"Yes." A pause. "I don't know what to make of this."

"Me either," Harper admitted. "Did the lieutenant tell you where they're going to begin?"

"He wants to talk to the Baylee and Emily. He mentioned you once told him they overheard him asking about you. Wondering if you were safe. Do you know what that's about?"

"I can't be certain," Harper said. "I was…out of town at the time."

"I don't know if I want the police to talk to the girls," Mr. Baldridge admitted distantly. "They already buried Ollie. I don't want them to be traumatized with questions."

"I understand," Harper told him. "But the police need to hear the details from them. Not me."

"They'll want to talk to you as well."

"All right, I'll go down to the station soon and talk to Lieutenant Quintos."

"You have no idea why someone would use you as an excuse to get close to my son?"

In truth, Harper did have an idea, but she wasn't willing to let it be known. Not yet, anyway.

"I don't," she said. "But whoever killed him probably knew he was friends with me. They knew Ollie would come to me in a heartbeat if he thought I was in trouble."

"But you don't have an idea who?"

Harper detected exasperation in his words.

"I'm sorry, I don't," Harper replied. "Do you want to meet for coffee and talk?"

A hesitation.

"I should be getting home. I'm just now leaving the station. I might get the girls a sitter and go into work. I need to think about something else for a little while."

"Okay, Mr. Baldridge, let me know if there's anything I can do to help out."

"Yeah, thanks. I believe we've got the situation under control."

She tapped the screen to call him.

"Quintos," the lieutenant answered almost immediately.

"Hi, it's Harper Matthews, Lieutenant."

"Yes, Miss Matthews, I was going to give you a call. I'm sure you may have heard; however, your friend's body had been exhumed. You were correct about him being poisoned. I would like to speak to you. Would you be able to come in for questioning sometimes today?"

"Yes," Harper told him. "Although I'm not sure what help I would be. Ollie was murdered while I was at Granger's house."

"It's standard procedure, Miss Matthews. I'll be questioning all of Mr. Baldridge's friends and his family."

"What time do you want me?"

"How's two o'clock?"

Harper glanced at the clock on the microwave as it went to noon. She would have two hours to kill before going to the police station.

She took a sip of wine.

"Two o'clock will be fine, Lieutenant. I'll see you then."

When she ended the call, Harper curled her feet underneath her body, turning on the TV. She flipped through the channels before settling on a movie on Hallmark.

She watched as the movie played, but her thoughts went to Ollie and his last moments. Did he know he was dying? Was he afraid? What were his last thoughts? His final words?

As Harper shook her head, trying to erase the thoughts filling in, she wiped away the tears that fell.

Forty-nine

The vibration on her cell phone jarred her from an unsettling dream. Harper fell off the couch, banging her head against the edge of the coffee table. She cursed underneath her breath as she held her forehead.

It took a minute for her to originate where the phone was ringing from. After discerning that it was still on the countertop in the kitchen, Harper tripped her way into the kitchen, her legs feeling sluggish.

"Hello?"

"Hey." Olivia's voice sounded faraway to Harper's ears. "You okay, Harper? You sound strange."

"I just woke up." Harper lowered her head to the counter, pleading for her headache to ease.

"Wow, you must have needed it. It's late."

"No, I'd fallen back asleep. I had the worse—wait. What time is it?"

"One forty-three," Olivia told her.

Harper cursed herself as she scanned the apartment for her handbag and keys.

"I'm supposed to meet Lieutenant Quintos at two. I'm going to be really late."

"He called me a little while ago," Olivia replied. "He wants to talk to me about Ollie. He said they found out he really was poisoned. I can't imagine what he must have gone through. It's so terrible."

Harper found her keys and handbag in her bedroom.

"I know," she said. "And to make matters worse, I think Mr. Baldridge blames me for Ollie's death."

"What makes you think that? You weren't even around here."

"I know, but he doesn't know that. Just the tone of his voice sounds a little…accusatory. The only thing is, Liv…Ollie's death *was* my fault."

"Stop it," Olivia huffed. "You had nothing to do with it. Don't go blaming yourself." She paused. "You sound like you've been drinking."

Harper locked herself out of the apartment and jogged toward the elevator.

"Geez, sometimes this elevator starts raising my heart rate," Harper evaded. "Can't they install windows?"

"Maybe you should call a cab," Olivia said.

"Why?"

"You shouldn't be on the road drinking," Olivia replied. "Especially going to the police station."

"So I had a little glass of wine. No big deal."

"Sounds like you had more than just a little," Olivia noted.

Harper frowned. "I'm allowed to drink, Liv. Stay off my back. You're not my mother."

"Ever since you came back, you seemed to drink more than ever before," Olivia pointed out. "I'm your friend and I'm getting worried."

"Well, you can stop," Harper replied. "I'm a big girl."

"Fine," Olivia breathed. "Are you on your way to meet Quintos now?"

"Yeah," Harper told her. "Pray I'm not late getting there."

"Call me after you leave him," Olivia said. "I want to know what to expect."

"Will do. Talk to you soon."

Harper ended the call as she broke into a run.

When she climbed in the car, she started the ignition, pulling out of her parking space.

The traffic in Atlanta was heavy. Time seemed to move fast as she moved slower. She'd begun to wonder if she should call Lieutenant Quintos and let him know she'd be late, but she finally was able to get past the accident holding up two lanes.

She reached the station a few minutes after two o'clock.

Before darting from her car, she found an Altoid mint container inside the armrest. She pulled two out and began sucking on them, hoping it'd help her eliminate the wine from her breath.

She hurried into the building, announcing her arrival to the desk sergeant.

She pulled in a sharp breath and pushed it out as she waited for Quintos.

"Miss Matthews, I can take you back now," the desk sergeant told her.

Harper followed her through the building, to Quintos' office. She felt her legs grow heavy as she walked.

They found Quintos at his desk, thumbing through his notes.

"I'm so sorry I'm running late," Harper said as the desk sergeant allowed her to enter the office. "I'd fallen back asleep. If it wasn't for my friend calling, I'd probably still be sleeping."

"It's quite all right, Miss Matthews," Quintos said without looking up from his papers. "Have a seat, if you will."

"Sure."

She waited, smoothing the wrinkles in her pant legs with her palms.

Finally, Quintos grabbed his notepad, turned to a clean sheet of paper and looked up.

"Thank you for coming today," he began. "I'm going to start with some basic questions about your relationship with Oliver Baldridge, then move on from there."

"Okay," Harper said. She cleared her throat.

"How long have you known Mr. Baldridge?"

"A while," she told him. "I met him in high school. I guess it's been about seventeen or eighteen years."

"What was the nature of your relationship? Just friends, did you date, or were you friends with benefits?"

"We were friends. He was my best friend. That's all." She hesitated, then decided she'd better be completely open. Harper had seen enough cop shows to know everything mattered. "Well, we did have feelings for one another, but we never acted on it. I don't know why he didn't, but I worried it could have ruined what we had."

She watched as Quintos scribbled into his pad.

"According to Mr. Baldridge's father and daughters, you had an argument before you…went undercover. Is that true?"

"It was stupid, really." Harper cleared her throat.

"So, you did argue?"

"Yes," she answered. "Someone broke into my apartment and attacked me. It scared me. I'd accused Ollie of doing it. But it wasn't him. It was only a reaction."

"How do you know?" Quintos questioned. "Did you see your attacker's face?"

"Well…no," Harper replied. "But Ollie would never have hurt me. Craig was smart. He knew what to say to rattle me without my realizing it. I'd become paranoid."

"What did he say?"

"That anybody involved with trafficking could be anybody. Even Ollie."

"'Even Ollie'? Is that verbatim to what Craig said?"

Harper nodded. "At the time, it never crossed my mind someone like Ollie could be involved. But, when I was attacked, he showed up right after the intruder left. I was scared. I took it out on him."

She frowned, looking down at her hands.

"I never got to apologize."

"Did you ever report the attack to the police?"

"No," Harper said. "I wasn't sure what to do. Craig had convinced me the police wouldn't help put an end to trafficking. After I was attacked, I was determined more than before to infiltrate them. So, I stayed at Olivia's for the night and the next morning, I went to see Craig."

Quintos nodded as his hands continued to scrawl with fervor on the pad.

"I was also told you had another argument. Before you were attacked. Do you remember?"

She nodded. "He wanted us to get together. To finally start dating. He was angry because I would choose relationships with men that wouldn't last."

"How did that make you feel?"

"Frustrated, I guess. I didn't want to hurt him."

"Were you in love with him?"

Harper hesitated a beat before nodding. "I think so. But I didn't realize it until after I found out he was dead."

"Did Craig ever meet Mr. Baldridge?"

"Not in person," Harper said. "Not that I knew of, anyway. He did admit to me that he saw Ollie and me go into the hotel after…after the shooting."

"Can you think of anyone in Mr. Baldridge's life who may want him dead?"

"Definitely not. Whoever killed him has to have some connection to human trafficking. I know."

Quintos looked up and studied Harper before continuing.

"Because they lured him out by saying something happened to you?"

Harper raised her shoulders and let them fall. "I don't know the answer to that. It's just a feeling I have. I just feel it's all a little too coincidental."

"While you were inside Granger's home, did you have any connection to Mr. Baldridge?"

"No, of course not. We weren't allowed to have a phone. The last time I saw or spoke to him was the night of my attack."

Quintos remained silent until he finished writing in his notes. He set his pen down.

"Is there anything about Mr. Baldridge you think may be important?"

Harper considered the question and came up with empty.

She shook her head in answer.

"I was also informed you went to New York recently," the lieutenant replied. "Tell me about the trip."

Harper studied him before speaking. She decided he probably knew the details but wanted to hear it from her. So, she once again relayed what had happened while in New York."

"Okay," Quintos said, setting his pen down. "I believe I have enough for right now, Miss Matthews. We'll be in contact about the investigation."

"What about Jenny Buford?" Harper wondered. "Are the New York police investigating her murder?"

"As of right now, Jenny Buford is a missing person. No body, no murder. They'll contact me if they find evidence of a murder."

"You'll find Ollie's killer, right?" Harper asked.

"All I can say is we'll do our best. I'm still interviewing his family and friends. I'll also re-interview the men we've arrested. I do plan to explore your theory that Mr. Baldridge's death was in some way involved. It's a long process. It may take days or even years to find out the truth. If we ever do. I'll let you know if we need anything else."

"What about the pathologist who autopsied him first? Are you going to question him?"

"We already did," Quintos said.

"What did he say?"

Quintos folded his hands on his desk as he stared into Harper's eyes. "I'm unable to tell you of what other witnesses have said during their interviews. I realize you've been through a lot, and the sudden loss of your friend must have taken its toll. The best thing for you to do is to go about your normal life. I recommend you also visit a therapist."

"Therapist?" Harper said, mouth agape. "I don't need therapy."

"It may help come to terms with everything," Quintos replied. "It's not a requirement. Just a suggestion."

"I'll think about it. Thank you, Lieutenant."

She rose and extended her hand. He accepted it with a nod.

After Harper left his office, she waited until she reached outdoors before pulling her phone from her pocket. Although it was Olivia she intended to call, it wasn't the one she reached out to.

She placed the phone to her ear, listening to the ringing.

"Hey."

"Hi, John," Harper said. "Are you still in town?"

"I am until early tomorrow morning. Then I fly to California."

"Do you want to meet for drinks? I promise I won't keep you out too late."

"Sure thing," Jonathan said. "Why don't you come by the hotel? We can meet at the downstairs bar."

"Sounds great. I'll see you then."

Fifty

"It's still hard to believe," Harper said into her wine. "I can't imagine Ollie not being around anymore."

"It is a shame," Jonathan said. "He was a father, right?"

Harper nodded. "Of twin girls."

"How are they doing?"

"I haven't really gotten to speak to them much. But, when I did, Emma seemed angry. I don't think it sunk in for Baylee yet. Not completely. Their mother died in a car accident a few years ago. They were with her."

"Jeez," Jonathan said, sipping his martini. "That's awful."

"How does one go on after this?" Harper wondered.

As she took a sip of wine, she began to feel the room spinning. She was on her third glass and didn't feel like she was ready to call it quits. She'd called Jonathan with the intention of talking through her pain without adding extra details, but it wasn't working. Even the wine didn't seem to deaden the ache she felt in her heart. If anything, the ache seemed to grow. Harper wondered if she should order something stronger.

"It takes time," Jonathan replied. "But you'll get through it, Harper. You're the most resilient woman I've ever had the pleasure to meet. If you ever wanted to know why I'm very attracted to you, that's the reason."

Harper lifted the corner of her lips to a smile. "You're attracted to me?"

"Very much so," Jonathan confirmed.

"Then why did you cheat?" she asked. "We could have been something more if I didn't catch you in bed with someone else."

Jonathan nodded into his drink. He tilted his head back for a sip before answering.

"It was a big mistake. One I've never forgiven myself for. I can't even begin to tell you how sorry I am."

"You can try," Harper told him.

Jonathan gazed at her.

"How?"

"That's for you to find out."

Harper finished her wine and tried to stand.

"Well, I should—"

Losing her balance, she fell into Jonathan's arms, inches from her face.

"I think you should stay here tonight," Jonathan told her, his voice husky. "At the very least, let me call a cab."

"A cab sounds like the smart thing," Harper muttered. Her heart thrummed in her chest as the room began to spin. She must have had more wine than she'd thought, but then again, she wasn't counting.

Jonathan held onto her and they walked out of the bar and he pressed his finger to the elevator button.

It seemed to take an eternity for the doors to slide open. After a group of people stepped out, Harper and Jonathan stepped in. He pressed the button for his floor.

"Ollie and I could have been an item," Harper said. "But, now, we never will be. And it's all my fault."

"I'm sure you're not to blame," Jonathan replied.

"I pick the wrong men," Harper admitted. "The right man was in front of me the entire time. But I never realized it until he died."

When the elevator opened, Jonathan half-carried her to his room.

He used his keycard and opened the door.

"Let me get you some water, and I'll call you a cab."

As Jonathan went into the kitchen, Harper found the couch and plopped down.

She closed her eyes until she felt the cushion bounce.

Opening her eyes, she regarded Jonathan.

"The cab will be here shortly," he told her. "Maybe thirty minutes."

Harper placed her palm on his chest with a smile. "Thank you for taking care of me."

"My pleasure," he answered.

She didn't move her hand away. Instead, she slowly worked her way up and to his neck. Harper moved slow, one reason, she wanted to be sure she didn't throw up all over him and another because she was unsure of what she wanted to do.

Jonathan waited, his eyes focused on hers. Once their lips were inches apart, Harper kissed him lightly. He followed her lead.

"Are you sure you want to do this?" he asked her, his voice full of desire.

"No," Harper replied. "And yes."

Before he could respond, she pressed her lips against his. His strong arms wrapped tight around her body, his fingers tangling in her hair.

He pulled her head back to nip her neck, sending a surge of fire inside her body.

She pulled him to the bedroom.

Harper sat on the bed, pulling him with her. She surrendered herself to Jonathan, willing to forgo bad memories for a night of lust.

Fifty-one

Harper ran her hand along the opposite side of the bed and opened her eyes when she realized it was empty. She sat up, noticing the sun was beginning to rise. Her head pounding, she looked across the dim room.

"Jonathan?"

She waited for his response. When there was none, Harper climbed out of bed, pulling on a hotel robe. She stepped out of the room as she tied the strings around her waist.

"John, are you still here?"

He wasn't in the living or the kitchen rooms, but the coffee was made and a piece of paper was propped against the maker.

She picked it up.

Harper, good morning—

I didn't want to wake you. I must fly to California. I'll be returning in a few days. I hope we can see each other then. In the meantime, would you mind checking me out? It needs to be done by noon. Thanks! Jonathan.

Harper found a mug and poured herself a cup of coffee. Then, she searched the rooms for something to ease her growing headache. When she found none, she decided to stop by the pharmacy on the way home.

She found her cell phone by the couch.

Olivia had called three times, left two messages and sent five texts.

The messages were asking how the interview session with Lieutenant Quintos went. The same was in her messages until the last message voiced her concern.

Harper checked the time. It was only seven fifteen, but she knew Olivia would be awake by now.

She pressed *return call* and curled on the couch, waiting for her friend to answer.

"Harper! Where are you? You never called me last night. I was getting worried."

"I'm sorry, Liv," Harper said. On the table were two empty bottles of wine. She picked one up and gazed through it. The television was distorted through the glass. "I meant to call you, I did. But I think I had more wine than I intended."

She rubbed her temple.

"Wine?" Olivia echoed. "You got drunk on wine? Again?"

"It was calming." Harper hesitated. "I needed it."

"Where are you, anyway? You didn't come home last night. I was worried, so I came to check on you. I've been in your place all night."

"I stayed with—" Harper stopped herself before she admitted she'd come to see Jonathan Parker. She didn't want Olivia to know about it. Not yet, anyway. Although Harper was willing to be with him last night, she didn't know if she wanted to even try with him. Olivia would only be disappointed in her if she admitted to sleeping with him. "I stayed at a hotel. I knew I'd drunk too much, and I didn't want to drive home. I'll be there shortly."

"As long as you're okay," Olivia told her.

"I am. Really."

"Good. I already fed Collier and walked him for you."

"Thanks, Liv." Harper sipped her coffee. "Did you see Quintos?"

"Yeah, he asked me a lot of questions about you and Ollie."

Harper released a groan. "Seems as if he's accusing me of killing him."

"But, that's crazy to even suggest," Olivia claimed. "You weren't even here."

"I know. But I guess these are questions he's got to ask. As much as I hate to say it, Liv, but I know Ollie's death has to have been connected to me. Lieutenant Quintos might see it." Harper pulled in a breath and pushed it out. "This is all my fault, Liv. I was stupid enough to fall for Craig's trap and now Ollie's death and my life is a whole different kind of ruin."

"But, without you, all of those girls would still be stuck. My father used to tell me good deeds often have bad outcomes. But, no matter what, the good deed can be worth it."

"Profound," Harper said, rising.

"Why don't we meet for breakfast?" Olivia suggested. "Maybe we can talk about something else. Get your mind off this situation."

"I'd like that."

"Good. Let's meet at J. Christopher's."

"It'll take a little bit for me to get moving." Harper looked at the clock. Seven thirty-three. "How's eight thirty?"

"I'll see you then."

When the call ended, Harper closed her eyes, putting her head between her knees. She rubbed the nape of her neck before standing.

She topped her coffee off and went into the bedroom. Unfortunately, she didn't have different clothes to wear, so she gathered her outfit and walked into the bathroom. She turned the shower on, adjusted the temperature and stepped under the spewing water when it was warm enough.

She waited until the warm water seemed to wash away the wine leftover before using the hotel's shampoo and conditioner to wash her body. After she felt clean enough, Harper got out of the shower and pulled on last night's clothes.

She finished her coffee, grabbed her handbag and the keycard Jonathan left on the counter.

Fifty-two

The next few days went by without incidence. Harper had tried to visit Ollie's daughters several times, but Oliver Baldridge had made an excuse each time, promising she could see them next. The last time she tried making contact, Thomas claimed they'd gone out of town.

She decided the Baldridges needed space, so she stopped trying for the time being.

She realized she was starting to rely more heavily on drinking wine, but it was the only thing that helped her fall asleep and calm her nerves.

She had been able to speak to Adaline and Blair a few times. Harper could tell in their upbeat voices they were doing much better since she last saw them. It would still be a long healing process for all involved, especially for her young friends. At times, Harper wondered if any of them would ever truly heal.

She decided only time would tell.

She made plans with the girls' parents for her to visit them.

In the meantime, Harper would call for updates on Ollie's murder and the search for The Ghost. Either they wouldn't tell her specifics on the investigation, or they didn't know anything new. As a result, Harper would find herself sobbing into her drink or in the shower.

Harper knew she had to face the fact that it was possible the questions would remain unanswered.

She continued to practice her violin, even writing new music. The sounds didn't have the same effect for her as it used to be in the past. Harper wasn't sure if it was her playing or the wine, but either way, she was beginning to lose interest. As a child, the violin had been an escape for her, which became a staple for her life.

Now, the times were changing.

Jonathan was due to return the following day. Harper found herself looking forward to it. She wanted a companion other than Olivia. Someone who could take her mind away from the real world. She didn't know if her relationship with Jonathan would go anywhere, but that was okay with her.

Harper decided to see a therapist, if nothing more than to end

Olivia's constant request that she do so, and possibly to end the nightmares she never could wake from.

Before their session ended the day before, her therapist had given her a brochure of a ministry whose purpose was to raise awareness of human trafficking. He mentioned his sister was the founder of the ministry and dealt with men, women, and children who were victims every day. Not only in Atlanta, but across the United States. He suggested it may do her good in helping others like herself.

Harper hadn't mentioned the ministry to Olivia. She wanted to make the decision on her own without input from someone else. While unsure whether throwing herself into a situation with human trafficking again would be a good idea, she decided it couldn't hurt to check it out.

She continued to hear Ollie call to her. He'd always told her to end her fear, she must face it head-on.

Harper sat in the parking lot, staring at an overgrown church, which housed a large sign reading: *Grace's Story: Where pain ends, and hope begins.*

After several minutes passed, Harper pushed open her door and climbed out of her car. She made her way into the building.

A woman walked by, then stopped, noticing Harper.

"Hello," she said with a smile. "Can I help you?"

"I'm Harper Matthews. Dr. Broderick gave me a brochure about this place."

"Oh, yes!" the woman said, her face lighting with amusement. She extended her hand and gripped Harper's with fierce. "Justin told me you might show up. I'm Joan."

"He did?"

"Yes, he said you were considering volunteering with the ministry. I heard a lot about you. I'm excited to meet you."

"Thank you," Harper said. She scanned the vast space. "What exactly do you do here?"

"We're big on fundraisers. A lot of people help out. Children, men, women, victims, or just good-hearted citizens. Cake sales are our biggest fundraisers. We're currently in the process of setting one up now. It'll take place at the end of the week."

"What do you do with the money?" Harper asked. She shook her head and snickered. "I'm sorry, I'm just clueless about it all."

Joan smiled. "Not at all. There are a lot of trafficking victims in the United States today. More than you can imagine. It takes a tremendous about of time for them to heal. We do our part by providing what they need to help the process. A lot of our rescued victims are hooked on drugs, so we give them shelter and rehab. Some are homeless. Again, we give them shelter. While there are quite a few with good, solid families, sometimes they don't have the money for therapy. Talking to someone is vital to being able to move past the ordeal. So, we pay for their therapy."

"That's amazing," Harper told her.

"I think it is. We've thrived since I opened it up five years ago."

"What made you open it?"

"I wanted to make a difference in the world. Not many people realize how big a deal it is being trafficked. They view it as more of a third world country kind of thing. In reality, it could be happening next door. When people donate, whether it's because they've heard how much of a trouble it is, or if they're just kind, once they learn about us…and they will learn…it's an eye-opener."

"I'm sure."

"Are you interested in volunteering? I can put you to work right away."

Harper nodded. "I'd love to."

"Great! Just follow me. I'll introduce you to a few of our volunteers."

Joan led the way to the sanctuary where they had set up tables for the cake sale at the front, near the altar.

Several men were setting up the tables while the woman covered the surfaces with a white paper cloth. Two teenagers decorated a table already set up.

"Everyone," Joan said as they walked down the aisle. "I'd like you to meet a new volunteer. This is Harper Matthews."

"Glad you decided to join us."

Harper turned to the speaker and saw her therapist heading in their direction.

"Dr. Broderick," Harper acknowledged, her cheek turning a shade of red. She hoped no one would notice. "I'm glad to see what this is all about. It sounds like an amazing ministry."

"It really is," Dr. Broderick told her.

"Why don't you go to Sara over there and help her decorate the pews?" Joan suggested.

Harper looked at the girl struggling to untangle a wad of decorative strings. She guessed Sara to be a few years younger than herself.

"Okay," Harper replied. "I'd be happy to."

She made a beeline toward Sara and sat in the pew behind her.

"Hi, I'm Harper," she said. "Joan told me to give you a hand."

Sara rolled her eyes with exasperation. "Thank goodness. These strings are a mess. Whoever threw them in the attic last didn't care enough to throw them neatly. I've already begun to tear them."

"Let me try," Harper said, reaching her hand out.

Sara passed the tangled mess to Harper. "Good luck. I'm Sara, by the way. Sara Williams."

"It's nice to meet you, Sara. How long have you been a part of this ministry?"

"Since Aunt Joan opened it." She smiled.

Harper arched an eyebrow. "She's your aunt?"

"Yeah, a few years ago I got myself into a mess," Sara explained. "I ran away from home because I got tired of my home situation. My parents fought so much and it wasn't easy to handle. I met a guy who promised to help me start a new life. As a sort of payment, he made me sleep with him. I was his pet, so to speak. He sold me to a few other men."

"You mean he trafficked you?"

Sara nodded. "For almost three years. I was lucky. This undercover cop came in. I think he could tell I didn't want to be there. So we just talked. The next day, the FBI comes in, busting the brothel I was at."

"Wow," Harper said. "You're very open about it."

Sara let her shoulders rise, then fall. "I didn't used to be. I was messed up for the longest time. I was in and out of rehab. Almost OD'd twice. I just wanted the pain to end. But, Aunt Joan and Uncle Justin wouldn't give up on me. After a lot of therapy, I felt comfortable enough to let them know most everything that had happened to me. They named this place after me."

"So, Grace is your first name? Or middle?"

"First. I've always gone by Sara. But Aunt Joan thought naming it Grace's Story was fitting. We do a lot of fundraisers, also play a lot of games. But I stand up in front of everybody that comes and tell them my story. I basically say 'it happened to me, so it can happen to you.' I've never been much of a speaker. But for me to get past the fear, I have to work through it, you know?"

Harper lifted the corners of her lips to a smile as she worked to untangle the strings. "I used to have a friend who always said that to me."

"It's true," Sara told her. She shook her head with a laugh, "But it's certainly isn't easy."

"No," Harper agreed. "It's not."

She'd finally untangled the string. Sara beamed as she took it.

"Awesome! You can take one of the strings and loop it on the other side of the pews." Sara demonstrated by taping the end of her string to the top of the pew, then looping a small portion into a bowl shape before taping it on another pew.

"I think I can do that," Harper said.

She grabbed an extra tape, a roll of decorative string, then started working on the opposite side.

Fifty-three

After Harper returned home from Grace's Story, she set her messenger bag on the counter, drew in a deep breath, and pushed it out. For the first time in over a month, she'd begun to feel whole again. A part of her continued to nab at her heart when she thought of how stupid and vulnerable she'd been or when she thought of Ollie's death.

But Harper was now beginning to feel as if maybe she can once again find the light in the darkness.

Her talk with Sara seemed to do the trick.

Will Harper ever completely heal?

She didn't know.

Even Sara admitted she still woke from nightmares of the abuse after being drugged and trafficked.

But Harper knew each person dealt with tragedy and pain in different ways. It was now a waiting game to see how she can bring herself to feel whole again.

It wasn't even her ordeal that worried her. It was the reminder that Ollie, her long-time best friend, would no longer be with her to help her heal.

Harper walked to the fridge, removed a bottled water and unscrewed the top. Collier sat on the couch, watching her, his head tilted as if he sensed his owner's pain.

As she took a sip, her mind drifted to Ollie's mysterious death.

He'd been poison.

It was unimaginable, no matter the circumstances.

She knew the police would likely not tell her any information. After all, as close as she was to Ollie, she still wasn't family.

Still, she didn't want to sit around waiting for answers.

Harper made a decision to call Lieutenant Rice.

"I want to speak to Granger," she said without announcing who she was.

"Miss Matthews," Rice replied, "I'd advise against that."

"I don't care," Harper said simply. "Please. Let me talk to him."

"He's in the FBI's jurisdiction now. I doubt they'll allow you to speak to him."

Harper frowned. "There's absolutely no way? What if I told them I was family?"

"Are you implying you want to lie your way into speaking to Granger?" Rice said, her words laced with surprise.

"Granger knows a lot of people, Lieutenant," Harper reminded her. "He'll likely know who Bruce Perry is. I ran a Google search on him, but I'm not sure which, if any, is him. I want to find Bruce Perry."

"I'm sure Quintos will speak to him," Rice said.

"Maybe," Harper agreed. "But who do you think he'd rather talk to? Me or Quintos?"

Rice fell silent.

"You know I'm right."

"You shouldn't be telling me this, Miss Matthews," Rice said.

"Would I stand a chance of talking to him if I claim I was family?"

Rice pushed out a long, heavy breath. "It's possible. I haven't heard that they put him in lockdown, so you may be able to speak with him."

"Good," Harper said. "Thank you."

"Don't mention it," Rice told her. "I mean it. If my captain knew I was helping you this much…who knows what he'd do. It won't be pretty."

"I do appreciate your help," Harper said. "More than you'll probably ever know."

"Watch yourself, Harper," Rice replied. "Take care of yourself."

"I will."

Harper grabbed her messenger bag and keys as she ended the call.

Fifty-four

Harper stepped inside the federal building and glanced around until she found someone she could speak to.

She widened her eyes and made her gait quick and frantic.

"Excuse me, but my name's April. April Granger," Harper exclaimed, breathless. "I found out you've arrested my brother. I need to see him. Please."

The agent looked down on her. "Who is your brother?"

"Mark Granger. Please, can I see him?"

"I'll see what I can do. Please have a seat and someone will be with you in a moment."

"Thank you. Thank you so much."

Harper took a seat and waited for someone else to come to her.

And she waited.

And waited.

Finally, a man about twenty years older than the first agent approached her.

"Miss Granger?"

Harper rose.

"That's me."

"Come this way, if you will."

Harper nodded and scurried after the agent who led her down a series of hallways until they finally reached their destination. He opened the door and allowed her to step inside.

She knew it was an interrogation room and wasn't surprised when she found he wanted to ask her questions.

"Have a seat, ma'am. I'm Agent Davison."

Harper remained silent as she watched him sit across the table from her.

"Your brother is in quite a bit of trouble, ma'am."

Harper narrowed her eyes. "What did he do now?"

"Well, he's being investigated for his involvement of a human trafficking ring for one," Agent Davison said.

"What?" Harper asked, her voice laced with surprise. "Come on. My brother may be a lot of things, but certainly not that." She waited a beat before she covered her mouth with a sigh. "He wouldn't, would he?"

"Do you know his friends? Maybe there's someone he's mentioned and may have confided in his….dealings?"

Harper shook her head. "I don't. I'm sorry. My brother and I don't always see eye to eye. But I still love him, you know? Oh, this is just going to break my mother's heart."

She rested her elbows on the table and covered her face with her hands.

When she lifted her head, she wiped away fake tears.

"My mother actually sent me to talk to him. Please, can I see him?"

The agent nodded. "Give me a little bit to set it up."

"Oh, thank you, thank you so much."

Harper sniffed as the agent rose and left the room. She stood to pace the floor, still remaining in character for anyone who may be watching. She knew they would be.

Finally, someone came for her and led her to the visitor's area.

A few families were already there, talking to their loved ones.

Harper sat and waited a few more minutes until someone brought a cuffed Granger into the room.

Their eyes met as he was led to the table.

Granger lowered himself to the seat, never wavering his gaze. The agent walked away.

Two more remained in the room, watching over the room.

"Sister, huh?" Granger said finally.

"It's the only way I could see you," Harper admitted, her voice low. "I need to ask you something."

"What makes you think I'll answer?"

Harper raised her shoulder to her chin and let it fall. "Honestly, I don't. But I had to try."

Granger's lips curved into a smile that made her feel sick to the stomach.

"You're a tough one, I have to give you credit for that. You don't give up."

"You can thank my parents for that. For different reasons," Harper replied.

"Oh? What are those reasons?"

"It's not your business, Granger."

"Maybe not," he replied. "But my information doesn't come for free. I give a little, you give a little."

Harper paused, then realized she didn't have much to lose.

"My mother was very strong-willed," she admitted. "She never thought twice about helping people.

"Ah," Granger said with a smile. "You wished to be like her. Where's Mommy now?"

"She's dead."

"Sorry to hear that," Granger said with no sorrow in his voice. "And your father?"

"My father," Harper muttered. "is somewhere in the world. I don't know where he is, neither do I care."

"Hostility," Granger noted. "Tell me why."

"He killed my mother," Harper said. "He was abusive to us both. He locked me in the closet for hours just because it made him feel good."

"That explains your fear of small places," Granger mused. "You're a flight attendant, aren't you? How can you handle being thousands of miles in the air? Enclosed space. No chance of escaping."

"Time for my questions, now," Harper insisted.

"All right. Fair enough."

"Who is Bruce Perry?"

Harper gauged Granger's expression, noting the flash of realization in his eyes.

"I can't say I know," Granger told her.

"You're lying," Harper asked, narrowing her eyes. She leaned forward. "You at least know of him."

Granger watched her watch him for a few seconds, but it seemed more like minutes.

"Bruce Perry taught me how to recruit. He's been in this business for years. He's also very dangerous. And very loyal to the one they refer to as The Ghost."

"So, what…he's second in command?"

"I suppose you can say that."

"How can I find him?"

"Miss Granger, time's up."

For a second, she didn't realize the guard was talking to her until he reached to touch her upper arm.

"What? No, I need more time."

"You can see your brother another time," the agent replied.

Granger rose as well and leaned in close to her cheek and planted a kiss. Before the guard pulled him away, he spoke to her.

"He'll find you."

She watched, forcing back a shudder as Granger was pulled away from the visitor's room.

Harper was led out to the front and before leaving the building, she made a trip to the bathroom to vomit, a reaction she knew would come, one she was afraid she'd have during the visit.

After she finished, she washed her mouth and scrubbed the spot where Granger had laid his lips.

Harper cried into the sink, feeling her legs almost giving out from underneath.

Fifty-five

Harper knocked on Olivia's door, then leaned against the wall. She closed her eyes, the visit with Granger haunting her. She wiped away a tear and knocked again.

Finally, after the third knock, the door opened.

"Harper!" Olivia exclaimed. She pulled at the thin robe as if afraid it'd come undone. "What are you doing here?"

Before Harper could answer, Olivia narrowed her eyes.

"Are you okay?"

"I just need to talk to someone," Harper said. She pushed by her friend and headed for the kitchen. "I just came from speaking to Granger."

"What?" Olivia exclaimed. "Why would you do that?"

"He knows Bruce Perry. I needed to find out where I can find him."

"Did you?"

Harper opened her mouth to answer when she spotted two wine glasses on the counter. She narrowed her eyes.

"Is this a bad time?"

Olivia's eyes skirted to the closed bedroom door, then back at Harper.

"I wish you'd called. Uh, why don't I dress, and I'll meet you at Starbucks?"

"What's going on with you, Liv? You're acting weird. Do you have company?"

"I—"

But she didn't get the chance to respond before the door opened.

Harper's eyes grew, and she took a step back.

"Jonathan."

"Hey, Harper," he acknowledged, pulling on a white t-shirt. He glanced down at Olivia. "Guess I'll see you later."

Olivia only nodded, her eyes still watching Harper, who watched him walk out of the apartment.

"I didn't mean for you to find out this way," Olivia said quickly.

Harper's attention snapped to her friend. "'This way'? You mean at all. How long have you been sleeping with him?"

Olivia's eyes dropped to the floor.

"It just happened," she said.

"How long?" Harper pressed, her voice tight.

"A few days after you went with Craig, Jonathan and I had some drinks. Then, one thing led to another. I didn't tell you because I didn't want to hurt you. I knew things ended badly with him."

"Yeah, because the creep cheated on me." Harper shook her head as if to shake all thoughts and memories free. "You should have told me, Liv."

"I know. I'm sorry."

Harper closed her eyes. "Sorry isn't good enough. I-I need some time to think."

"Harper," Olivia said.

Ignoring her friend, she walked away, hurrying outside to her car. She got inside and drove home, all the while fighting back the tears.

When she reached her complex, she parked and dragged herself to her floor.

She stared at Ollie's door, cursing him for leaving her.

She walked in the apartment, slammed the door, cursing herself for being willing to go under, for doing something that was better left for the police to handle.

Harper poured herself a glass of Merlot. With bottle and glass in hand, she curled up on the couch. Collier hopped next to her, climbing into her lap.

"How do things get so messed up, buddy?" Harper wondered, rubbing his neck. She focused on her drinking the wine, trying not to let the tears to fall.

Eventually, after the third drink, Harper settled herself in a laying position and fell asleep.

When she woke up next, Collier was barking. The room was dark and Harper realized it was nighttime.

Sitting up, she rubbed her eyes and rose with the idea of walking him.

It was then, she realized she wasn't alone.

The silhouette of a man stood in the kitchen, watching her.

"Who—"

He lifted his finger to his lips to silence her.

"This is your first and only warning," he said.

It was a voice she didn't recognize.

She blinked, trying to erase the sleepiness enough to see his face, but soon realized he wore a black ski mask.

"Stop looking into our business."

"Who are you?" Harper forced out.

"You've been warned, Harper Matthews. Your friend is dead because of what he found. Do you want the same fate? Stop getting into our business. Because your death won't come as easy as his."

He continued to gaze at her for a few more minutes before he walked to the door.

"Don't forget to lock your doors. You never know who might break in."

After the door shut behind her, Harper stumbled to it, then locked and deadbolted, feeling her chest tightening.

She grabbed her cell phone and called Lieutenant Rice.

She answered, her voice groggy with sleep.

"Someone just broke into my apartment," Harper stated. "I don't know how long he'd been here or what he did, but when I woke up, he was there."

She spoke quickly, grabbing her hair and paced the floor. Collier continued barking. She yelled at him to be quiet, but when he didn't, she went to her room and shut the door.

"Someone was in your apartment? What did he look like?" Rice asked, sounding more awake.

"I don't know. He wore a ski mask. I didn't recognize the voice. He spoke low, but it sounded rough."

"Are you okay?" Rice asked, concern in her words.

"I-I think so." Harper sat on the edge of her bed. "Just rattled."

"You said he spoke to you. What did he say?"

Harper hesitating, biting her bottom lip.

When she told the lieutenant, Rice released a curse.

"I told you to stop it," she replied. "Maybe now you'll heed my warning."

"He just admitted Ollie found something, Lieutenant," Harper exclaimed. "That means my suspicions are true!"

"And the police are looking into it, Harper," Rice said sharply.

Harper fell quiet, listening to the muted sounds of Collier's barking.

"How could I have been so careless?" she wondered aloud. "I've been so careful about making sure my door was locked. I'd been so upset coming back from Olivia's I just didn't think."

"What happened at Olivia's?" Rice prodded.

"It's stupid," Harper said. "I went over there to tell her about visiting Granger found out she'd been sleeping with my ex for a while."

"Wait," Rice said. "Back up. What happened with Granger?"

"He didn't say much, just that Bruce Perry is close in rank to The Ghost. Granger said Perry would find me, not the other way around. I think if we can figure out where Bruce Perry is, Lieutenant, we might find the ghost."

"There is no 'we,' Harper," Rice said sternly. "I admire your tenacity, I do. But you are not the police. You have no training. Do you realize how easy it would have been to kill you tonight? You have to stop. Don't make me call Quintos and tell him to put a detail on you. I don't want to have you arrested for interfering in a federal investigation."

"But I'm so close!" Harper complained.

"Live your life," Harper," Rice instructed. "Go back to work."

Rice ended the call and Harper fell back onto the bed.

Of course, she knew the lieutenant was right, but she also knew very often, in real life, the police and feds may not solve the mystery.

The only question was: can Harper do what the police might not?

Fifty-six

Harper knew that before she did anything else, she needed to regroup. She needed to gather her thoughts and focus.

When morning came, she drank her coffee, staring at the wine bottles she had left in the holder. She knew she'd had a whole lot more of the spaces filled in her rack, but somehow she was down to one and a half. She didn't realize she'd put herself on a destructive path.

She was on the road to becoming just like her father.

If only Ollie could see her, he'd be disappointed in how she'd handle her life as of late. Harper realized something had to be done.

Life was full of disappointments, but she didn't want to rely on alcohol to diminish it. Alcohol didn't solve her problems. It only prolonged them, if not made them worse.

She reached underneath her kitchen counter for her trashcan and pulled it out. Harper poured the remaining liquids down the sink then dropped the empty bottles into the trash.

Next, she removed the bag from the can, set it aside to place a new one inside, then put the leash on Collier.

"Come on, buddy, we're going for a short walk."

Collier was only too happy to oblige.

He barked and twirled as she opened the door, then made sure it was looked behind her.

They strolled to the elevator, trash bag in tow, and headed for the ground floor.

Harper allowed Collier to do his business as they trekked to the garbage bin, and without further thought, she tossed it inside.

"Well, Collier," she said to the Sheltie. "Here's to a new start."

Collier was too busy sniffing at trash scattered around the garbage bin to pay her much attention.

She pulled him away and returned to the apartment.

As she opened her door, she heard her phone ringing.

Olivia.

Harper frowned.

She knew she wouldn't stay mad at her friend forever but, still, she didn't feel much like talking. She didn't want Olivia to be hurt by Jonathan in the way Harper was, but she knew it wasn't her place to tell Olivia who she could date or sleep with. If Olivia wanted to spend her time with Jonathan Parker, Harper made a silent promise to be there to hold her hand when, or, rather, if, he hurt her.

Of course, Harper hoped it wouldn't be the case. She decided even men like Jonathan Parker may turn a new leaf and find love.

For Harper, her true love had been murdered while she was trying to survive.

Leaving the phone to ring, Harper undid Collier's leash and made sure he was fed.

She grabbed a granola bar, her messenger bag, and phone, then left the house.

Olivia had left a voicemail, so as Harper made her way to the car, she listened.

"Harper, I hope you're okay," Olivia said, distress in her voice. It sounded as if she didn't earn much sleep. "I didn't tell you because I didn't know how. Jonathan initiated it first. I'd had too much to drink that night. From then on, I just felt like I needed a man to hold me, you know? He made me laugh. It'd been such a long time that I felt that way. But seeing you so hurt last night, it just isn't worth it. I called Jonathan and told him we couldn't see each other anymore."

Olivia paused and sighed before she ended the message.

A feeling of guilt seeping into her gut, she climbed in her car and headed for Grace's Story.

Halfway there, she glanced to see the same truck behind her, realizing he'd been tailing her since leaving her apartment.

He kept two car lengths away, so she was unable to see his face, but he was definitely the same red truck.

Harper turned at the next light, keeping a close watch in the mirror.

Sure enough, it turned with her.

Her heart beating faster, she pressed her foot on the gas to speed up just enough, hoping to lose him. The truck matched her speed.

Harper fumbled with her phone to call someone, but it slipped through her fingers, falling in between her console and passenger seat.

She slapped her palm against the steering wheel with an angry curse.

Panic was now in full mode.

She pressed her gas closer to the floorboard and maneuvered around two small cars and a van. She turned another corner, the back end of her car swinging along the street.

No one else was on the street, but she was still being followed.

Only now, the driver was closer, tailgating her.

She whispered a silent prayer, which was soon answered when the truck abruptly turned, speeding down another road.

Heart pounding, Harper turned down a street, slowing to a stop.

She allowed herself the time to sob onto her steering wheel while trying to steady her heavy breathing.

Her hands shook as she tried to find her phone, but when she couldn't manage to grasp a hold on it, she gave up and pushed her door open. She stepped out to stretch her legs and get her bearings.

When she finally felt calm, she got back into her car and pulled away.

On the way to Grace's Story, she continued looking behind her, watching for the red truck or anybody else that may have taken up the task in following her.

Arriving with no other incident, Harper again fished for her phone, grasping hold with her thumb and index finger. She pulled it out to see a text notification from Olivia.

Plz talk to me.

Harper opened the messaging app to reply.

I'll call u later.

The three dots popped up, notifying her Olivia was responding.

R u still mad?

A knock sounded on her window, and when she looked up, she saw Sara smiling at her with a wave.

Harper responded in kind as she pushed the door open.

"I'm glad you're back," Sara replied, reaching out for a hug.

"Me too," Harper said. She slipped her phone in her back pocket. "I really enjoyed the time I spent here. It was therapeutic. I needed it."

Sara smiled. "I'm glad. How are you?"

Harper scoffed. "That's an open-ended question."

"Did something happen? Do you want to talk about it?"

The truth was, Harper did want to talk. But did she want to talk to Sara? She barely knew her. On the other hand, Sara would probably understand why Harper was so invested in finding Bruce Perry.

"Well, it's a long story. I don't know if you'd be interested."

"We're friends, Harper. Friends talk, and they confide. But you don't have to. I'm here when you're ready."

Harper smiled at her.

"Thank you, Sara."

"Until that happens, we'll put you to work."

Fifty-five

After a busy couple of hours, Harper and Sara sat in the corner, drinking tea.

"You going to tell me what's going on in that head of yours?" Sara asked, lifting her cup to head her smirk.

Harper laughed. "It's not easy for me to talk about."

"Take your time," Sara said. "I won't judge. Maybe I can even help sort out your problem."

Harper paused, then decided she was in a safe enough place to talk to her new friend.

"I told you before my best friend, Ollie, was killed in a car accident, right?"

Sara nodded.

"I never thought it was an accident, so I went to speak to the original coroner. He told me he found traces of aconite in his system, but someone changed the report somehow, and left a note for the doctor, threatening to kill his family if he said anything."

"Wow," Sara said. "That's terrible."

"So I've been trying to find a way to prove Ollie was murdered."

"Did you?"

She nodded. She told Sara about her trip to New York and Jenny Buford's murder.

"In Daniel's file," Harper said, "there was this name that sounded to me like he was really high up. Like he might know who The Ghost is."

"What was the name?"

"Bruce Perry."

Sara's cup slipped from her fingers, her eyes widening. Harper saw undeniable fear.

"Sara?" Harper narrowed her eyes. "Do you recognize the name?"

Tears filling her eyes, Sara nodded.

"I dream of him every night. He…he broke me in."

"You mean he forced you to sleep with him?"

Again, she nodded. She leaned forward and spoke in a harsh whisper.

"I've never spoken that name before. To anyone. The things he made me do, it's shameful."

"How did he approach you?" Harper asked.

Sara wiped the corner her eyes with her knuckles.

"He was so nice. I was having a lot of trouble at home. Going through a lot of issues. He made me a balloon animal, telling me a funny story while doing so. He made me laugh. I thanked him and told him that I felt so much better. He smiled and said he was glad he could help."

Sara pulled in a shaky breath.

"I don't remember how he convinced me to really talk, but eventually, I mentioned I was planning on running away as soon as I got the money."

"He offered to help you?"

Sara shook her head.

"The opposite, actually. He told me things would get better. He asked me to stick with it for a few days. So I did. But eventually, he 'helped' me escape from my parents," she continued, using air quotes. "By then, he had me, and he knew it. I didn't want to sleep with him, but he said I had to for payment since I didn't have money. He said he'd care for me. He made me do things I didn't want to do, but I couldn't escape. I wanted to go home."

"I'm so sorry," Harper said.

"I felt helpless," Sara replied. "I remember one girl who tried to run away. He caught her and shot her in front of me and the others. He said that's what happened if we didn't follow the rules. Then we had to dig a grave and bury her. Almost like it was meant to seal the deal."

"Did he ever mention the name, The Ghost?"

Sara wavered her head. "No."

"Do you know how I might find Perry?" Harper asked.

"I don't know. I don't know if he has a house or not. He travels a lot for work. I went with him quite a bit. He left me alone most of the time, but I couldn't ask for help because I was afraid he'd find out. And there was no way to run."

"Thank you for telling me this," Harper said. "I know it's not easy to talk about this."

"You're right, it's not." Sara pushed out a breath. "But you, unlike my aunt, understand what I went through. We're in this together."

"Yes, Harper agreed. "We are."

"Look, I know you want to find out who killed your friend, but I don't know it's worth your life. Bruce Perry is a dangerous man. He'll kill you. Or have you killed."

"You sound like Lieutenant Rice. She keeps telling me to stop." Harper let out a small laugh.

"You should listen to her," Sara said with a frown.

Harper placed a hand on her new friend's shoulder. "Don't worry, I'll be fine. I'll see you later. Thanks for today."

Sara nodded. "I'll see you later, right?"

"Count on it," Harper replied. She reached out to hug Sara tight, and when she pulled back, she walked away.

Fifty-seven

"I just want you to be happy," Harper said when Olivia opened the door. "And if Jonathan Parker makes you that way, then good."

Olivia forced a smile.

"I'm sorry I didn't tell you about us. I really am."

Harper waved her hand in the air. "Let's move on from that, okay? I have so much to tell you."

"Right," Olivia said. "You went to see Granger. What happened? Oh, come on in."

Harper stepped into the apartment, telling Olivia everything.

"Wow," she said when Harper finished. "It's either a small world or fate that you met Sara."

"Maybe it's both," Harper said, with a shoulder shrug. "I know I have a lot of new information, but at the same time, I feel like I haven't learned anything. I still don't have leads on The Ghost and I don't know how to find Bruce Perry."

"You should give the FBI everything you know. It might help," Olivia suggested.

"I wonder if Granger knows Sara?" Harper mused. "It's very possible."

"You can't be serious," Olivia said. "You want to talk to Granger again? You have more balls than you give yourself credit for. He seriously gives me the creeps and I've never met him."

Harper positioned herself on the couch to look at Olivia better.

"I'm in so deep, Liv. How can I quit?"

"You're obsessed," Olivia accused. "You've already been through such an ordeal when Craig *tricked* you. And now someone broke into your house and followed you in the car? Those are just scare tactics. Next time, they won't be so nice."

"I know," Harper said. "But Ollie found out something that ultimately got him killed. I can't let that slide. I really can't."

Olivia pushed out a disappointed breath, resting her head on the back of the couch. "I don't want to go to another funeral so soon."

"I'm going to visit Granger again," Harper said with finality. "I'll let you know what happens. I'll call you later."

It was obvious Olivia knew she didn't have a say in the matter. Instead, she rose and walked with Harper to the door.

"Just be careful. That's all I want you to do."

"I will."

Harper leaned in to hug her friend before walking away.

For the second time, Harper lied her way in to speak to Granger.

She sat across the table from him, watching his expression as she spoke. "Do you know a girl named Sara Williams?"

Granger shook his head. "Should I?"

"She and I recently met. I found out earlier today that Bruce Perry trafficked her. It was a few years ago."

"I don't know all the girls Perry recruited."

"Let's be real, Granger," Harper said, narrowing her eyes. "Recruiting is too much of a friendly word. Kidnapping is more like it. He kidnapped Sara. Craig kidnapped me."

"Like I said: I don't know all the girls Perry *kidnapped.*"

"Sara said he traveled a lot for his job. What did he do?"

"He flew planes."

"Bruce Perry is a pilot?" Harper said. Now she understood what Sara meant. She wondered if Jonathan knew who he was. She decided to call him after she left Granger.

"For what airline did he work?"

Granger shook his head to say he didn't know.

"Tell me something, Harper," Granger said. "What's your secret?"

"My secret?" Harper asked, off guard. "Why do you care?"

"I can see you're a deep person, Harper Matthews," Granger replied. "I want to know something nobody else knows. Remember, I give a little, you give a little."

"Seems to me I've given a lot," Harper pointed out.

Granger frowned. "I don't owe you."

Crossing her arms over her chest, Harper leaned back in her chair. "I think differently, Granger. But to answer your question, I don't have any secrets."

He smiled, leaning over the table, stretching his neck, as if he were trying to move in close. "We all have secrets. It's a part of life. I sense yours is, you don't want to be alone. You're scared of aloneness."

"That's…" Harper trailed off, trying to think of a rebuttal, but came empty.

"I hit the nail on the head, did I not? You want love, but you look for it in all the wrong places. When you were shoved in that closet as a kid, you only faced the darkness. You had no one to share your fears with. But you don't have problems flying…do you?"

Harper narrowed her eyes, refusing to admit part of what Granger rang true within herself.

"You want to know my secret, Granger? I dream every night about killing you and others like you. I dream that you die a horrible death. Because that's what you deserve."

Ending the conversation, she rose, her eyes never leaving his. She announced she was ready to go. She was escorted out of the building.

At her car, she called Jonathan Parker.

"Harper," he said when he answered. "I didn't expect to hear from you so soon."

"I need to see you," she said, cutting to the chase. "Can I come over in…" she glanced at the clock on the dashboard. It was getting late, but she was too eager to wait. "Can I come over in an hour?"

Silence fell over the line.

"Sure," he said finally. "I'll pour us some wine."

"I don't need a drink," she protested. "Actually, I'm backing away for a while. I've found it clouds my judgment. I'll see you soon."

"I'll be here."

"See you soon."

Harper started her car and headed in the direction of Jonathan Parker's apartment.

Fifty-eight

Jonathan opened the door with a smile and ushered her in.

"I'm glad you're here," he said.

"I'm only here for business, she said, facing him.

He bobbed his head and walked to the kitchen. "You said you didn't want a drink, but have you changed your mind?"

"No. Thanks," she said. "I'm actually trying to back off for a little while."

"Do you mind if I have one?" he asked.

"Of course not," she said.

Harper waited for him to pull a beer bottle from the fridge. He leaned against the counter, eyeing her with curiosity.

"What's up? What did you need to talk about?"

Harper paused, considering what she wanted to ask him. Surely, he'd want to know the reason why she was asking about a random man, but she certainly didn't want to tell him everything.

"I was wondering if you've ever heard of a pilot named Bruce Perry?"

He blinked and looked away, before returning his gaze to him.

"I don't recall that name," he said. "Who is he?"

"His name's just come up a few times," she admitted. "I figured it was possible you could give me some information about him. That's all."

"Sorry, Harper. The name doesn't ring a bell. I could ask around, though. I'll start asking tomorrow. I have a flight in the red-eye to California."

"Don't let it seem suspicious," she said quickly.

"Now I'm really curious," he chuckled.

Harper heard a cell phone ringing in the distance. Jonathan excused himself to his bedroom.

While she waited, she looked out the window at the skyline of Atlanta's night.

Harper needed to go to the bathroom, so she went in search of it, hearing Jonathan's angry, hushed voice on the line.

"…Bruce Perry. Who told her about that name?"

Harper stopped walking and listened closely.

"I told him to kill her," Jonathan was saying. "No, I don't care what Granger thought! Daniel told her way too much. She needed to be done away quickly and cleanly…Yes, I know about your scare tactics, but obviously, she's not taking the hint." He released a curse. "She's here now, asking about Bruce Perry, you worthless scum…fine, take care of it tonight. I'm leaving in a few hours."

Harper heard a bang and, her heart started as she hurried to the living room. She grabbed her messenger bag from the countertop and draped it around her neck. She proceeded to the door as Jonathan reentered the room.

"Are you going somewhere?" he asked.

"I just got a call," Harper said. "From Olivia. She's upset. I think I better go see how she is."

Jonathan studied her as she walked to the door. As she twisted the knob and pulled it open, he ran to shut the door.

"I can't let you leave, Harper," he said.

"Jonathan, I have to go," she insisted.

Jonathan grabbed her neck, pulling her from the door. He pushed her to the floor.

She fell to her bottom with a grunt and looked up at him, her eyes wide.

Jonathan cursed, rubbing his hair.

"I can't believe this is happening," he said with an agitated groan. "It's going to look too suspicious. But what choice have we got?"

"Jonathan, what's wrong with you?" Harper asked, playing the innocent victim.

"I saw your shadow," he said. "When I was on the phone. You know."

She bit her lip.

"You're involved," she whispered. "You tried to have me killed. I didn't know anything, Jonathan. Why did you try to have me killed?"

"Because I know you, Harper," Jonathan said. "Once you have something in your mind, nothing would stop you from getting to the truth."

"Did you kill Ollie?" she asked, fearing the answer.

"He came to me, asking about Bruce Perry. I knew it was only a matter of time before he found out the truth. So, yes. I killed him. It had to be done, Harper."

Tears clouded her vision and she shook her head.

"He had two girls," she cried. "You didn't have to kill him."

"Don't you see?" Jonathan asked. "There's a lot of money to be had. And there are bonuses to go with it. I couldn't let him ruin it."

Harper gaped at him while fighting back the tears. She had known Jonathan Parker for almost five years. She'd even dated him for almost an entire year. Now, she was seeing a whole new side of him. She felt her stomach churn, tightening within her.

"Harper," he continued. "I've always liked you. When that idiot Daniel started to involve you…" He shook his head. "You should have just given me that envelope the first time I asked for it. I've given you many times to stop. Why wouldn't you?"

Harper cursed him. "How could you do this, Jonathan? These are people's lives you're messing with. You abuse them, murder them…It-it's not too late. You can pull out now. Turn yourself in."

Jonathan shook his head. "No. I'm sorry it had to be this way."

"What are you going to do to me? Kill me?"

"I have no choice."

"There's always a choice," she pointed out. "You're just choosing a bad choice. I once cared about you, you know."

He frowned. "I know. I cared about you too. You were a good lover, Harper. But, you know what they say. There comes a time when all good things must come to an end."

Harper glanced around the room again, working out a way to escape. She was trapped between Jonathan and furniture. She'd have to move quickly.

"Who is The Ghost?" Harper asked, trying to keep his mind otherwise occupied.

Jonathan snickered. "The Ghost doesn't exist, Harper. He's a figment of those girls' imagination. But, in a way, I suppose we are all ghosts. We are unable to be caught. Sure, some of us will be, but our business will thrive. Money will come. We will remain long after you're dead."

"What about Bruce Perry?" Harper continued. As Jonathan inched forward, she edged to the side, toward the couch, cutting off the open kitchen. "Who is he?"

He paused as if thinking on what it was he wanted to say.

"I'm Bruce Perry," he admitted. "After I was caught the last time, about five years ago, I knew I needed to change my name. I needed a whole new identity. So, I got my pilot's license and got a job with the airline. What a perfect cover, don't you agree? Hide in plain sight. I get the girls and fly from place to place. Drop them off for the buyer. Exchange money right there at the airport."

He smiled at her, making Harper's stomach churn more.

"You make me sick."

"You wouldn't understand," Jonathan replied.

"I don't need to," Harper said. "You won't be able to keep this up."

"I—"

Harper didn't give him a chance to finish speaking. She stepped on the cushion of the couch and flung herself to the other side. Once she maintained her composure, she grabbed a knife from the block and faced Jonathan.

He held a gun at her, his eyes narrow and dark. He had a ghost of a smile curving on his lips.

Harper's heart skipped several beats as the barrel seemed to zoom in toward her. Harper held the end of the knife as if her life depended on it. Maybe it did.

"You won't shoot me, Jonathan," Harper said, hoping she sounded convinced. "The other guests will call the police and you'll be in custody before you know what's happening."

"And you'll be dead," Jonathan replied, matter-of-factly.

Harper tried to swallow, but her throat felt too dry.

"Drop the knife, Harper," Jonathan instructed, stepping forward, his movements slow. "And toss me your bag."

Her hands shaking, Harper let the knife slip through her fingers before removing her messenger bag from around her neck. She tossed it over the couch, holding her hands for him to see she wouldn't try anything.

Jonathan gestured with his gun for her to proceed out of the room.

She obliged, stopping when he put the gun at her throat. The metal felt cold and heavy against her skin.

"Try anything, I'll kill you. And I'll do the same to anyone who tries to get in my way."

With a tilt of his head, Jonathan instructed her to continue walking.

Her legs feeling like lead, she proceeded for the door, twisted the knob and pulled it open. Jonathan swung the door shut as he followed close behind her.

"Where are we going?" she asked.

"Just walk."

The hallway was clear, except for a room service wagon waiting by a room three doors down. There was a wine bottle sitting on top. A means of opportunity.

As Harper walked, she pulled in a shaky breath, preparing a daring escape.

She walked closer to the wagon.

Jonathan was still close enough for her to throw her elbow back, digging into his stomach. He keeled over slightly with a soft grunt, but not enough to keep him down. Harper sprinted to the wagon with Jonathan hot on her heels. As his fingers brushed against her arm, she grabbed the neck of the wine bottle and broke it over his head.

He released a surprised scream, and Harper shoved the cart in his direction.

She didn't wait to see how long Jonathan would remain down.

Harper ran toward the elevators but took the stairs instead. She ran up the steps, slipping on the one that would lead her to the sixth-floor door. Her left ankle twisted and she cracked her knee as she fell to the hard surface.

A cry of pain flew from her mouth.

Feeling breathless and pained, Harper used the railing to pull herself to her feet. She limped to the door, open it, and stepped out of the stairwell.

She looked around, trying to find a safe place to wait Jonathan out, but she still needed to find a cell phone to use to call the police.

Harper limped down the hall, knowing Jonathan would likely have a difficult time finding her, but she couldn't allow him to escape too far.

She turned down another hall where she saw a maid entering a room.

"Help me!" Harper exclaimed.

She favored her right leg as she moved quickly.

The maid stuck her head out of the room, her eyes narrowed.

"Help me, please," Harper exclaimed.

"Need help?"

Harper leaned against the wall, her hand over her chest as if to steady the beating.

"I need a phone. I need…to call the police."

"You want police?"

"Yes," Harper said. "Do you have a phone I can borrow?"

"You use phone in room," the maid said, watching as Harper nodded and passed by her to the room. "You need doctor?"

"Probably," Harper breathed.

She picked up the phone and dialed 911.

Once the operator picked up, she requested to be directed to Lieutenant Quintos.

Minutes passed before Quintos answered.

Harper told the lieutenant in as few words as possible what had transpired.

When she finished, Quintos instructed for her to remain where she was and he'd send his men to her.

Fifty-nine

The paramedic wrapped Harper's ankle but insisted on sending her to the doctor, so after she finished telling Quintos and another officer what had happened, she rode in the back of the ambulance.

At the hospital, she called Olivia to tell her where she was, but she left out how she came to be there. Such conversations weren't for a phone call.

An hour and a half had passed before Olivia arrived, wild-eyed.

"Goodness, Harp!" she said, studying the wrap her friend had on her ankle and knee. "What happened?"

Harper positioned herself to sit upright.

"You'd better have a seat, Liv."

With a pause, Olivia sat on the edge of the hospital bed, her eyes never leaving Harper's.

"So, you know I went back to see Granger, right?" Olivia nodded. "Well, he told me Bruce Perry was a pilot. So I called Jonathan. I wanted to know if he'd ever heard of him before."

"Geez, Harper!" Olivia exclaimed. She pushed herself off the bed and paced the room, throwing her hands in the air. "Maybe now you'll be careful. How many times do you have to get yourself—wait. You were with Jonathan?"

Harper nodded. "He claimed not to know who Perry was, but then I overheard him over the phone talking to someone. Then, I knew."

Harper's voice began to quiver as she reflected on what happened only hours before.

"Jonathan's involved, Liv," Harper forced out. "He tried to get Granger to kill me, but for some reason, Granger didn't want to."

"I can't believe it," Olivia said after the room fell into a long silence.

"He-He killed Ollie, too," Harper said, her voice quivering. "He killed him because Ollie found out about Jonathan's true identity."

"Oh, Harp, this is terrible," Olivia said. She walked to the side of the bed to lean in for a hug.

Harper gripped her tight, finding herself unable to let go.

Olivia stayed with Harper until the doctors released her. She signed the papers and, with the help of crutches, she left.

The sun was peering over the horizon, and as Olivia drove them home, Harper could hardly believe everything had happened in one night. It seemed an eternity since she first arrived at Jonathan's hotel room.

In the hospital, she had tried to rest for a little bit, but she seemed to wake up every hour. She wasn't sure if it was from the nurses coming and going, the machines beeping, or her own insomnia.

Either way, she decided she'd be happy to reach her own bed.

She knew Quintos had his men searching for Jonathan, as well as the FBI and neighboring counties, but she had to force herself to realize maybe Jonathan was right. Maybe he and the others would never be found. All of them were ghosts.

Olivia pulled into a parking spot at Harper's complex and shattered Harper's thoughts.

"Would you like me to stay with you tonight?"

Harper considered the offer and decided it would be good for her to have someone else there. She would feel safer.

She nodded.

"Thanks."

"Anytime."

Harper pushed the door open and stepped out. She opened the backseat and pulled out her crutches.

They made their way into the complex and up the stairs.

Olivia had Harper's keys in her hand, so she unlocked the door, pushing it open. Inside, Collier spun his usual greeting, barking with excitement.

Harper went inside and laid her crutches against the counter. She made her way to the couch, trying not to let Collier push her down.

She sat and Collier jumped up next to her, lapping his pink tongue against her face. Laughing, she pushed him away.

"Calm down, boy," she said.

"Why don't I go walk him for a few minutes?" Olivia suggested.

"That'd be great, thanks," Harper told her.

Olivia got the leash and latched it on his collar, pulling the Sheltie away from his owner.

Harper swung her feet on the couch, closed her eyes, reflecting on what had happened in the last two months. The words of Craig echoed in her mind: *the fact is, in this business, anybody can be involved.*

It was a scary thought knowing she worked with Jonathan closely without knowing he had a whole other side of him. The thought made her sick.

It was worse not knowing where he was. Did he manage to escape? Would he ever be caught? When will it come to an end?

Harper didn't know, and she probably would never know.

What she did know is Jonathan was out there somewhere, and the feds were searching for him. They likely would continue to search for him until the day he dies. She supposed that'd have to be good enough.

Ever since she first entered Granger's house, Harper had felt as though she was a victim. But, she would no longer think of herself as such. Her mother taught her to be strong.

And strong she will be.

Tomorrow was a new day, and Harper vowed to uncover the injustice of the world.

Some day, somehow, the pain will end.

If you or someone you know may be a victim of human trafficking, do not hesitate to get help now!

USA: 1-888-373-7888
Georgia Cars (Minors 12-17): 404-602-0068
Out of Darkness (18+): 404-941-6024

For more information, other resources, or to donate, visit rescuinghope.com.

CPSIA information can be obtained
at www.ICGtesting.com
Printed in the USA
LVHW080058130120
643319LV00012BA/522/P

9 781733 789615